THE LOST KESTREL FOUND

BOOK SIX OF THE SYLVAN CHRONICLES

PETER WACHT

The Lost Kestrel Found
By Peter Wacht

Book Six of The Sylvan Chronicles

Published in the United States by Kestrel Media Group LLC.

ISBN: 978-1-950236-10-7

eBook ISBN: 978-1-950236-11-4

Library of Congress Control Number: 2020900243

✹ Created with Vellum

ALSO BY PETER WACHT

THE REALMS OF THE TALENT AND THE CURSE

THE TALES OF CALEDONIA

(Complete 7-Book Series)

Blood on the White Sand (short story)*

The Diamond Thief (short story)*

The Protector

The Protector's Quest

The Protector's Vengeance

The Protector's Sacrifice

The Protector's Reckoning

The Protector's Resolve

The Protector's Victory

TALES OF THE TERRITORIES

A Fate Worse Than Death (short story)*

Stalking the Red Ruby (short story)*

Death on the Burnt Ocean (Forthcoming 2023)

Monsters in the Mist (Forthcoming 2023)

The Dance of the Daggers (Forthcoming 2023)

THE SYLVAN CHRONICLES

(Complete 9-Book Series)

The Legend of the Kestrel

The Call of the Sylvana

The Raptor of the Highlands

The Makings of a Warrior

The Lord of the Highlands

The Lost Kestrel Found

The Claiming of the Highlands

The Fight Against the Dark

The Defender of the Light

THE RISE OF THE SYLVAN WARRIORS

Through the Knife's Edge (short story)*

* Free short stories can be downloaded from my author website at www.PeterWachtBooks.com.

YOUR FREE SHORT STORY IS WAITING

THROUGH THE KNIFE'S EDGE

This short story is a prelude to the events in *The Sylvan Chronicles* and is free to readers who receive my newsletter.

Sign up and get your free copy at www.PeterWachtBooks.com.

1

A STIRRING

The strong gusts of an early morning wind lifted the raptor as it winged its way around the Highland peaks and into the valley. On most mornings, the raptor hunted. But not today. Today the raptor felt an unfamiliar urgency. Its strong wings, spanning seven feet, propelled it a thousand feet above the ground. The white feathers speckled with grey on the bird's underside blended perfectly with the sky. When visible, the raptor was a dangerous predator. When hidden, it was deadly, shooting down through the thin air like an arrow, its sharp claws outstretched for the kill.

Today it searched for different prey, yet it did not know why. It knew only to obey the urge pulling it to the east, an urge so strong it drowned out its instinct to hunt.

The sun radiated off the orange, black, and brown feathers covering its back. As it dodged around the mountaintops, a monstrous shadow trailed along, darkening the ground as it passed over the Highlands. A beautiful sight, but also treacherous. The rugged land hid untold riches -- gold and silver, precious jewels and more. But, as the old saying went: If the Highlanders don't get you, nature will. For centuries, many in search of treasure stole into the Highlands, hoping a few days' work would lead to a lifetime of luxury. For most, these dreams of fortune shattered before their eyes, the hard steel of the Highlanders or the rugged terrain bringing these adventurers back to a cold, stark, and unforgiving reality.

The raptor knew that this age-old story played out even now. For almost a decade the Highlanders had battled against reivers seeking to take the treasures of the Highlands as their own. Fighting for their homes and their homeland, they had waged a losing struggle, the invaders' greater numbers and use of Dark Magic inexorably crushing the people's spirits as their populace dwindled and they were forced into the higher, more inaccessible passes for their own safety. Until now. For though defeated, the Highlanders had refused to be conquered, hoping for better days. Hoping they would be given the opportunity to repay the debt they owed the reivers who had taken so much from them. Hoping that perhaps the legend would come to life. Hope was a powerful thing. It had sustained the Highlanders during even the darkest of days during the last decade. And now their hope was becoming something more. It was taking shape and solidifying. It was becoming tangible. Becoming real.

The raptor could sense the change occurring within the Highlands, for the mountainous Kingdom was the raptor's domain; now its only home. Once, not too many years in the past, raptors lived in every Kingdom from the Western Ocean to the Sea of Mist. But no more. Nobles and wealthy merchants paid dearly for the feathers of the mighty bird. Rumors of their magical powers abounded. Some believed the feathers, when ground down and mixed with a few select ingredients, served as an aphrodisiac. Others insisted that drinking the strange brew gave wisdom. Still others thought it brought luck or riches or strength.

Although no one had ever proven the truth of these myths, the old beliefs died hard. As the years passed, so did these majestic birds, until none remained except those in the Highlands, protected by the harsh weather, the rough landscape, and the Highlanders themselves, for the raptors had a special place in their hearts. The raptor represented all that it was to be a Highlander: strength, resilience, resolve, fortitude.

The raptor gazed at the lush valley of green that stretched between the mountains for more than a league. A dark smudge appeared in the very center. Skimming over the treetops, the raptor's strong wings drew it closer, until the smudge became a huge rock that rose hundreds of feet into the air and dominated the valley. From a distance, it resembled a small mountain cut off from its brothers and sisters by encircling forest. But as the raptor approached, riding the warmer air currents with its outstretched wings and gliding slowly upward, the markings of man became clear.

To the untrained eye, the monolith appeared to be no more than a huge rock thrusting out of the earth. In truth, it was the Crag, the stronghold of the Highlanders. The Crag had never fallen to an attacking army. Many had learned that lesson the hard way, leaving behind broken bodies and crushed spirits. Carved from the mountain, it was a formidable sight. The Highlanders had built their fortress on top of a long-dead volcano, taking great slabs of black stone from the plateau to form its walls. During the night, the citadel receded into the darkness, undecipherable from the gloom.

Eight towers formed the Crag's perimeter, joined together by the outer curtain. Or rather, they once did. Half the towers had crumbled, now nothing more than piles of stone. The wall was a hundred feet high and forty feet thick, yet along its base half a dozen holes that were wide enough for several draft horses to walk through standing next to one another had been blasted through the stone into the inner courtyard.

In the center of the outer ward stood the central stronghold. Built in the shape of a square, its inner curtain stood fifty feet higher than the outside wall, its corners again supported by towers. All these towers had been destroyed except for one, which stood on the eastern side closest to the sea. Known as the Roost and rising higher than all the rest, on a clear day it was said that from its great height the Highlanders could peer halfway across the continent and gaze upon the shores of the Heartland Lake.

True, the Crag had never fallen to a foreign army. But it had been betrayed almost ten years before. Delivered by one of their own like a lamb being led to slaughter. The Marchers attempted to fight off a surprise attack of not only reivers, but also Ogren, Shades, and warlocks. Despite their staunch resistance, the Marchers were too few against an overpowering force, and they had no way to defend themselves against the Dark Magic of the warlocks. Talyn Kestrel, Lord of the Highlands, perished while defending the Crag. Though many Highlanders escaped thanks to the efforts of the doomed Highland Lord, none had returned to this place since the fall of the Marcher fortress.

The massive raptor began to circle what was left of the Crag, enjoying the warm sun on its back. Normally a solitary creature, the raptor was surprised to see a handful of other raptors settled onto the broken towers of the Crag or drifting on the gusts of wind that swirled around the keep. The raptor landed gracefully on the open window at the very top of the Roost, remembering the last time it had been here on that final night that the Highlands had been free so long ago.

A small boy had lived in the room. The raptor had felt a connection to the boy immediately, yet it did not know why. It had watched the boy escape two assassins that night, eventually making his way safely out of the Crag and into the surrounding forest. The raptor had stayed with the boy until he had met two people it knew would protect him. And since then the connection to the boy remained, growing stronger with each passing day.

The raptor had found that same boy several times in the intervening years. Each time the predator did, it felt pride for what the boy had become. There was a strength to the boy, a determination, which it recognized within itself. The boy was the Highlands, and the Highlands him.

For a time the raptor perched on the Roost watching, waiting. For almost a decade the Crag had sat abandoned, the once mighty fortress quickly covered by moss, ivy, and undergrowth, the forest trying to reclaim its stolen territory. But the raptor didn't think that would be the case for much longer. It sensed a new beginning. Blood was beginning to flow in the Highlands once again, a people beginning to stir.

With its sharp eyes the raptor glimpsed something in the distance that triggered a territorial response. The raptor launched itself from its place on the Roost, using its powerful wings to draw closer while also finding the warmer drafts of air to gain height on the intruder. The raptor followed its instincts, as it was known for attacking from above in a blinding display of speed and skill, much like the Highlanders themselves who were known as the most fearsome fighters in all the Kingdoms. It was said that to risk the wrath of a Highlander was to risk death. The same could be said of the raptor.

When the raptor identified the encroaching beast, it flexed its sharp claws in anticipation. This was a creature worthy of its attention. A blood enemy. Raptors had not seen a Dragas for centuries, since the time of the Great War, yet through the collective memory of the species the raptor knew every inch of the flying dark creature; its strengths, its weaknesses, its preferred method of attack. Therefore, the raptor knew how to combat the larger animal, seeking to ignore the thick scales across its back and focus instead on its soft underbelly. All while trying to avoid its long, spike-like claws and sharp teeth.

To invade a raptor's territory immediately invited a challenge, but to be a creature such as this invited a swift death. Raptors had no patience for creatures of the dark. Judging the time was right with the sun shining brightly behind it, the raptor dove silently toward the dark creature, extending its claws. At the last second, the Dragas sensed the attack, halting its progress in the sky and trying to dodge the raptor as it hurtled past. The massive dark creature proved largely successful, though the raptor did succeed in catching one of its claws across the beast's belly, slicing deeply into its flesh, a dark black blood pouring out.

The Dragas instantly pursued the raptor, roaring in anger, its cry of rage reverberating off the mountain peaks. Though the raptor was faster over short distances, the Dragas used its larger wings to stay close to its attacker, snapping at its tail feathers with its serrated teeth. In a quick burst of speed and a tilt of its wing, the raptor caught the Dragas by surprise as it looped underneath the dark creature, again running a claw along the beast's belly, leaving another long, bloody wound in the monster's hardened hide. Incensed, the Dragas roared once more in fury. The Dragas turned swiftly to hunt its prey, but its pain mixing with rage blinded it to what was occurring around it.

It was then that the monster learned its mistake. The dark creature had thought it was fighting one raptor, not realizing that there were more in the sky. The first raptor had distracted it, giving the other raptors the time to position themselves for their deadly attacks. When the Dragas sought to turn on its first tormentor, a second raptor swept by, its claws tearing into its thin, leathery wing. Before the Dragas could respond to that attack, another raptor dove down and sliced a gaping hole in its other wing, followed by two more raptors that plunged their sharp claws into the wreckage that was once its belly.

Against one raptor, the Dragas stood a chance. Against five, the conclusion was already determined. The dark creature roared its defiance a final time as it plummeted down toward a Highland peak, its tattered wings no longer able to keep it aloft. The raptors circled above it, watching the dark creature's back break against the hard stone, before lazily turning in the sky, enjoying the warmth of the sun before settling back onto the Crag.

The raptors would protect their territory as they had for centuries. But this time, the large raptor that took its place once more on the Roost sensed a difference. Change was coming. A reckoning was coming. And the raptors would be ready. Until then, they would watch and wait. They would protect the home of the Highlanders from the creatures of the dark, just as the Highlanders protected them.

2

———

A DIFFICULT PATH

Rynlin Keldragan stood atop the Breaker, the harsh, cold wind seemingly trying to tear away the cloak he had pulled tighter around himself. Carved from massive blocks of granite, the Breaker rose well over three hundred feet in height and was one hundred feet wide, stretching from the western Highlands to the coast and the Winter Sea. It gave the defenders the space they needed to repel any attack from the north. But there were no defenders now, and there hadn't been for quite some time.

The tall Sylvan Warrior, dark hair and short beard speckled with grey, hated being here. The memories always returned, a continuous stream running through his mind. Nightmares, in all honesty. It had been the most important battle of the Great War, the most important event in the history of the Kingdoms. He could recall the events of a millennia ago as if it were yesterday.

The Sylvana were first called together one thousand years before to fight an evil in the far north, which had invaded the Charnel Mountains. At the time, those mountains were known as the Northern Peaks and were a beautiful sight to behold.

Little did they know how the world would change now that the Shadow Lord had appeared, seeking to conquer the Kingdoms. In the beginning, the rulers of the different lands didn't view this new threat at the very edge of the Kingdoms as a serious threat, the mountains and the Northern Steppes standing in the way. So only a small army made up of soldiers from the closest Kingdoms marched into the Northern Peaks to defeat this new danger. The fighters did the best they could, but were heavily outnumbered by the Dark Horde, composed of the creatures the Shadow Lord had twisted for his primary purpose: desolation and destruction. The soldiers fought valiantly, yet could only delay the inevitable advance of the Shadow Lord's servants and hope that help would come.

The other Kingdoms soon realized the great peril they were in, but it would take weeks, if not months, for them to call together their armies and march to the north. At that time, druids still held sway over the land, and often served as advisors in the courts of the different kings and queens. The chief druid, a woman named Athala, suggested that the Kingdoms send their best warriors to her, and they would fight the Dark Horde until the massed armies of the Kingdoms could take the field.

The other rulers thought it was an excellent idea, and the greatest warriors of that time met Athala on the Northern Steppes, as the Dark Horde was pushing hard for the south and would soon break out of the Northern Peaks. When that happened, the Kingdoms would have little chance of stopping them. Athala called her small army of only several hundred Sylvan Warriors, naming it after a mythical band of legendary soldiers who, the stories told, appeared in times of need and fought for those who had been wronged.

The Sylvan Warriors met the Dark Horde at the edge of the Northern Peaks, fighting desperately to hold back the Shadow Lord's advance as they battled for three days and three nights.

Despite the overwhelming number of terrifying creatures that swept down from the north, the Sylvana refused to yield, giving the Kingdoms the time needed by sacrificing their blood, sweat and tears. In the end, the Sylvan Warriors succeeded. They forced the Dark Horde to retreat. Before the Shadow Lord could recover, the armies of the Kingdoms arrived and drove him even deeper into what was then already being described as the Charnel Mountains, the verdant, green landscape having begun to turn a sooty black as the Shadow Lord's presence started to corrupt the land.

But the Kingdoms couldn't destroy the Shadow Lord. They could only defeat him. So the rulers of the Kingdoms again followed the advice of Athala and made the Sylvan Warriors a permanent fighting force with no ties of allegiance to any Kingdom. The sole purpose of this elite group was to fight the Shadow Lord no matter the odds, and they had done so ever since.

Rynlin wiped at his eyes, telling himself that the tears that had formed came as a result of the biting wind, though he knew the truth of it. So many good men and women had died fighting against the Shadow Lord and his monstrous horde of warlocks, Ogren, Shades, the lightning fast Fearhounds and Mongrels, and other hideous creatures that had come from the north seeking to conquer the Kingdoms. So many friends. Gone. And virtually none remembered by those who had benefited from their bravery and constancy.

Yet even with the formation of the Sylvana, the Kingdoms still feared the Shadow Lord's return. Therefore, after the conclusion of the Great War, they had built the Breaker and formed the First Guard, soldiers from the different Kingdoms charged with serving a year on the towering barrier, watching, waiting, and preparing for the next attack so that when the Shadow Lord once again sought to claim the Kingdoms for his own, and all assumed that he would, the Kingdoms would be better prepared to defend themselves and able to muster their armies and march north. But as the years passed no attack had come, and the Kingdoms began sending fewer and fewer soldiers to serve in the First Guard until, eventually, no one stood atop the Breaker anymore.

Rynlin shook his head in frustration, recalling the sacrifices made so long ago to ensure that the Shadow Lord and his Dark Horde did not conquer the Kingdoms. The Sylvan Warrior believed the truism that those who forget their history are doomed to repeat it. So seemed to be the case now with the Shadow Lord and his dark creatures stirring once more. Many of the Kingdoms failed to recognize the danger or willingly ignored it, worried more about the happenings in their own Kingdom thanks to the machinations of the High King rather than, at least to their own eyes, a yet to be confirmed threat to the Kingdoms as a whole. Myopic fools. By the time most realized the danger it would be too late.

Under Rynlin's gaze, the Northern Steppes stretched for leagues into the distance, the dark smudge of the Charnel Mountains far to the north. Though Rynlin couldn't see it, he could feel the evil pulsing from the very center of the begrimed, jagged range of towering peaks. Blackstone. The lair of the Shadow Lord. The Sylvan Warriors were weaker than in any other time since their formation, several falling prey to the creatures of the Shadow Lord during the last year and thereby reducing their ranks even more. Would they be able to hold back the Shadow Lord as they had in the past? Would the Kingdoms heed their call to arms? Would the Breaker hold back the Dark Horde?

So many questions. So many worries. To say nothing of the fact that his wife had taken on a task both critical and dangerous, and he was in no position to help her. And what of his grandson? He continued to take risks, more than he should or, in fact, needed to take, never considering the possibility that eventually he would pay the price for doing so. But there was nothing Rynlin could do about that. His grandson had started along a certain path, reluctantly at first, but with courage nonetheless. With each step his grandson took along that road, Rynlin felt as if the boy's ability to choose diminished, his fate having already been sealed.

His wife's favorite saying came to mind: *"You do what you must do."* He had hoped that his grandson could avoid what the prophecy suggested would happen. But all the signs pointed to the prophecy's inevitable, deadly conclusion. The final battle between the light and the dark, his grandson in the very middle of it pitted against an opponent with unimaginable power who had never been defeated in single combat. An opponent who was the very source of Dark Magic in the Kingdoms. How could he expect his grandson to overcome that?

Rynlin pushed his maudlin thoughts from his mind. There was nothing he could do for Thomas right now, but there was something else that he could do. And taking action clearly was a better alternative than standing on top of a frigid wall allowing his fears and worries to consume him.

Taking a quick glance to the east, he saw several large kestrels circling above the northern peaks of the Highlands. The massive birds called the Highlands their home. They represented not only the Highlands, but the people living there. The people his grandson now led. They were tough, resilient, and they did what was needed even when that wasn't the easiest path.

Rynlin grinned. That certainly applied to his grandson. Thomas would, indeed, follow his own path. If that led him as the prophecy predicted to a final contest against the Shadow Lord, so be it. His grandson would do what was necessary. His people would expect no less of him, just as he would expect no less of himself.

In the meantime, Rynlin would see if he could offer some

assistance to ease the burdens weighing on his grandson. A bright flash of white light engulfed the Sylvan Warrior. When the blinding radiance cleared, a giant hawk gripped the crenels of the Breaker with its sharp talons. With a screech that echoed through the Highlands to the east, the bird launched itself from the black stone, its powerful wings driving it steadily toward the Charnel Mountains.

3

WORRY AND FEAR

Rodric Tessaril, High King of Armagh, sat upon his uncomfortable throne as a young child would when required to pose for a portrait, fidgeting, unable to remain still. His thick fingers drummed on the arm of the throne incessantly, his right leg bouncing nervously. Not the most regal of poses, he realized, but he also knew that most only perceived him as king because of the power he wielded, despite his constant attempts to put forward a regal image. He often wore a purple cape that dwarfed his small stature and dragged across the polished stone as he stomped through the halls of Eamhain Mhacha. The much too large golden crown, perched precariously on his head and always in danger of clattering to the floor, also did not have its intended effect.

Rodric hoped to make up for his lack of stature and plain appearance with the accoutrements of his rank. But try as he might, the fear he attempted to instill came not from his appearance, as had been the case with the warrior High Kings of old, but rather because of the harshness of his rule. He had learned at an early age that a king could be loved or feared, but not both. He recognized quickly that he would never be loved, so Rodric had put all his energy into being feared. In his mind, respect was respect, regardless of whether it came from fear or love.

He ignored his perpetual insecurity for the moment, his thoughts centered instead on a matter that had plagued him for months. A matter that put his carefully crafted plans at risk. A matter that threatened his very rule.

His worry and trepidation so consumed Rodric that he failed to notice the tall lord enter the chamber. The man wore a shining steel breastplate that obviously had just been scrubbed to a blinding sheen, a white cloak draped over his shoulders. The lord would have been described as handsome, if not for the very large nose that seemed to precede him into the throne room.

It was only after the tall lord bent to his knee and cleared his throat that Rodric emerged from the shackles of his own mind. The nervous tics finally came to an end as the High King stared at Johin Killeran, Lord of Dunmoor. Rodric's irritation rose quickly, seeking an outlet, but he did his best to contain it for now. Though he blamed Killeran for many of his current problems, he still had a use for the often incompetent, always pompous fool.

"Anything?" asked the High King in a voice that threatened to crack, already suspecting the answer he would receive.

"No, my lord."

Killeran's response was obsequious, as he recognized the danger of the situation. He had linked his fortunes with the High King. If Rodric were to fall, so would he, the only difference being that Rodric would have farther to fall than he would.

Rodric's gaze bore into Killeran, who refused to raise his eyes from the stone floor. The boy had escaped them in Tinnakilly, leaping from the battlements of the keep rather than face the crossbowmen arrayed around him.

Watching the boy step off the edge, Rodric's heart had felt free for the first time since his enterprise began at the Crag those many years before. The boy had been a thorn in his side for too long. Yet the next day no body was found broken on the rocks far below. Nor the next day. Or the day following. Rodric ordered Loris, the obsequious King of Dunmoor, to expand the search well down the Gullet, thinking the body may have been carried away by the swift current south toward Stormy Bay. Yet as the days passed and the search continued, there was no sign of the boy. Now months after the incident, his worries and fears had taken up residence in the back of his mind. Always there. Whispers of failure threatening to overpower him. No one could have survived a fall like that. Could they? Or were the stories of what the boy could do true? Was he truly the Raptor? Could he still be alive?

"I need proof, Killeran. Proof!"

"I know, my lord." The sharpness of the High King's demand released a trickle of sweat down Killeran's back.

"Our plans depend on it and time is running short."

"I know, my lord."

"Then why can't you find the body!" Rodric had meant to yell, but instead it came out as a shriek, reverberating off the walls of the throne room.

"We've tried, my ..."

"Enough excuses, Killeran. We have no more time for failure. We must have success."

Rodric took a deep breath, steadying himself. Though deserved, his anger would gain him nothing at the moment. He must regain his focus and keep his larger goal in mind.

"Make sure Loris continues the search," said Rodric, struggling to regain the calm that so often alluded him. Killeran nodded his acquiescence. "Now what of the rumors, Killeran? Are they connected to our missing boy?"

"I don't know, my lord."

"Then what do you know?" wailed Rodric, only able to contain his fury for so long. "The Council of the Kingdoms approaches! There can be no surprises! Everything must go to plan! Our ally expects nothing less."

Killeran cringed at the words. Though he took the High King for a fool, for the first time he feared Rodric, if for no other reason than his erratic behavior. In Armagh, Rodric could do as he wanted with little or no consequence. Nevertheless, death by Rodric's hand was nothing compared to what their hidden ally would do to them if they failed to do as commanded.

Killeran stammered out his response as quickly as he could.

"Nothing has been confirmed, my lord. But the Highlands are unsettled. There are few, if any, Highlanders in the lowlands. As a result, all mining has stopped. The reivers are afraid to hunt in the higher passes, and for good reason. Small groups of reivers are disappearing with nary a trace, and even large patrols are coming under assault. The attackers are no more than shadows, rarely seen, striking quickly and then fading back into the countryside. Although Dinnegan promised to address the matter while I was called back to the west, apparently things have not worked out as we expected. I'm told as well that the haunting lilt of the bagpipes echoes constantly through the Highland peaks, my lord. But no one knows why."

Rodric smiled coldly. At least one small good had come from this debacle. His partner, Norin Dinnegan, foisted upon him by his ally, had failed to hold up his end of the bargain, to extract the wealth of the Highlands no matter the cost to those who lived there. That was a fact that he could use in the future. But a frown quickly replaced his smile. What Killeran said threatened to multiply his barely contained fears.

For the past ten years his reivers had ruled the Highlands, forcing the Marchers into the higher passes and enslaving any Highlanders unlucky enough to be caught in the open, putting them to work in the mines. But that had changed with the destruction of the Black Hole, the reivers' primary fort and base of operations in the Highlands. Burned to the ground by the boy who should have died on the Tinnakilly rocks, production from the mines had ground to a halt. Now there was nothing being dug from that cursed land. With no gold or precious minerals, how was he to prepare his army for what was to come next? How was he to grasp the power that was so rightfully his?

Worrisome indeed. And unable to forget his hidden ally, potentially deadly. His fingers began tapping on the armrest once more, his right leg again bouncing furiously. He ignored Killeran for quite some time, retreating into his thoughts as had become more common these last few weeks, retreating into his fears. Had the roles been reversed in the Highlands? Had the hunters become the hunted?

4

A PLAN

Just days before the Highland chiefs gathered at the Pinnacle they had been a somber lot, beaten down by almost a decade of continuous warfare against reivers and dark creatures. Yet it wasn't the constant fighting that had almost broken them as a people. No, they were born fighters. They excelled on the battlefield. All the other Kingdoms acknowledged their superiority as a military force; all the other Kingdoms had gladly made use of their martial services before the Highland Lord had ended that practice decades before after several Marchers were betrayed by their employer; and all the other Kingdoms were thankful that the Highland Marchers only had a small army, because if they were more numerous, they likely would have ruled the entire continent if they so desired.

The number of Marchers had dwindled after the assassination of Talyn Kestrel, Highland Lord, just ten years before. Pursued by their enemies into the higher passes of their homeland, they had struggled to keep their families safe and their rugged land free. In the beginning they had clung to their hope, believing the stories about the Lost Kestrel, Talyn's grandson. When the Crag fell, the grandson's body was never found. Had he survived the assault? Would he appear in their time of need?

Several Marchers, led by Coban Serenan, Swordmaster of the Highlands, had searched for the boy after the surprise attack, following his trail through the forest surrounding the Crag until they lost it in the untamed mountains of the eastern Highlands. The boy had made it to a clearing that held barely visible signs of a small fire. But from there the trail disappeared with nary a trace of where he might have gone. Try as Coban and his Marchers might, there was nothing for them to track. They had lost the last Kestrel.

A few Marchers still continued to search, having faith that their fortunes had to turn at some point. But as time passed their struggles worsened. Although the reivers were no match for the Marchers, Killeran's warlocks and their use of Dark Magic negated the Marchers' superiority in arms. As a result, the Highlanders' hope had deteriorated with each passing year, almost disappearing entirely. Until just a few days ago when their hope had been rekindled and then set ablaze.

Because the Lost Kestrel was no longer lost. The Lost Kestrel had been found.

The rough encampment encircling the Pinnacle had been transformed into a military camp. Coban had taken charge, immediately sending out runners to spread the word. Soon the signal fires that dotted the Highland peaks, dormant for so long, sprang back to life. And as the bagpipes played, their strong notes extending to the farthest reaches of the Kingdom, the Highlanders learned that Thomas Kestrel, grandson of Talyn, had returned. The boy had assumed his grandfather's place on high as Lord of the Highlands. Moreover, he had gained some measure of revenge, killing the traitor who had betrayed the Highlands and unlocked the Crag, ensuring its fall and the misery that followed, in a duel. By nightfall more

Marchers had begun to appear. First in ones and twos, then in droves as the chiefs called to their villages, and their fighters, men and women, responded with vigor and hope.

As they arrived, Coban and the chiefs were there to greet them, directing them to marked locations as the army camp took shape and the training began. The Highlands felt alive once more, and the Marchers had a purpose. They would reclaim their homes and their homeland. Although the last ten years had weakened the Highlanders, their desire and will to earn their freedom had never died. Yet they understood that achieving that objective required completing one task, and the Marchers acknowledged that it would be a challenge, possibly an insurmountable one, for their freedom depended on eliminating the reiver army.

"We don't have enough Marchers to defend the whole of the Highlands," complained Renn, a stout Highland chief with a flowing mustache that dropped almost to his chin. "The reivers are too many and we are too few."

It had been a constant theme for much of the morning, as Thomas sat quietly, listening to his chiefs voice their concerns. Seneca and Nestor had had their say. Renn felt the need to repeat the primary issue. The Marchers did not have enough fighters for a major push against the reivers.

"We can't protect every village," continued Renn.

He was about to list his concerns once again, but Thomas had heard enough. He tamped down his growing impatience and spoke in an even, clear voice. Though not very tall, his blazing green eyes and stoic strength added to the weight of his formidable presence.

"Then we won't."

Renn stopped in mid-thought, surprised by Thomas' unexpected comment.

"We won't?"

"No, we won't," Thomas confirmed. "We must think differently. We must act differently. We need to concentrate our people and force the reivers to come to us. Then we can fight them on our terms. We decide when we fight and where we fight."

"You have something in mind, Thomas?" asked Coban, a knowing grin lighting up his normally grim visage.

"When I was a boy, Talyn used to tell me stories before going to bed at night." Thomas smiled at the memory, recalling one of the few times during his days as a child that he had felt comfortable in the Crag, as if he actually belonged there. "Sometimes he would talk of the great generals. One in particular comes to mind right now. Chen Tzu taught that you must fight the enemy on your own terms. You must dictate the circumstances of each battle, not your opponent. That's what we're going to do. We'll form the Marchers into a handful of raiding parties with the freedom to act on their own. But they will have a single duty. Engage the reivers, inflict casualties, then melt away into the Highlands. We whittle down Killeran's so-called Army of the Black Sword, improving our odds, until we're ready to challenge him directly. The more men he loses the more desperate he will become. Then we can take advantage of that."

"What of all the villages in the lower Highlands?" asked Seneca, the gleam in his eye suggesting that he liked Thomas' approach, but he was still worried about the potential impact on the Highland people.

"We can only defend so much of the Highlands as Renn said, so we move everyone to the upper Highlands, beyond the higher passes, to the larger villages centered on the Crag. That will be our base for our raiding parties."

"A good plan, Thomas," agreed Seneca. "But what of our northern border? More and more Ogren are coming into the Highlands. If we allow them to get a foothold we will never dislodge them."

"A valid concern," agreed Thomas. "I already have some friends watching the northern Highlands. I will ask them to take a more aggressive role regarding the Ogren war parties coming across the Northern Steppes."

Seneca nodded, evidently satisfied with Thomas' response. "For this to work we need to know where Killeran's men are going before they do. Otherwise, our raiding parties will fail."

"Don't worry," said Thomas with a sly grin. "I think I can help with that."

5

SOMETHING NEW

Kaylie Carlomin, Princess of Fal Carrach, followed after the cowled figure who had saved her, the woman requiring her to stay silent as they worked their way cautiously through the streets and alleys of Ballinasloe. She was the princess of Fal Carrach. This city was in her blood. It was her city. Yet she skulked through her home like a thief in the night.

The last few hours had been a blur. Upon learning of the plot to assassinate her father, she had decided to take matters into her own hands, thinking that she could ferret out the culprits on her own. She admitted now that sneaking out of the Rock and then trying to learn the identity of the suspected assassin had been a mistake. If not for her unknown rescuer, she would be lying gutted in an alley right now or worse. Still, though thankful for the help, she was irritated with herself for not thinking things through. Instead of rushing off, she should have taken the time to develop a real strategy.

Arriving at the docks without incident, the woman grabbed her arm, pulling her deeper into the shadows. Several minutes passed, the woman as still as the night as the silence deepened. Diminutive in size and wearing a dark cloak with a hood that hid her features, she seemed to be waiting for something. Kaylie looked out from the alley at the empty square in front of her. On its far side was the long bridge that led out into Ballinasloe's harbor and would take her to the Rock and safety. Why not just go across now? They could make it if they moved quickly.

Kaylie was about to suggest just that but held her tongue, a bolt of fear striking her heart. The men who had taken her, as well as several others, noiselessly emerged from several alleys, meeting in the square in front of them. She heard whispers and muttered curses before the men separated into smaller groups and crept off in different directions. Thankfully, none of the groups selected the alley in which they hid. The woman waited several minutes more, standing still as a stone, allowing the time to drag on until she was absolutely certain that the way was clear before giving Kaylie a light tug on her sleeve.

They walked quickly and quietly across the square. Kaylie shifted her gaze from one alley to the next, scanning for any movement behind them, fearful that some of the men searching for them would find them once they walked onto the span that connected the harbor to the fortress. But the woman didn't seem the least bit concerned, striding purposefully across the bridge. It was several minutes before the closed gates became visible.

Kaylie expected that they would have to attract the attention of the guards on duty to gain admittance to the castle, but when they reached the end of the bridge, the gates looming before them, the woman didn't stop. Instead, she bore to the left across the rocky ground that dropped off into the sea until they were some distance along the wall from the gates.

"What are you ..."

Before Kaylie could complete her question, the woman shushed her. Standing in front of the wall for several long seconds, she ran her hand along the stone then pushed in on a barely detectable indentation. A small door-size section of the wall swung inward on silent hinges carved into the stone.

Kaylie could barely contain her shock. "How did you know ..."

The woman pulled her through the doorway quickly, making sure it closed behind them before grasping the lamp that Kaylie had seen in the then dim now complete darkness. The woman lit the lamp and began walking up the musty staircase. Kaylie knew there were hidden passageways throughout the Rock. She had used many of them, most frequently as a child because of the fun of sneaking through her home, hiding from her father, trying to scare the guards. But she had never found this hidden path.

For several minutes Kaylie followed the woman through tunnels she never knew existed. Finally, her rescuer stopped, shining the lamp so that she could examine the rough-cut stone that appeared to their front. Looking behind them, Kaylie realized that their travels through the castle walls had taken them higher within the keep. They had reached a dead end with nothing but blackness around the top steps upon which they now stood. The woman reached out and touched a notched stone, then stepped back, letting the hidden door open toward them without a sound. They stepped through quickly and the stone slid shut on their heels.

Kaylie looked around in amazement. They had arrived in her private chamber, a single lamp burning brightly by her bed just like she had left it before heading out on her ill-conceived adventure. How did this woman know who she was? How did she know how to sneak through the castle's hidden passageways? How did she help her escape a gang of roughnecks through alleys and streets that she assumed those men knew better than her? A dozen other questions ran through her mind, making it hard for her to know where to begin. She decided to start with the most relevant.

"Who are you and why did you help me?" Kaylie asked, finally getting a question out as the woman dropped her hood.

Though petite in size, Kaylie sensed an inner strength within her rescuer, a presence that made Kaylie catch her breath. The woman's sparkling blue eyes, set off by her dark, chestnut-colored hair, mesmerized her, making her think of Thomas. The only difference was the color.

The woman stared at Kaylie for several long moments, seemingly taking in everything about her. Kaylie felt as if she were being stripped apart and put back together by the woman's gaze. That her rescuer was evaluating every good and bad decision she had ever made, every mistake and success, every hope and dream.

So this is the girl who has captured the attention of my grandson, the woman thought. The young princess had blue eyes the color of the sea, her long, raven-black hair, held by a silver clasp, reaching to her waist. She could understand how this beautiful young lady had caught his eye, the mischievous gleam in her gaze likely hard for him to resist. But the cloaked woman also sensed a strength in the girl, a resilience and courage, which no doubt would attract her grandson, as well as an impetuousness and strongmindedness that reminded her of her own daughter. She pushed that thought from her mind, not having the strength or desire to follow down that sad road at the moment.

"I was curious. And a good thing, too."

"Curious? You helped me because you were curious?"

The woman ignored Kaylie and stepped out on to the balcony, head cocked to the side, apparently listening for something before coming back into the room, satisfied by whatever she had discovered.

"What were you doing following dangerous men at night in the city?" the woman asked sharply. "It's not something a princess should be doing. It's reckless and irresponsible."

"How did you ..."

"I'm not a fool, girl. Now answer the question."

The woman's penetrating gaze almost overwhelmed Kaylie. But she fought against it.

"Why should I trust you?" she asked, ignoring the woman's question and struggling to keep the nervousness from her voice.

The woman's startling blue eyes hardened for an instant, then softened. "That's the first question you should have asked."

"Nevertheless, my question stands." Kaylie was pleased with herself, able to muster an imperious tone.

The woman smiled, liking this young woman's verve. She reached beneath her cloak and pulled out a silver pendant. The metal shined brightly in the light of the room's single lamp.

"Do you know what this represents?"

Kaylie stared at the triangular silver amulet, its corners smooth, the gently curling horn of a unicorn carved into the metal. "I do. But I never thought ..."

"Most people will never see its like. But for now it should tell you that you can trust me. Now back to my original question. Why were you following those men?"

Kaylie realized that there was no use in lying to this woman, so over the next several minutes she revealed her purpose and all she had discovered about the plot against her father.

"Well, then, we'll have to do something about it, won't we?"

Kaylie stared at the small woman, not expecting her to accept her explanation outright. Moreover, her rescuer's presence unsettled her. Most queens could dominate a gathering. Sarelle Makarin, Queen of Benewyn, immediately came to mind, as she had the ability to capture every eye and silence every conversation just by walking into a room. But none could compare to this woman.

"What do you mean we'll do something about it?"

"We'll talk more later. Now get some sleep."

"But how will you…"

"I said sleep, girl."

The woman walked out on to the balcony. Kaylie quickly followed after, wanting an answer to her question, but as the cool nighttime breeze struck her, she realized her rescuer was gone. She had simply vanished into the late-night gloom.

Kaylie stood there for a moment, shocked that the woman had disappeared into the darkness. She leaned over the ledge, noting that there was nothing under the balcony but a drop of a hundred feet to the courtyard below. Then again, having seen the amulet, she shouldn't have been surprised, remembering the tales her father had told her. A strange, unnerving, and extremely competent woman. Kaylie didn't know what she would have done and what would have happened without her assistance.

She decided to take the strange woman's advice and get some sleep after failing to stifle a yawn. Why did that woman seem so familiar? That thought continued to play through her mind as she lay on her bed and finally drifted off to sleep just as the sun began to peek above the horizon. Her dreams brought her back time and again to Thomas' sparkling green eyes and when she had seen him for the first time in the Burren.

6

FIRST LESSON

The following day seemed to drag on, time barely moving. Woken up early and not having slept well because of the late hour she went to bed, Kaylie had barely made it through the day. Sitting at the desk in her chamber and going through some of the materials she needed to review now that her father was away from the Rock, ranging from proposed contracts to legal claims that needed to be settled, she had a difficult time concentrating on the various matters that demanded her attention. Instead, time after time, despite her best efforts, her focus drifted to the plot against her father and the woman who had rescued her. How had she found her in Ballinasloe? Had she followed her when she snuck out of the Rock?

"I tracked you through your ability in the Talent."

Kaylie almost fell out of her chair, astonished to see the diminutive woman from last night walk through the open doors leading to the balcony. Her rescuer appeared refreshed, energized, as if the events of the previous night had had no effect on her. Her commanding presence filled the room, and Kaylie felt a small twinge of jealousy in that she could not yet do the same.

"What are you talking about?" asked Kaylie, unwilling to confirm or deny the woman's assumption about where her mind had wandered.

The woman appraised her with a knowing smile, appreciating the girl's stubbornness.

"Come now, Kaylie. If we're going to work together, then we need to trust one another."

"Can I trust you?" she asked. Even after all the woman had done for her the night before, even after recognizing the amulet that signified that the woman was a Sylvan Warrior, doubts remained.

"You can't," the woman replied. "Not completely. Not yet. Better to be wary until we've worked together a bit more. Trust is earned, not given. I'm sure in your position you're aware of that."

"Yes," Kaylie replied. "My father says much the same thing."

"A smart man, your father."

"You know my father?" asked Kaylie, the possibility surprising her.

"Yes, though it's been some time since we last saw one another. Some time, indeed. I've always liked him, you know. A good head on his shoulders, but he also knows when to follow his heart. The mark of a good king."

"How do you know my father?" The woman's revelation had aroused Kaylie's interest.

"A question for another time, young lady. Now I don't have all day, nor do you. You have two more questions. Ask them quickly, then we can begin."

The longer Kaylie engaged in conversation with this woman, the more unsettled she became. But there was something about her that she liked even with the woman's hardened exterior. Something that suggested she could be listened to and trusted. She didn't come across as one of the many hangers-on who circulated through her father's court, more interested in what Kaylie, as heir to the Fal Carrach throne, could do for them rather than building a real relationship or friendship. Trusting her instincts, Kaylie decided to take a risk.

"What's your name?"

"Rya."

Kaylie waited expectantly, wanting more. Instead, the woman's sharp gaze remained on her, a quick motion of her hand suggesting she get on with it.

"Work together? What do you mean work together?"

"If you're to learn the Talent, then you need a teacher. I'm your teacher." The diminutive woman stood in front of Kaylie, an inner strength emanating from her, a challenge in her eyes.

Kaylie took some time to consider the situation. The woman had saved her life last night. Moreover, she knew the inner workings of the Rock and had done her no harm, and she had shown her an amulet that was still valued here in the Rock. But with all that had happened, the fear of an assassin still in the back of her mind, what was she to do?

"Why should I trust you?"

"You're growing tiresome, child," replied Rya sharply. "It seems we've stepped back to last night. We've already been through this. As I said, better to be wary. Trust is earned, not given. We can begin your training in the Talent now and after a time we can both decide if we trust one another to continue the lessons, for if I don't trust you to follow my instructions and heed my warnings our work together will end."

Kaylie sighed in resignation, admitting to herself that she had already made up her mind. The thought of touching the natural magic of the world again thrilled her. "How do you know I can use the Talent?"

"You tell me."

Kaylie bit back an angry retort, thinking for a moment rather than allowing her irritation to get the better of her. She knew that interacting with Rya would require patience, certainly not one of her stronger qualities. "Because you can use the Talent as well."

"Correct. And so our trust between one another begins to build."

"How did you disappear off the balcony last night? That is a skill I would really like to learn."

"A question to be answered on another day. We have much to do and not much time so let's get started."

Rya stepped into the room, taking off her cloak and settling herself in a chair facing Kaylie's desk. She stared at the young woman for several minutes, seeming to take in everything about her in that one glance just as she did the night before. Then for the first time since Kaylie met Rya, the older woman smiled.

"You've acquired some basic skill in the Talent," said Rya. "And that's a good thing. It gives us something to build on. But if you're truly going to reach your potential, which I believe could be substantial, you need more consistent instruction."

Kaylie smiled as well. Substantial skill in the Talent sounded very appealing to her.

"So tell me, Princess, how did you first learn you had some ability in the Talent?"

"I met a boy in Tinnakilly at the last Eastern Festival," Kaylie started, hesitating for a moment, a catch in her throat, but realizing there was nothing to be gained by holding back, and then everything poured out. "He won the archery contest. There was something about him that caught my attention. He wasn't like the boys here in the Rock, the sons of lords and wealthy merchants who see me as a prize rather than as a person. And I had met him before when I was in the Burren with some friends. He saved us from two Ogren. Well, it wasn't just him, but also his friend, this massive wolf that's as large as a small horse. It was the most incredible experience."

Kaylie continued on, offering more details about her

encounter in the Burren, until Rya held her hand up, signaling for her to stop. Rya smiled to herself, remembering that evening when Rynlin and Thomas had returned to the Isle of Mist after spending time in the Highlands. So much had changed since then, except for the fact that Rynlin, her husband, as usual had failed to provide her with a full explanation of what had happened that day. Typical. So typical. They'd have to have another long talk about that when next she saw him.

"Let's focus on my original question, Kaylie."

"Oh, yes, sorry," Kaylie said, somewhat chagrined. "Anyway, I met this boy at the Festival. After he won the archery contest, we went for a walk in the woods surrounding the tournament fields. He showed me some of the things he could do with the Talent, and then he showed me how I could do it as well. Before we parted, he also gave me some lessons on how I can try to improve my skills, at least to a certain extent, on my own. So I've been doing that a bit as time allows. But nothing more than that."

Rya struggled to control her temper before responding. She should have expected as much. Sometimes that boy was more trouble than he was worth. Playing at the Talent without competent instruction was too dangerous. Taking a deep breath to calm herself, she turned her attention back to the young woman sitting before her.

"I see. And Thomas didn't mention the rules or consequences for the use of the Talent, did he?"

"No," she replied, surprise evident in her voice. "How did you know his name?"

"That boy will be the death of me some day," said Rya, shaking her head in dismay and ignoring Kaylie's question.

"You know him?"

Kaylie was surprised, but then also pleased. This might be an opportunity to learn more about the young man she continued to think about and mourn, the events in Tinnakilly still weighing heavily upon her.

"I have some history with him, yes. Sometimes more than I would like. But that's not relevant to our discussion right now. Is there anything else I need to know?"

"I betrayed him," she replied, tears beginning to form in the corners of her eyes.

Kaylie explained what had happened when she and Thomas went on a picnic the next day. How Ragin had appeared with soldiers and captured Thomas, but not before Thomas, even though heavily drugged, killed several of the soldiers.

"I swear I didn't know what was going to happen. I don't even remember anything from when Thomas and I first sat down to eat and then arriving back at the fortress and seeing Lord Chertney standing there smiling in the rain as they dragged Thomas off to the dungeon."

"Wait a moment," said Rya, leaning forward in her chair, the intensity of her gaze making Kaylie uncomfortable. "Chertney was there?"

"Yes, he was particularly pleased. He came across as just having won the golden goose at the local fair."

Rya sat back, taking a moment to contemplate this new information, but not surprised by it. She should have expected as much. Her grandson was impetuous, but not stupid. And he was also very good at forgetting key details when asked for explanations. If Chertney had set the trap, that would explain quite a bit.

"Everyone makes mistakes, girl. But you need to let this one go. It wasn't your fault."

"What do you mean?"

Kaylie had carried this burden ever since Thomas had been taken. When he escaped, and apparently died doing so by choosing to jump from the battlements rather than be skewered by the crossbow bolts shot at him by the guards, her anguish had been extreme. She was the cause of his death. Thinking of her betrayal tore her heart apart.

"I mean you were caught in the middle of something over which you had no control."

"Still, it's because of me that he's ..."

"You, Thomas and I have the ability to use the Talent," cut in Rya. "Did Thomas explain where the Talent comes from?"

"He said that the Talent was a magic that came from the world around us. Those who can use the Talent are harnessing the power of nature."

"Correct. Did Thomas tell you about others who can make use of this natural power but for their own ends?"

"No."

"That fool boy," said Rya, huffing in disbelief.

She rose from her chair, needing to walk in order to release some of her pent-up exasperation. You'd think with all the training that she and Rynlin had given Thomas, he would have been smart enough to teach Kaylie properly if he was going to reveal the power lurking dormant within her. She stopped to study Kaylie one more time. Perhaps there was a reason why he hadn't gotten very far. She could see how quickly Thomas could have become smitten with this beautiful young lady.

"When I first arrived, you asked how I found you."

"Yes, you said it was because I could use the Talent."

"Yes. I could sense your ability in the Talent. What Thomas didn't explain was that there are others who can use a similar power, but in this case Dark Magic, granted to them by the Shadow Lord. It's an affront to nature and it comes at an unimaginable cost, but there are those who are willing to do anything, to sell their very soul in fact, in order to gain power. These individuals can also sense Dark Magic or the Talent, as the two powers are closely related, how they are used, for what purpose, being their primary distinction. And that's what I mean by consequences. If I can find you, so can someone who can use Dark Magic, unless you learn how to shield your Talent from those with the ability to find you."

"Can you show me how to do that?" asked Kaylie, fearful of what might happen if she ran across someone who could use Dark Magic.

The fact that there were some people who could use Dark Magic didn't unsettle her in the least. With all that had happened to her in the past year, she didn't think anything could fluster her anymore.

"You can count on it. In fact, I'll teach you how to mask your ability before I leave tonight. But let's go back for a moment. Chertney can use Dark Magic. You said Thomas had been drugged. That was to dull his senses so he couldn't use the Talent."

"That makes sense," said Kaylie. "But if Chertney could use Dark Magic ..." She stopped for a moment, her mind working quickly.

"Go on, girl. Tell me what you're thinking."

Kaylie had kept the thought to herself, not wanting to appear foolish, but Rya wanted her to take a risk. So she did.

"I was thinking that if Chertney could use Dark Magic, he could have used it against me so that I wouldn't know what I was doing."

"Well done, girl," said Rya. "Thomas being taken wasn't your fault. You probably had no control over your actions. You were simply being used as a way to get close to Thomas. You had no choice in the matter. No control over your decisions or actions."

Kaylie felt as if a huge weight had been lifted off her chest, yet she still felt responsible. And angry at being used.

Rya sensed the emotions roiling within her. "Everyone makes mistakes, girl. You must move on."

"But, he's dead because of me. I ..."

Rya's voice turned unexpectedly harsh. "From what you said, his death was never confirmed. Did you see a body?"

Kaylie was shocked by the fire in Rya's words, not knowing how to respond.

"Strong tone for a lady, yes? But I'm trying to make a point. Dead or alive, Thomas isn't the issue here. What's done is done. What we need to focus on is your father. Now, what do you plan to do about these assassins?"

"Me? But I ..."

"You already started, girl. With your father away, you rule the Rock and Ballinasloe. Your plan from last night, though brave, was a foolhardy and dangerous first step. We can chalk that up to inexperience. Now, examining the challenge and the threat more thoroughly and with greater forethought, what are we going to do next?"

Kaylie stared at Rya for a moment, then collected herself. Rya was right. She ruled Ballinasloe while her father was away. It was time for her to act like it.

"Where do we start?" asked Kaylie, looking at Rya with both anticipation and consternation. She felt overwhelmed and hoped that the strong woman sitting before her would help to guide her.

Her fears threatened to get the better of her. She feared for her father, and for her city and Kingdom as well. Yes, she had been trained since a very young age to assume her father's place on the throne, but this was all too real. Too unexpected. Too fast. She didn't feel ready to handle so much responsibility. And the consequences of failure were more than she could bear to consider.

"You tell me," replied Rya. "One day you will rule Fal Carrach. You will be responsible for this Kingdom. This is your problem to solve."

The petite woman sat calmly in the chair facing her, an expectant look on her face. Kaylie sensed that Rya could tell her exactly what to do, but had no intention of doing so. She growled in irritation, her aggravation threatening to get the better of her. She realized that this, in itself, likely was her first lesson with her new instructor.

Fine, she would approach it as such. Kaylie tried to remember all that she had learned, particularly from her father, the many times he had attempted to educate her in the intricacies of power and ruling a Kingdom, despite her being more interested in chasing after vapid boys at the time. As several of her lessons came back to her, with greater confidence she began to put the pieces together.

"With Kael Bellilil away with my father, call on Garlan, Captain of the Guard. Have him increase the guards for each rotation, but quietly. Charge them with searching the Rock for any additional secret passageways that we may not be aware of. Send out loyal soldiers to the waystations on the roads extending from Ballinasloe so that they can warn my father before he returns. Disperse some trusted men throughout the castle and the town to see if they can discreetly root out more information before the assassin can strike. The more information we can obtain now, the better our decisions will be in the future."

Rya nodded approvingly. "That's a good start. Let's go meet this Garlan."

7

CHANGE IN PLAN

The Shadow Lord stood on a balcony that allowed him to peer out over the windswept, broken, and deserted city. He had waited so long, so long that his patience wore thin. But he could wait a bit longer. He needed to if he wanted his plans to come to fruition.

His long black cloak didn't stir despite the breeze. He seemed impervious to the elements, such as the wind that blew great gusts of blackened dirt into the air, creating small dust storms that spun through the abandoned streets of Blackstone. Through it all, he stood there calmly, still as the dead stone of the city he had made his own. The shadow seemed to follow him, swirling around him, hiding him. At times only his blood-red, blazing eyes gave him away, burning with a malice and hate centuries old.

Chertney's efforts had disappointed the Shadow Lord. He had never failed like this before. With the power that Chertney wielded, the power that the Shadow Lord himself had deigned to give him, he couldn't understand how a boy yet to reach his full potential could continue to escape him. And this boy was becoming more and more of a problem. The Shadow Lord still needed time before setting the final parts of his plan in motion. He wasn't strong enough to step out of the shadows. Not yet. This boy had to be removed before he revealed himself, and the time for that to happen continued to slip away much like sand through an hourglass.

"I must change my plans, Malachias. We must move faster, before the boy can interfere again."

The raspy voice of the Shadow Lord, barely a whisper, carried to the back of the chamber. A tall, thin man stood in the shadows, his sable robes hiding his shape. His bald pate reflected what little light trickled into the room, nevertheless his mesmerizing black orbs were visible despite the gloom.

"Yes, Master. I understand."

"You will not fail me, will you, Malachias?"

"No, Master. I will not."

"For if you do, you will pay a price. A price you will not want to pay."

"Yes, Master. If I must, I will."

"Then go and do as I have commanded, Malachias. Show me that you deserve better than Chertney. Show me that when the time comes for the Dark Horde to descend on the Kingdoms, you deserve a place at my side."

"Yes, Master."

With barely a sound, Malachias faded into the mist surrounding him and disappeared. The Shadow Lord continued to stare out over the desolate landscape. After waiting all these centuries, he was ready to reclaim what belonged to him. He had been denied the Kingdoms once. It would not happen again. Yet a boy stood in his way. He found the entire notion inconceivable, almost humorous. But if matters progressed as he expected with Malachias, the boy wouldn't be a problem much longer. And if Malachias stumbled as Chertney and so many others had, perhaps the traitor who could get close to the boy would succeed. Either way, he could finally lay his worries aside. For the boy finally would be dead.

$$8$$

TOUCH OF SHADOW

Rodric Tessaril grimaced with distaste as he walked into his son's room. Despite the brightness of the day, the heavy drapes remained closed with just a tiny slit open to allow a thin line of light to illuminate the gloom. Once the High King had taken pride in his son, believing that he resembled the High Kings of old. Tall. Handsome. Regal. All the characteristics that he himself seemed to lack. All the perceived shortcomings that drove him in his quest for power, in his quest for the respect he felt others perpetually denied him, yet would never be denied his son. But no more. Now when looking at his son he experienced only disgust and regret. Ragin's pride and arrogance had cost him dearly. Not only his son, but also himself, for Ragin's stupidity had made Rodric's task all the more difficult.

Ragin stood at the window, peeking through the open slit. Hearing the door open, after several long minutes, he turned reluctantly toward the sound, knowing who the visitor would be as no one else came to his room anymore. Ragin's failure had taken from him more than his good looks. It had also threatened his path to the Armaghian throne. Ragin faced his father, his lips curling into a sneer. A horrible, weeping scar ran down his right cheek to the base of his neck. An eye patch covered his ruined right eye. Yet more frightening than his disfiguring injury was the glint of feverish madness that sparked in his good eye.

"This obsession is quickly becoming insanity!" screamed Rodric, his face red with rage, spittle flying from his lips. "You were a fool to challenge the boy, even in his weakened state. You'd seen his abilities, his skill with a blade. You paid the price for your own arrogance! You have no one to blame but yourself."

Ragin's sneer grew larger, the scar cracking with the movement of his cheek muscles, making his appearance all the more difficult to look at. His father felt the need to have the same argument every time he deigned to enter his son's apartment, as if the first dozen times hadn't been enough.

"You forget yourself, father. If I had succeeded we wouldn't be having this conversation. And your plans almost would be complete."

"Maybe so. But you didn't succeed, Ragin. You failed. And now we both must pay the price for your foolishness and incompetence."

Rodric stared at his son awhile longer, expecting a response but receiving none, wanting the argument to continue so that he would have an outlet for his rage. Instead, Ragin ignored him and turned away, having tired of the game. He stared out the window once more, mumbling to himself too quietly for Rodric to make out the words.

With nothing more to say, the High King turned on his heel and slammed the door behind him as he left. Rodric sensed a change in his son. The arrogance and feeling of entitlement remained, yet a shadow resided in him now. A darkness had seeped into his heart, and that unsettled Rodric. Although he wouldn't admit it to himself, it also made him afraid.

Ragin waited impatiently for his father to leave, taking small pleasure in the fact that he had irritated him so easily. Alone once more, he relished the quiet, the opportunity to think, to plan, to scheme. He knew. He didn't know how, but he knew. He knew in his heart the boy survived. He didn't die on the rocks as everyone said. He knew the coward who had scarred him survived the fall. And he knew they would meet again.

But when they did, he would need to be ready. For his father was right. The boy surpassed him with a blade and apparently had abilities Ragin had never considered. If Ragin were to have any chance at success, he needed to even the odds any way that he could. And he would. He'd do anything necessary to obtain his revenge. Even sell his soul.

9

———————

SPIDER'S WEB

Rodric left his son's chambers unable to shake the sense of foreboding that had buried itself within his gut. He knew his son's weaknesses and had ignored them for years, thinking that as he matured sense would replace his impetuousness and conceit. Clearly it had not. But now, his son's failure appeared to have changed something within him, as if those weaknesses had been pushed closer to the surface and had taken control of Ragin's decision making, whatever clarity he had once had now replaced by an unmitigating drive for revenge.

He started to walk down the dimly lit hall, darkened alcoves lining the walkway for as far as the eye could see. His thoughts wandered as they always did upon visiting Ragin, seeking some solution to this latest setback yet failing to find something to grasp hold of, when he stopped abruptly, sensing a presence to his right.

"Lurking in the shadows once again, daughter?"

With a smirk Corelia Tessaril, her blonde tresses fashioned into a series of ever more intricate braids, stepped out of an alcove.

"Good morning, father."

"I have little patience, Corelia. Especially after speaking with Ragin."

"I understand, father. It was not my intention to bother you as I know how difficult it is for you to come to terms with my brother's shortcomings. I was simply ..."

"Doing as you normally do," finished Rodric. "Gliding to and fro, picking up information here and there, all so that you can put it to use at some later date."

Corelia could have denied it. But she chose not to, deciding that this was her opportunity to perhaps gain an advantage over her now damaged brother.

"Indeed I was, father. It seems that Ragin's failure on the battlements has affected him in a way that could harm your plans."

"What do you know of my plans, Corelia?" Rodric's voice came out in a hissed whisper. Normally he enjoyed conversing with his daughter. She challenged him constantly, though never going too far. But now she was heading into potentially lethal territory.

Corelia noted the change in her father, but she ignored it. Realizing this may be her best opportunity, she stepped closer to him, the intensity of her gaze forcing her father to step back.

"More than you probably want me to know," she replied. "Yet that's not something to fear. In fact, it could perhaps work to your advantage."

"How so?" an intrigued Rodric asked, suddenly wary but also remembering his daughter's aptitude for untangling, or tangling, intricate schemes as her goals required.

"I know that you have certain allies who are assisting you in your adventures," she began.

Rodric stepped forward as quick as a striking snake, squeezing her wrist. "Better not to speak of my partners, Corelia. Better not to know more than you already do."

Corelia could have cowered, playing the frightened girl, in response to her father's action. Instead, she decided that now was the time to step forward and challenge her father, to show him her true mettle. Yanking her wrist from his grasp, she spoke in a low, commanding tone.

"I know what I know, father. I know about your allies. I know about your arrangements with the various Kingdoms that support you. I know your plans for the Highlands. But most of all, I know that I can help you."

The strength and certainty of his daughter's words surprised Rodric, but also secretly pleased him. Perhaps this was an opportunity that could benefit him. Perhaps he had been focusing too much of his attention on the wrong child.

"Tread carefully, Corelia. What you talk of harbors a danger you cannot even imagine."

"And yet you continue on your course, despite that danger."

Rodric nodded. "To achieve great power often ..."

"Great risk is required," completed Corelia. "I recall your teachings, father. Remember, I am your daughter, after all. We, two, are much alike. Perhaps we are even more alike than you and Ragin."

Rodric stepped back from Corelia, looking at her from a new perspective, seeing her in a different light. He realized that she was no longer the young girl who constantly struggled for his attention, competing with her brother in anything and everything. No, she had grown into a clever woman who clearly knew what she wanted and likely knew how to obtain it.

"What did you have in mind, Corelia?"

"An alliance, of sorts," she replied, chin held high, her voice strong. "I have ways of obtaining information that can be of use to you in achieving your plans. And I can be of use to you as well in other ways. I know that originally Ragin had an important role to play, possibly with respect to Fal Carrach and Gregory's daughter. That strategy seems to be unraveling as I doubt King Gregory will look kindly on an unstable prince as a match for his precious daughter."

"Continue," prodded Rodric, the gleam in his eyes calculating.

Corelia smiled, realizing that the risk she had taken was bearing fruit, that she was succeeding. With renewed confidence, she forged on.

"Ragin appears to be ... broken. His failure on the battlements has damaged him, and in turn that has harmed your plans. Assuming that things work out in the Highlands as you wish, I believe there are other ways that we can gain control of Fal Carrach through Kaylie Carlomin. It just requires a little more work and a slightly different tack."

Rodric eyed his daughter shrewdly, weighing her. He had always viewed his two children as tools. For him, love was never a consideration. Ragin and Corelia had purposes to serve. If Ragin could no longer play his needed role, perhaps Corelia could step into his place.

"It appears that not only have you identified many of the webs I've been weaving, but you've also been working on several of your own."

"Yes, I have," she replied. "But only with the goal of helping you. After all, like father, like daughter."

For the first time in days, Rodric laughed. Not so much at his daughter's attempted humor and obvious lie, but rather it appeared that although one door had closed, another had opened. With it, a new opportunity had come to the fore.

"We will speak more of this later this evening, Corelia. You will tell me your plans and we will see what can be done about them."

"Yes, father," she replied, her smile radiant. She had won the first skirmish! She had taken the first step toward gaining her father's trust and, perhaps, supplanting her brother.

Rodric pivoted abruptly, beginning to walk down the hallway once more, before turning back a final time.

"Corelia, a word of advice?"

"Of course, father."

"Just be careful of the webs you weave. You never know what you might catch. You might not like it."

10

HOMECOMING

For the first time in a very long time Thomas felt some trepidation. He stepped through one of the massive holes that had been blown through the Crag's forty-foot thick outer wall almost a decade before, one of the many paths the Ogren had used to assault and conquer the home of the Highland Lord. His home once again.

He stood there in the quiet of the late afternoon, the sun slowly setting in the west and splaying shadows across the stone. Half of the eight towers, joined together by the now pock-marked outer curtain which formed the Crag's perimeter defense, had been destroyed during the attack that night, now no more than piles of rubble. The central stronghold, except for the gaping maw left by the torn and twisted portcullis, appeared to be in better shape, even with the tops of three towers having been destroyed. The squared walls were unmarked other than for the ivy and vines that had taken advantage of the time the Highlanders had been forced to hide within the upper passes of the Highlands. Putting his hand to his face to block the sun, Thomas stared up into the sky, noting the handful of kestrels drifting on the warm breezes, before focusing his gaze on the Roost, the tallest tower in the Crag. The tower in which he had lived before his grandfather had been killed.

Why he was nervous, he didn't know. He was the only one here, after all, other than the kestrels drifting in the sky and the ghosts of those who had perished here. Perhaps it wasn't the place that bothered him so much as the challenges he now faced. When he lived here in the Crag, despite being the grandson of the Lord of the Highlands, he had been an outsider, or at least was treated that way. Because of what the Highlanders took to be his mother's strange abilities, those same abilities that had begun to materialize within himself at an early age, for the most part he had been ignored at best and shunned at worst. No matter what he tried, no matter what he did to fit in, he couldn't change the perception that he was different. That he was something other than what the Highlanders wanted or expected. Only his grandfather and a few Marchers, such as Coban, had accepted him for who he was, his own father always finding some excuse to be away from him.

Benlorin Kestrel had claimed that he couldn't be with his son because he had responsibilities elsewhere, Talyn having charged him with defending the northern Highlands from the more frequent incursions of dark creatures. But Thomas knew the truth. His father blamed him for the loss of his wife, Thomas' mother Marya, who had died giving birth to him. He had overheard his father in an argument with his grandfather once confirming it, one of the few times that Benlorin had returned to the Crag from his camp in the Highlands.

After hearing that, Thomas had given up, realizing that trying to fit in wasn't worth the effort, realizing that he had no control over others' perceptions of him. He could only be who he was meant to be, not what others may have wanted him to be. So instead he focused on what he enjoyed doing, reading, spending time with his grandfather when time permitted, and exploring the forests surrounding the Crag. At times he was lonely, spending more time by himself than with others. But he had grown used to it.

Thomas tried to jolt himself from his reverie, wondering if his decision to return to the Crag if only for a little while was a good one. There were few good memories for him here, yet for some reason he felt the need to return, if only for a short while. He had become the Lord of the Highlands, taking his rightful place as the successor to Talyn Kestrel. And though his abilities in the Talent still seemed to put many of his Marchers on edge, uncomfortable with the power he controlled, they were practical men and women and they recognized the value of having someone like him in the lead. Someone who could combat the Dark Magic of the warlocks that had tormented them for almost a decade.

Remembering how his grandfather Talyn liked to remind him that there was no point in dwelling on the past, he pushed his thoughts to the side and walked with more confidence into the central keep, slipping between the broken steel pieces of the portcullis with ease. The remnants of the Marchers' last defense as they sought in vain to protect their Highland Lord were everywhere. Scattered, rusted blades, some partially covered by piles of stone caused by the warlocks who had accompanied the reivers, Ogren and Shades in the assault on that fateful night, littered the stone floor, though the remains of the defenders who had likely fallen here were nowhere to be seen. Knowing the proclivities of the Ogren for human flesh, he guessed at their unfortunate fate and promised their spirits that they would have their revenge.

Shouldering open the large, oak door that led into the keep, he stepped over the piles of stone rubble and splintered wooden beams that had fallen from the ceiling, heading to a darkened entrance, the door torn from its hinges and rotting on the floor. He began to climb the circular stairway that led up into the heart of the Roost, not needing a torch as his green eyes glowed brightly in the gloomy turret, giving him the capability to see easily in the encroaching darkness.

Almost to the top of the Roost, he came out of the circular staircase that lined the side of the tower into a small hallway. The dim light of an open doorway at the far end beckoned. Taking a deep breath, he moved on light feet down the hallway and stepped into the room. A fine dust covered everything. Yet, it was exactly how he remembered it. His bed with its tumble of blankets, now moldy and rotting away. His clothes pulled from his dresser, the one he had to climb in order to reach the very top shelf. His many books strewn about the floor. He smiled briefly at that. His messiness had saved his life when the assassins came for him that night. If not for the book the second assassin slipped on, allowing Thomas to scamper by and out into the hallway, thankfully running into his grandfather, he likely would have died that night. Such was the twist of fate.

He closed his eyes for just a moment, taking it all in, steadying himself. Coming here again, after so much time, he had hoped that he would feel like the Highland Lord in more than name, but he knew now that it wasn't to be so, at least not on this day. Doubts still plagued him. Doubts about whether he had done the right thing by returning to his homeland. Doubts about whether he was strong enough to do what needed to be done. Doubts about whether his strategy would work, for if it didn't it would mean the demise of the Marchers and the destruction of the Highlands all the sooner.

Thomas jumped back, hand going for his dagger, as a loud squawk echoed off the walls of his former chamber. He breathed a sigh of relief and felt a sense of wonder as he took in his guest. The massive kestrel had alighted on the windowsill of his room, its orange and white feathers sparkling in the waning light of the day. The bird perched there majestically, its sharp talons digging deeply into the stone.

For several minutes, the two stared at one another, Thomas almost losing himself in the sharp gaze of the kestrel. For some strange reason he felt like he knew this kestrel, as if their paths had crossed before. Perhaps when Rynlin and Rya had taught him how to use the Talent in order to shape change so that he could take on the trials to become a Sylvan Warrior. This kestrel resembled the one that had flown by his side after he had taken on the form of a kestrel himself and flown among the peaks of the Highlands for the first time. There were other times as well that he remembered encountering a kestrel similar to this one, so maybe it was the same predator. Maybe there was some strange connection between them. If so, he was glad for it.

The kestrel with its strong gaze infused him with a sense of calm, a sense of purpose. It was almost as if this majestic bird sought to share its strength with him, knowing of the challenges to come. As he continued to stare at the kestrel his confidence began to grow. He knew the risks he took, the dangers to be faced, and he would go forward as expected and as needed. He would do all he could to free his people, to give the Highlands hope and belief once more. He was the Highland Lord. The only way to feel like it was to act like it, and so he would.

The large kestrel lowered its sharp beak once, as if the bird had served its purpose, and then it used its talons to push itself backwards off the windowsill. Thomas rushed to the window, watching the kestrel as it glided down toward the ground, then with a single flap of its powerful wings launched itself up into the sky and toward the peaks of the Highlands.

Thomas took his time circling back down through the Roost, the darkness of the evening beginning to settle on the Crag. When he reached the main entrance he hesitated just a moment before pushing a door split in two, the damage obviously done by an Ogren battle axe, out of the way and entering the Hall of the Highland Lord. Scorch marks covered the back wall, and a few thick, charred ceiling beams reached down to the floor. Pieces of colored glass lined the eastern and western walls, the intricately designed windows that had allowed streams of color to shoot through the chamber shattered during the attack. Thomas turned his attention to the northern wall, pleased to see the throne of the Highlanders still in place. Though calling it such was a misnomer, for the throne was not a chair but actually was a large, smooth, raised stone upon which the Highland Lord stood when circumstances or his office required it. The Highlanders had never had much need of thrones or the other accoutrements of rank enjoyed and demanded by many of the other rulers in the Kingdoms. They viewed the Highland Lord as someone charged with serving them rather than the other way around.

He closed his eyes and took hold of the Talent, then extended his senses within the hall. His grandfather had died here to give him the time he needed to escape. For a moment, he thought that he could sense his grandfather's spirit in the room, a feeling of warmth and love spreading over him. But then, strangely, that feeling transitioned to something else, something cold and deadly.

Thomas opened his eyes and dove to the left, tumbling down behind one of the fallen beams as a burst of black energy shot through the air where he had been standing just a second before and struck the southern wall with a deafening boom. Peering over the beam, he saw a black-cloaked figure standing in the doorway to the hall, inky energy spinning between his outstretched hands. With a flick of his wrist, another burst of black energy shot toward Thomas, and then another, and another. Thomas rolled further to his left, allowing the fallen beam to take the brunt of the attack, but knowing that his strategy would eventually lead to his death if he remained where he was. The cowled figure had entered the hall, cornering Thomas.

A memory of training with one of his instructors in the martial arts came to mind. Antonin, First Spear of the Carthanians, was a simple and direct man. Over and over he had drummed into Thomas a basic philosophy. Attack. Always attack. Even when you should defend, attack. You will never win by defending. Although Thomas had spent hours arguing with Antonin regarding the logic of his advice, he thought that now was an excellent time to put that advice into practice.

Pulling in more of the Talent, Thomas formed a shield of white energy and stepped out from behind the fallen beam. His attacker had shifted to the left, seeking to take Thomas from behind. Momentarily surprised that Thomas had emerged, the cowled figure resumed his assault, balls of black energy streaking from his hands. Thomas raised his forearm, the shield of white energy deflecting the attacks. Then he stepped forward himself, maintaining his shield but with his free hand spinning shards of white, hot energy across his fingertips.

His assailant quickly became the defender as Thomas threw the shards of white energy toward him, the cowled figure raising a shield of swirling black mist to protect against the attack. But it wasn't a single assault as the shards of white energy became a steady stream, Thomas inexorably stepping forward to close the distance on his attacker, taking Antonin's advice and never giving the black-robed figure a chance to do anything else but defend. With each step, Thomas pulled in more of the Talent, increasing the intensity of the stream of white energy. And with each step, the black-cloaked figure took a step back. As Thomas continued his advance, pulling in more and more of the Talent, he reached a critical conclusion. He was stronger than his opponent. Smiling with that realization, Thomas released his shield and pushed forward, adding a second stream of white energy to the first.

It was then that the cowled attacker comprehended the enormity of his predicament. The boy was stronger than he was. The two streams of white energy had begun to eat away at the edges of the shield of black mist, the white energy slowly consuming the black tendrils, reducing the size of the shield by the second. The cowled figure's thoughts quickly turned to escape. Needing a distraction, Thomas' assailant flicked his wrist, a bolt of black energy blasting into the ceiling, several of the already splintered wooden beams breaking apart.

Thomas leapt to the side, barely avoiding the massive broken joists that crashed to the stone floor. A fog of dust and debris enveloped the hall. Nevertheless, with his sharp vision Thomas saw his attacker rapidly form a portal of swirling black and then step through it. With a crack, the portal closed and silence reigned once more in the Hall of the Highland Lord.

Thomas stood there in the grey cloud, having released his hold on the Talent. His attacker had escaped, though just barely. That fact annoyed him, but what bothered him more was the sense that there was something about his attacker that had been familiar. That he actually knew his attacker though he saw no more than a black-cloaked figure. He growled in irritation, feeling as if the hint to his dilemma remained just beyond his grasp.

Letting the problem go for the moment, as the dust finally settled Thomas turned his gaze once more to the stone upon which the Highland Lord traditionally stood. The last Highland Lord to step onto that stone had been his grandfather, Talyn Kestrel. Perhaps one day he would as well. But not yet. Not today. No, he had more pressing matters to attend to. He needed to move faster, thinking that this latest attack was one of desperation. Whether directed by Rodric or the Shadow Lord, he didn't know and he didn't care. But clearly whoever had set this latest assassin upon him was nervous. No, now was the time to strike. Now was the time to follow Antonin's advice, which had just proven useful, once again. Now was the time to attack.

11

THINGS TO DO

Garlan rubbed absently at the rough scar that marred his face. It ran from his ear down the right side to his chin and even after all these years continued to irritate him, the perpetually dry skin a constant bother. Once he had been handsome, some would even say debonair, and many of the young ladies living in Ballinasloe welcomed him, but not anymore. Now they said he grew violent the more he drank, and as the years passed he drank more and more. But he ignored what they said, knowing the truth. Knowing that the wound he had received so many years before had destroyed more than his once handsome visage.

He had served Fal Carrach faithfully for years, risking his life for the Kingdom. Yet all he had received in return was pain. He should have been the Swordmaster by now, but that path had been blocked by Kael Bellilil, that Highland usurper who had multiple reasons to return to his homeland but still chose to remain here. Garlan had earned that position, deserved to be Swordmaster, at least in his own mind, through years of hard work and sacrifice with very little given in return.

Garlan pushed these all-too-common thoughts away, a

constant nag that never seemed to leave him. The anger that often followed these recurrent, bitter reasonings would be a detriment, as would the drink that he so desperately desired but temporarily resisted, to what he needed to do next.

He had never expected to be called into the presence of the Princess of Fal Carrach. Much less be told that there was a threat to the crown and that he must take certain steps to prevent this threat from becoming reality. He grinned ruefully. And he had never expected the princess to have such strength and determination. There was more of her father in her than he had imagined.

Perhaps this was the opportunity he was seeking. A way to improve his position after years of unsuccessful and unnoticed attempts at demonstrating his value. After all, often loyalty could be bought at the right price.

Yet the audience with the princess worried him for other reasons as well. Who was that other woman standing behind the princess? She was striking. No, striking didn't do her justice. There was something quite appealing about her, in a dangerous sort of way.

Garlan shook his head, clearing his thoughts as he strode quickly down the hallway toward the guards' quarters. No matter. And no time to ponder. He had things to do. Then once they were completed, he would walk into Ballinasloe to his favorite tavern and have that drink he so desperately needed and deserved.

12

SURPRISE ATTACK

More than one hundred reivers stepped carefully through the woods, avoiding the crunch and crack of broken branches or dry leaves as much as possible, silently closing in on the small Highland village with the goal of springing their trap before the inhabitants awoke. The sun had just begun to brighten the sky to the east, the night-time dew soaking into their boots and leggings as they tread through the long grass and underbrush. They wanted to hurry, knowing that time worked against them and that they may have already lost the advantage of surprise. Still, they hesitated. The reivers had ruled much of the Highlands as their own for almost a decade, but in just the last year their supremacy had begun to disintegrate.

As a result, to a man they were wary, spending as much time scanning the village for movement as the forest surrounding them. They had heard the stories from their comrades. The sudden strikes. Marchers attacking lightning fast and without mercy, before sliding back between the trees and disappearing, rarely giving the reivers an opportunity to fight back.

But today, though still nervous and a little on edge, they felt more confident. They had spent the last hour approaching the village and their attempted stealth appeared to have paid off. All remained quiet among the Highland homes that lined the beaten down path leading into the hidden valley. In addition, just behind the reivers stood two short men draped in black cloaks. The cloaks covered them so completely that only their eyes, black orbs that glowed in even the slightest light, were visible. Warlocks. The warlocks were the reason the reivers had succeeded for so long in the Highlands, stealing the hidden riches of the land and enslaving its people. The Marchers had no defense against their Dark Magic.

Two scouts emerged from the forest just in front of the largest reiver, a broad-shouldered, hardened soldier with a scar that ran the length of his forehead down the right side of his face and continued beneath his collar. He viewed the scar as a mark of honor and ability. The man who had caused the gruesome injury had died, and he had not.

"Anything?" asked the tall reiver, gripping the hilt of his sword in anticipation.

Smoke had begun to rise through the chimneys of several of the small homes, the village beginning to awaken as the Highlanders started their morning cook fires. But no one had emerged onto the small village green yet. For a brief moment a pang of worry rushed through the reiver captain. He had expected at least one or two guards, yet none had been seen.

Perhaps this close to the taller peaks of the Highlands the Marchers didn't expect the reivers to make an appearance. Admittedly he and his men preferred the relative safety of the lower Highlands, as it was too easy to get cut off in the higher passes, giving the Marchers the opportunity to hound them and whittle down the reivers' superior numbers one by one. But the easier pickings to be found in the lower Highlands had dried up. It was as if the Highlanders had simply disappeared in the fog and mist that continually plagued these mountain peaks. Thus, the reason the reiver captain had been forced to take his men higher into the mountains in search of more slaves.

"No, Boru," answered one of the scouts. "All quiet, but likely not for long."

"Then let's get to it," said the reiver captain, motioning for his men to tighten the noose.

The warlocks stepped forward as well, standing behind Boru and sending a shiver through his body. Courageous to the point of being fearless in battle, Boru nevertheless feared the two creatures at his back. They felt like predators breathing down the back of his neck, and that unnerved him. At one time these creatures may have been men. But he didn't think they were now. They had become something else, something to fear, something less than human. Stories being what they were, he assumed that some of the tales about how they had obtained their Dark Magic had to have a few kernels of truth in them. But even if these stories contained just a few kernels, that was enough to keep a constant prickle of alarm flowing up and down his spine as he made use of their nefarious but useful skills.

Reaching the very edge of the clearing, Boru raised his sword, then slashed it down through the air. The reivers immediately charged into the Highland village, yelling and screaming, brandishing their swords, maces, and axes, hoping to terrorize the Highlanders and create chaos, thereby making their victory all the easier. Well versed in their task, the large raiding party broke into small groups as they stormed into the houses, knocking down doors and setting several of the homes on fire. The attack lasted only a few minutes, and as soon as it began Boru concluded that something was wrong. With exclamations of surprise and angry curses, the reivers assembled once more on the small village green at the center of the clearing, not a single captive in hand.

"Not a soul, Boru," said one of the reivers, spitting into the grass in anger. "It was made to look like the village was inhabited, what with the cook fires and all, but no one's here."

The arrows flew through the early morning shadows with a terrifying hiss before Boru could give any thought to that fateful discovery. Wave after wave, whistling through the air, darting between the trees and slicing into the reivers. Boru, the largest and most obvious target, felt the brunt of the attack. Three arrows sprouted from his chest in quick succession, driving him backwards. As his strength left him, he fell onto his back on the soft grass, watching his men drop around him, cries of pain, anguish, and fear rising up all across the green. Although even the smallest of movements proved a struggle his mind continued to work, telling him that the Marchers had planned the ambush well, pulling it off perfectly.

Boru glanced up as the two warlocks walked forward seemingly unafraid of the attack. A hail of arrows fell upon them, yet not a single one struck home, deflected by swirling shields of black mist that had formed around them as soon as the first arrow had punctured Boru's chest. He held out hope that the warlocks could regain control of the situation and give his few surviving men a fighting chance.

Then to his shock two bolts of white energy burst from the edge of the clearing, blasting through the warlocks' shields and driving through their bodies, their Dark Magic instantly disintegrating into a black dust that slowly disappeared. The two cowled figures stood their ground for a moment longer, steam rising from their chests, small fires beginning to burn on their cloaks and shirts, before they pitched forward, dead before they hit the dirt.

As darkness encroached on Boru, a coldness seeping into his body, he realized to his chagrin that his friends had been correct. Something stirred in the Highlands. Something deadly.

13

HELPING HAND

Catal Huyuk grunted from the strain, the corded muscles in his arms bulging from the effort of keeping the rusted blade from slicing into his chest. He had tracked this handful of Ogren for the entire day, waiting for them to make camp for the night. Then, once they had settled in for the evening, he had planned to sneak into their midst and slit their throats. Not the most gallant approach, but certainly the most effective. Moreover, it would mean five fewer Ogren killing and rampaging through the countryside.

He had left the Ogren to their tasks, moving a good distance away to wait until nightfall. But his plan had fallen apart when two other Ogren had appeared behind him out of the brush. They were as surprised to see him as he was to see them. He should have expected as much, knowing that the Charnel Mountains were filled with Ogren and other dark creatures, many seeking to cross the Northern Steppes and cause havoc in the Highlands. But he had been so focused on the group that he had been tracking that he had let his guard down.

The mountain of a man had acted instinctually, drawing his

dagger and stabbing one creature in the eye, killing it instantly. At the same time he swung his massive battle ax in a deadly arc, trying to disable the other Ogren by taking its leg off at the knee. The Ogren had shown unexpected dexterity, jumping over the strike and lunging at him with a growl. The beast's momentum knocked Catal Huyuk to the ground, which had led to his current predicament. He had managed to get his battle ax up in front of him, holding it like a staff when the Ogren swung its massive sword down, seeking to cleave him in two. He had caught the blow with his battle ax's handle, but the advantage remained with the Ogren, which used its bulk to continue to push down on Catal Huyuk, forcing the breath from his body as the hilt of his battle ax came closer and closer to the tip of his nose, and with it the pitted and corrupted steel of the Ogren's sword.

The Ogren roared in triumph, sensing victory, its sword slowly, ever so slowly, inching its way toward its target. Catal Huyuk struggled for breath, spots beginning to dance in front of his eyes. He heard the answering roar of another Ogren off in the distance, and he assumed that the party of dark creatures he had been following were hurrying this way to join in the fun. Catal Huyuk berated himself for allowing his overconfidence to get the better of him. This was not how things were supposed to work.

Close to losing consciousness, and knowing that if he did so his fate was sealed, he gathered his legs beneath him and with a last burst of strength pushed off the ground, dislodging the Ogren and sending it flying into the brush. Before the Ogren could disentangle itself from the thorns and grasping vines common to the Charnel Mountains, Catal Huyuk lunged at the beast. He twisted the grip of his battle ax so that the half-moon blade faced away and the long spike that protruded from the other side of the weapon faced downward. Then, using the last reserves of his strength, he raised the battle ax above his head and swung down, the spike impaling the Ogren to the rocky ground.

Gasping for air, Catal Huyuk took several deep breaths to steady himself. That damn Daran! The red-haired Sylvan Warrior, always ready with a joke and never seeming to take anything seriously, was supposed to have met him here among the southern peaks of the Charnel Mountains several days ago. But he had never appeared. What could have happened to him, he didn't know. If that scoundrel hadn't died making his way here, Catal Huyuk would make him wish that he had.

Hearing a rustle in the trees behind him, the Sylvan Warrior pulled his ax free and turned to face his next opponent. As he feared, the Ogren he had been tracking had heard the roar of its now dead ally and had decided to investigate. The first of the Ogren rushed forward, sword held above its head for a quick killing downstroke. Rather than hold his ground, Catal Huyuk charged toward the beast, rolling beneath the strike and with a backward swing slicing through the thick muscle of the beast's hamstrings with his battle ax. The Ogren howled in pain and surprise as it toppled to the ground, unable to push itself back to its feet.

Catal Huyuk rose to his feet faster than a man his size should be able to and continued his rush forward as a second Ogren stomped from between the stunted trees. The beast blocked the Sylvan Warrior's overhead strike, catching the ax's blade on its shield, but it missed the foot-long dagger that Catal Huyuk drove into its gut. The Ogren's strength quickly evaporated as Catal Huyuk pulled his dagger free. The beast sank to its knees, blood gushing from the puncture in its belly as it collapsed face first onto the uneven ground.

The Sylvan Warrior quickly stepped back to the center of the small clearing to gain room to maneuver, hearing more rustling among the trees. Much as he expected, the remaining three Ogren stepped into the glade. But these three were less impetuous than their now dead fellows. They had demonstrated rare caution and entered the clearing from three different sides, effectively encircling him. One Ogren let out a roar of triumph. The other two stared at him, intent on their prey, hunger in their eyes.

Catal Huyuk shook his head in resignation. Perhaps he would be dinner after all. His battle ax had grown heavier in his hands, his already diminished energy ebbing as the fight continued. He had killed four Ogren, but the effort had taken a toll. He was exhausted and his strength was waning. But he refused to be easy meat. He turned slowly as the three Ogren circled around him, taking their time, enjoying the chance to play with their prey. As the Ogren went round and round, calling to themselves in grunts and a guttural language that Catal Huyuk couldn't understand, the circle tightened. Wiping the sweat from his brow with a sleeve, he gripped his battle ax tightly in one hand, the dagger in the other, waiting for what he knew would come next. The three Ogren would attack at the same time, giving him no chance to evade his former prey. He was fast, but not fast enough for such an onslaught. He knew how this fight would end. Still, he wanted to take at least one more Ogren with him before he died. Hoping for two would likely be too much.

One of the Ogren roared, and Catal Huyuk took that to mean that the final attack was about to begin. The two Ogren on his sides charged forward, their speed surprising for creatures of such size. He turned to face the first, axe and dagger ready to strike, when a spear-like bolt of white hot energy sizzled through the air, striking the Ogren in the chest and burning its way through its body. Silence descended on the glade as the two Ogren stared in disbelief as their comrade fell dead into the underbrush with a loud crash.

Catal Huyuk grinned, then spun around and charged the Ogren that had planned to attack him from behind. Another bolt of energy slashed through the air, but Catal Huyuk ignored it, having eyes only for the Ogren that stood before him. The beast was too slow, its surprise at the quick turn of events hampering its movements. The Ogren tried to raise its sword in time but failed to do so, as the Sylvan Warrior drove the half-moon blade of his battle ax into the creature's chest and almost out through its back. The Ogren collapsed, dead before it struck the sooty soil.

"Thank you, my friend," rumbled Catal Huyuk, looking to his left and seeing that the former leader of this small troop of Ogren had met the same fate as the other dark creature, a large, smoking hole appearing where its chest once had been.

"You're welcome," said Rynlin with a dastardly smile, stepping out from between the trees. "You look a bit winded."

Catal Huyuk chuckled, simply glad to be alive. "You would as well if you had fought four Ogren before meeting these three."

"Probably so," he agreed. "I had expected Daran to be here with you."

"As did I," said the large Sylvan Warrior, who had bent over a dead Ogren, wiping the blood from his dagger and ax on the beast's dirty clothes. "I haven't seen him."

"A worry for another day," said Rynlin. "I have no doubt that roar at the end was heard for leagues. If there are other Ogren about, and I'm sure there are, they'll be heading in this direction. Shall we move to a safer location?"

"An excellent idea, my friend," replied Catal Huyuk, rising to his feet and then following after Rynlin as they disappeared among the trees.

The tall Sylvan Warrior had been correct. As they walked silently across a ridge, staying below the crest to avoid being seen, they could hear the roars of Ogren to their north and west, the beasts drawing closer with each passing second.

14

———

POLITICAL NUANCE

"What's the next step?" asked Kaylie.

After dismissing Garlan, she and Rya remained in her chamber, continuing to discuss the threat. The Princess of Fal Carrach felt more comfortable now as she sought to reveal the plot against her father, gaining strength from Rya and energy from the fact that she was making decisions rather than just reacting.

"Let's talk politics," suggested Rya. "Someone wants your father dead. So the first question is ..."

"Who stands to gain?" interrupted Kaylie. "Who wants Fal Carrach?"

"Correct. Follow that thought."

"After my father I'm next in line ..."

She suddenly realized that she could very well be a target as well. Eliminate her and there was no heir to the throne. Her conclusion frightened her.

"Are you all right, Kaylie?" Rya knew what the young princess was thinking, but better to let her discover it for herself and learn to control her fear.

"Yes, I'm fine." She took a deep breath, settling herself. Her ability to regain her composure so quickly pleased Rya. "Obviously, Rodric would stand to gain."

"Yes, but he can't take the throne openly. He would need a puppet."

"Agreed. After the Carlomin line, no other noble house has a clear claim."

Kaylie let her mind wander back to all of her instruction, the many tutors her father had forced upon her, until she found what she was looking for.

"It would be a free for all with several houses competing for the throne."

"Which house would have the greatest chance of success?" prodded Rya.

"My guess would be Norin Dinnegan. He's got the wealth and the political allies."

"And the ambition," concluded Rya.

"Yes, that as well." Kaylie rose from her seat, feeling the need to move. "But what can we do? He may or may not be the one behind the attempted assassination. He certainly has motivation. If my father dies, he would have two options. Kill me and attempt to seize the throne on his own, which is certainly a possibility given his wealth and connections. Or ..."

Kaylie's face grew pale as she reached a conclusion that clearly did not appeal to her and seemed worse than death.

"Or what?"

"Or he could force me to marry his son, Maddan, thereby becoming the power behind the throne."

"And once you're married to his son?"

"That will never happen. Maddan is a conceited, arrogant, mean ..."

"Continue with your original thought, Kaylie," Rya prompted patiently. "Don't get distracted. Keep your emotions out of your reasoning."

With some effort, Kaylie pulled herself back to the matter at hand. "If Dinnegan forces me to marry his son, he has nothing to worry about from any other claimant. There would be no other claim. Besides, none of the other noble houses would be foolish enough to challenge him. And once the marriage occurred, after a period of time ..."

Kaylie stopped pacing, the full scope of the potential deceit finally becoming clear.

"Tell me, Kaylie."

"After a period of time, he could eliminate me as well. A fall from a horse or some strange illness would be offered as the excuse. The Dinnegans would have the throne with no one to dispute the claim."

"An accurate assessment," agreed Rya, pleased at the speed with which Kaylie had worked through all the potential political nuances.

"But what are we to do?" demanded Kaylie. "Just sit around and wait? There is no way ..."

"No, girl," cut in Rya, standing up. "We do not wait. It's time for us to take the initiative. It's time to visit Dinnegan and see if we can determine what game may be afoot."

15

GROWING CONFIDENCE

Highland archers killed half the raiding party before the surviving reivers realized that they were even under attack. Some of the reivers tried to escape, but none made it back into the forest as the Marchers cut them down quickly, those few not struck down by arrows meeting their fate through sword and spear as they were unable to break free from the Marchers' noose at it closed around them.

Many of the Marchers had heard of Thomas' unique ability, but had never seen him make use of the Talent. Some now looked at him in awe. The bolts of energy tearing through the warlocks had shocked some and terrified others. But then their confidence grew, for now they had a weapon for the first time in a decade to combat the Dark Magic used to enslave them. They could take on the bastards who sought to take away their freedom without having to worry that the warlocks, despite the Marchers best efforts against the reivers, could still guarantee victory.

Thomas and Oso slipped out of the woods followed by the other Marchers, who moved quickly to gather up the bodies and bury them. Renn and Coban approached from the other side of the clearing, meeting them in the center of the village green where the body of the large reiver lay. After briefly admiring his men's handiwork with their bows, he strode over to the two dead warlocks. He flipped over the body of one with his foot, the cowl of the warlock falling away as he did so. The warlock's sightless, filmy black eyes stared up at him, its pasty skin looking more like melted wax. Thomas shook his head in disbelief, not understanding why someone would be willing to pay such a price for greater power.

"It shouldn't take us more than an hour to clean up this mess," said Coban, coming to stand next to Thomas, the sight of the warlock unsettling him. "The villagers will stay hidden in the glade until then. They can return home once we've removed the bodies."

Thomas nodded, pleased with the result of the skirmish, though somewhat sickened by the carnage. Nevertheless, it was necessary if the Highlands were to be free once more.

"This plan is working better than I thought," said Renn, the normally irascible Marcher grinning wickedly. "More Marchers are coming in from the farther passes every day, and more of the Highlands is free of Killeran's reivers."

"Yes, but I have a feeling that it won't always be this easy," replied Coban.

"You're probably right," said Thomas. "But no need to worry about that at this very moment. That's a problem for another day."

Oso grunted his agreement.

"Very true," said Coban.

"Besides, there's another group of reivers about five or six leagues from here," said Thomas quietly, his unfocused gaze staring off toward the northwest.

The Marchers recognized that look, still somewhat intimidated by the fact that Thomas could search the Highlands through the use of his Talent with such accuracy, but pleased by how it gave them an advantage in their fight against Killeran's so-called Army of the Black Sword.

"Do we march?" asked Renn, his grin widening and his hand massaging the hilt of his sword in anticipation of what was to come.

Thomas came back to himself, releasing his hold on the Talent. The raiding party was no larger than this last one. Another easy target.

"We do," replied Thomas. "Back to the hunt."

16

WEIGHED AND MEASURED

"Who's here?"

Norin Dinnegan, richest man in all the Kingdoms, sat comfortably in a large, straight-backed chair before the fire in his private office. Upon closer inspection, some could claim that the chair bore a striking resemblance to the actual throne of Fal Carrach, but none had ever offered such a perspective before, at least not openly. Why risk the wrath of a man known for holding grudges, remembering slights and having the capacity to gain his revenge whenever he so desired? Besides, almost all of the Fal Carrachian noble houses suspected Dinnegan's ambitions. He had attained more wealth than any other lord through both legitimate and nefarious means, so should not the trappings of those extravagant riches in the form of the power that could be wielded follow after? Should he not have the opportunity to demonstrate that he could easily apply how he ran his many business interests to how he would rule Fal Carrach?

But it was not to be, at least not while the Carlomins remained on the throne. At first he told himself that he would bide his time, waiting for the right opportunity. But as time passed he realized that his natural impatience would not allow him to wait for what had become an obsession for him. He had never waited for anything in his life. When he wanted something, he took it. Simple as that. And he wanted, he needed, the Fal Carrachian throne. Therefore, he would have to engineer the opportunity on his own. He certainly had the means to do so, and his incentive increased with each passing day.

Dinnegan had achieved his wealth, and thus his power, at the expense of others. At the expense of those he deemed weak or foolish. And that's how he viewed the world. There was Dinnegan, a man of intelligence and strength, of focus and unstoppable drive, and then there was everyone else. Woe to any who crossed him or offered a suggestion that might be contrary to his wishes or perhaps placed him in a bad light. There were always consequences for one's actions and words, and Dinnegan relished meting out the harshest of punishments when he deemed it necessary. Not only was it good business, but admittedly he also enjoyed it, allowing him to harness the normally suppressed, sadistic side of his personality.

"The Princess of Fal Carrach," replied Dinnegan's steward.

"To see Maddan, of course."

Dinnegan returned to the papers laid out before him. His silent partner had given him the primary responsibility for extracting as much wealth from the Highland mines as possible. Yet the unrest in that forsaken mountain Kingdom had made an already difficult task almost impossible. Mining had come to a stop and he had begun receiving reports that the Marchers were coming down from the higher passes, having declared open season on Killeran's reivers. He needed to find a way around this current difficulty, and quickly. Knowing his partner, more than his fortune or his reputation were at stake.

His irritation rose rapidly upon seeing the steward still standing before him, something that his steward recognized and rightly feared. Corporal punishment for a mistake or a slight in the Dinnegan household was the least of his concerns at the moment. His master's temper was short to begin with, even more so now that several of his most important business ventures struggled at best and threatened to collapse at worst.

The steward gulped, anticipating a burst of Dinnegan's notorious temper, but he continued on in a shaky voice. "No, my lord. To see you."

Dinnegan pushed himself to the edge of his massive chair, his escalating anger forgotten. His look of bewilderment was quickly replaced by one of worry. This was more than odd. Did they suspect? It had to be more than a coincidence. But what to do?

"Send her in," he replied, his mind working furiously in an effort to determine why the young princess would want to speak with him.

Dinnegan rose to greet Kaylie Carlomin as she swept into the room. She was accompanied by a lady in waiting he had never seen before, an older woman in the place of the several inconsequential girls who normally tagged along with the princess. Dinnegan sensed that something wasn't right, that he was missing an important piece of the puzzle, but he didn't know what. The older woman displayed a confidence and composure that unsettled him. Those piercing blue eyes seemed to bore into his very soul, searching for his most private and revealing secrets.

"Princess Kaylie, what a pleasure. If you would allow my steward to take your riding cloaks so that your visit here could be more comfortable?"

Kaylie smiled, then shook her head almost imperceptibly.

"Thank you, but no, Lord Dinnegan." The Princess of Fal Carrach surveyed the room, taking in Dinnegan's many tangible displays of his fortune. Her eyes were drawn to a locked glass case that enclosed a diamond larger than her fist and a string of pearls, each of which was twice the size of a marble. She assumed that these and the many other physical examples of Dinnegan's success were there not only to remind him of what he had achieved, but also primarily to remind others. "I don't expect we'll be here for long. We don't want to intrude any longer than necessary."

Dinnegan stood there, his surprise obvious. The seconds passed slowly as he waited for the Princess to continue. But she simply stood there, a mischievous smile on her face. He began to fidget when he glanced over at her companion. The older woman's face was barely visible with the cloak drawn up over her head, but her blue eyes sparkled faintly in the dim light. He felt as if this strange woman had weighed and measured him in an instant, and clearly she had found him wanting.

"I would have thought you came here to speak with Maddan," said Dinnegan, seeking to gain control of a situation that made him exceedingly uncomfortable. "I understand you and he have been spending a good bit of time together, perhaps with a mind toward the future."

Kaylie chuckled almost contemptuously at the suggestion, dismissing it with a wave of her hand. "I am not here to see Maddan," she declared forcefully. "You can be certain of that."

She would spend time with Maddan only if forced to do so, finding his arrogance and privilege insufferable. In fact, she'd rather spend time with an Ogren than with Dinnegan's son.

"If you're not here for Maddan, what can I do for you?"

"I simply thought now would be a good time to visit some of my more important subjects and supporters." As she spoke, she continued to take in the opulence of the room, the obvious conceit and materiality, and cringed inwardly. "As my father often tells me, 'Better to keep those who could have a real impact on the Kingdom, for good or bad, close to you.' With my father traveling, and the responsibilities of Fal Carrach falling to me in his absence, I thought I would put his words into action."

Dinnegan stood there, shifting his weight from side to side. He was a man of industry, a man of power and prestige, yet this wisp of a girl had sent a chill down his spine.

"Very good advice from the King, Princess," said Dinnegan, a light sheen of sweat appearing on his forehead.

"Indeed," agreed Kaylie. "As my father likes to explain, life is all about loyalty. For if there is no loyalty, then what do we have?"

"A good question," said Dinnegan, his sense of discomfort increasing as he forced himself to ignore the beads of sweat that had begun to trickle down the side of his face.

"Indeed. But do you know, Lord Dinnegan? Do you know the answer to the question?"

Dinnegan shuffled a bit more, feeling like a schoolboy called out in front of the class. Unable to control himself any longer, he pulled a handkerchief from his coat pocket and dabbed at the droplets of sweat that marred his normally calm and commanding demeanor.

"With respect to loyalty?"

"Yes, Lord Dinnegan. If there is no loyalty, what do we have?"

"I'm sorry, Princess, but I don't know the answer."

Kaylie laughed softly as the piercing gaze of the woman standing just behind her remained fixed on Dinnegan, much like an eagle deciding when to launch at its prey.

"If there is no loyalty, then there is no trust. And with no trust, there can only be betrayal."

A ball of cold fear settled within Dinnegan's roiling stomach. He grasped his hands behind his back in an attempt to stop his fidgeting. He needed to calm himself. What was the Princess suggesting? What did she know? He had been more than discreet. There was no way she could have any idea what he had planned. But she was here now with this woman who made him feel as he did when meeting with the representatives of his silent partner. She couldn't know. Could she?

"Uh, yes. Quite right, Princess," said Dinnegan, not knowing what else to say.

"I'm glad you agree, Lord Dinnegan. Thank you for speaking with me."

With that, the Princess of Fal Carrach swept from the room, her companion waiting just a moment, her sharp gaze taking in everything about him a final time before she turned on silent feet and left as well.

After almost a minute had passed, Dinnegan took a gulp of air, realizing that he had been holding his breath. He dropped back into his chair, his shaking legs threatening to collapse beneath him. He had met and negotiated with unsavory, dangerous men for years and had done so from a position of confidence and certainty. Yet this experience, at the hands of a girl no less, had left him frightened. He felt stripped to the bone, his innermost secrets open for all to see. It was not a feeling he enjoyed. But try as he might, he couldn't escape the sparkling, knowing eyes of the woman who had accompanied the Princess of Fal Carrach. A woman who was clearly a threat to his carefully constructed plans.

17

———————

FEARSOME ALLIES

The battered and scarred reivers, normally unafraid in battle, cringed as Lord John Killeran, his immaculate white cape draped across his back, tore into them for their ineptitude. The large tent that served as the Dunmoorian lord's base of operations in the lower Highlands did not compare to his quarters in the fort that that blasted boy had burned to the ground. Able to salvage only a few singed carpets, a stool, and a cot, all the other trappings and comforts he deserved and had earned as the Regent of the Highlands had been destroyed when that boy led the Highlanders' escape from the Black Hole. Almost a decade of carefully acquired possessions, almost all obtained as part of his efforts to enslave the Highlanders, gone in a matter of hours.

That's when it had all begun. When his future and fortune, once so promising, had taken a drastic turn for the worse. He should have killed the boy when he had the chance rather than force him into the mines as an example to the other Highlanders. For almost ten years he had enjoyed an iron grip on the lower Highlands, and now in just a few months he and his reivers hung on by a thread. The latest reports had soured his mood even more. In the last two weeks he had lost half a dozen raiding parties. Worst of all, the raiding parties he had sent out to find his missing reivers, the few that had returned, had found nothing. The missing reivers had simply disappeared. Now he didn't know what to do, other than scream at the men serving him. He had lost control of the Highlands. He had lost more than a third of his reivers. He had no information about what was going on. And, most importantly, he had no good excuse he could offer to the High King or Dinnegan for his failure.

Killeran prepared to launch into another tirade when a dark shadow glided through the open tent flap. Lord Chertney, dark hair and eyes giving him a menacing appearance, to say nothing of the hidden power that palpably lurked within him, cut off Killeran's nasally whine before he could begin berating his men once again.

"You may leave us," rasped Chertney, motioning to the tent's entrance with his hand.

Killeran's sergeants quickly made their escape. With the soldiers gone, Chertney turned his frightening gaze to Killeran.

"The High King isn't happy. You were supposed to have absolute control of the Highlands years ago. With the Council of the Kingdoms just a few months away, you had to demonstrate your ability to rule the Highlands in the High King's name. Yet you have utterly failed to do so."

Chertney said the last with a sneer, obviously enjoying his rival's lack of success.

"And don't forget our real master, Killeran," continued Chertney. "He has plans for the Highlands as well. I would be more worried about him than the High King."

"Don't you think I know that," whined Killeran with repressed anger, his squeaky voice making his rage almost comical. He knew better than to reveal his temper to Chertney. Though Killeran hated Chertney for the power he possessed, the power that Killeran believed should be his, he needed to tread carefully because of that very same power. "But what am I to do? The Marchers have stirred once more. They're destroying my raiding parties. I can't catch them in a large enough group so that I can apply my superior numbers for greater impact. The Marchers have vacated the lower Highlands, turning them into an open killing ground for anyone who is not a Highlander. And now many of the reivers will look for any excuse not to enter the higher passes."

"Then allow me to offer one last bit of assistance," said Chertney, a small smile pursing his lips. "But our master has informed me that you will receive no more aid after this. This is your last chance in the Highlands."

Chertney pulled back the tent flap.

"I'll leave a few friends here with you. Perhaps even you could figure out how to put them to good use?"

Killeran stepped out of the tent, his large, aquiline nose leading the way. He ignored Chertney's last dig. Several hundred Ogren stood before him, tightly controlled by a handful of Shades. Though the dark creatures terrified him, he knew well the value they brought to the battlefield, despite the fact that his men spent much of their time cowering in fear whenever required to fight alongside the beasts. Too often the dark creatures lost themselves in their battle lust, killing not only those opposed to them, but also those fighting with them. And then if hunger came upon them eating what they killed, whether friend or foe.

"These should do nicely," whispered Killeran, his eyes glittering with anticipation even as a shiver of fear ran through his body. "I've been hearing rumors of a new Highland Lord, but I've yet to see any evidence that this Lord actually exists. In my opinion, it is likely just the one the Highlanders call the Raptor. With these additional forces we should be able to eliminate the Raptor once and for all."

The Lord of Dunmoor strode off quickly, telling himself his speed came from his desire to find his sergeants so that he could once again gain control of the Highlands. He didn't want to admit to himself that his fear of the dark creatures massed in front of him gave an added jolt to his step.

18

NEXT STEP

"What did you think?" asked Kaylie. She and Rya sat in the back of a small coach as they returned to the Rock. "I must say that was fun. The man is twice my age, yet I clearly made him uneasy."

They had planned on conducting an unorthodox visit with Dinnegan, one designed to keep him off balance. Their approach seemed to do just that, perhaps even pushing him close to the edge.

Rya smiled, pleased with what had transpired. While Kaylie conducted the conversation, she had focused her full attention on the richest man in the Kingdoms, and she had learned a great deal.

"You did well," Rya replied. "He's hiding something."

"I thought so as well. Do you think he's behind the assassination plot?"

"You tell me."

Kaylie sighed in frustration. She had known this woman for no more than a few days, yet it seemed that every moment with her contained some lesson.

"Dinnegan has the motive and the means. He certainly has

the ambition. Based on his behavior just now, the nervousness, the fear just beneath the surface, yes, I do believe he is orchestrating this. But how do we confirm our suspicions?"

"Leave that to me," replied Rya, smiling grimly.

While in Dinnegan's mansion, in addition to using her Talent to read the man, she had extended her senses to get a better feel for the palatial structure. For all its outward appearance, it seemed the standard home for a rich man. Ostentatious. Showy. Built to impress. But her deeper evaluation suggested something else. She had sensed a muted wrongness. A darkness that shouldn't be there. And she meant to find out the cause.

19

———

USEFUL LEGEND

"Tell me, Oso. What's with all this talk about the Raptor? I have a sense you have a hand in it."

Thomas and Oso had walked away from the other Marchers onto a promontory that jutted out from a tall northern peak. A misstep would lead to a fall of almost a thousand feet. But the view made it worth the risk. To the west, at the very edge of the horizon, Thomas thought he could just make out the dark smudge of the Breaker, the barrier separating the Northern Steppes from the Clanwar Desert.

Many of the Marchers had taken to Thomas' nickname of the Raptor. Upon joining the Sylvana, Thomas had been charged with protecting the Highlands from dark creatures before he had become Lord of the Highlands. Much to his grandparents' chagrin ... well, as he thought about it, his exploits appeared to please his grandfather, Rynlin. Only his grandmother seemed bothered by the risks he took. Thomas had taken to the task with gusto. His grandparents had spent so many years trying to protect him on the Isle of Mist that when given this responsibility upon becoming a Sylvan Warrior, he relished the freedom it provided, as well as the opportunity to strike back at the creatures of the Shadow Lord. The dark creatures that had killed his other grandfather, Talyn Kestrel.

Assuming the charge with a vengeance, Thomas spent as much time in the Highlands as possible, eliminating Ogren, Fearhounds, Shades and other dark creatures whenever he came upon them. That's how he had met Oso, helping to free him and a group of Highlanders from his village. Of course, in the end John Killeran, nominal regent of the Highlands as declared by High King Rodric Tessaril, had captured them during their attempted escape.

Given the title of regent, Killeran was anything but, functioning as a sycophant seeking to claim the riches of the Highlands for himself and the High King. Finally escaping from Killeran after several months' forced labor in the mines and destroying the reivers' primary fort, known as the Black Hole, had cemented the legend of the Raptor among the Highlanders and created an unbreakable bond between Thomas and Oso.

"Someone asked me about it," the large Highlander explained with a shrug. "I said you were the Raptor and spoke of some of the things you've done. I was just telling the truth, not spreading any rumors."

Oso thought the moniker particularly apt. Thomas was applauded for his fighting skill, but even more so his prescience on the battlefield, knowing exactly when and where to attack with greatest effect, swooping down for the kill like a raptor, which played such an important role in the history and culture of the Highlands.

"Look in the sky," continued Oso, as he sat on a large rock at the edge of the promontory that gave him a tremendous view of the northern peaks of the Highlands. Wanting to use the few minutes of rest to his best advantage, he ran a grindstone across his blade slowly and with care.

Three raptors circled lazily above them, the large predators twisting and turning at the whim of the mountain breezes.

Every now and then one of the raptors swooped down as it would if it were seeking prey. But Oso suspected their actions were driven more by the desire to keep an eye on the Highland Lord.

"When was the last time two or three raptors didn't appear somewhere around you. It's like they're watching over you or waiting for something to happen. The Marchers see that. They know what the raptors represent. They know what you represent. You may not like being called the Raptor, but it's important to them and to our people. It gives them strength. Courage. Belief. It's what they need right now."

Words of wisdom from Oso. Thomas hadn't expected that. And he couldn't think of anything to say in response. Though the acclaim made him uncomfortable, Oso was right. Thinking about it for a moment, he began to realize the value of having such a reputation, much as his grandfather Rynlin made use of the myths he had so carefully constructed regarding the Isle of Mist.

While growing up on the island just off the eastern coast of the Highlands, his grandparents had used the Talent to hide his presence there from the dark creatures hunting him. His grandparents also valued their privacy, so to keep unwanted visitors away, Rynlin had crafted stories of the ghosts and other terrifying beasts that haunted the isle, using his skill in the Talent to offer some depth to his concoctions anytime anyone was foolish enough to set foot on the island.

Stories, real or perceived, could prove useful when told to the right people in the right way. So why not make use of it? Perhaps it was time for the Raptor to take flight.

"You're right, Oso," said Thomas, nodding his agreement. "There is value to this legend. We can use this to our advantage."

"What do you have in mind, Thomas?"

"Killeran's Army of the Black Sword is already afraid to

enter the higher passes. Their production from the mines has come to an end. They have no miners. Eventually they will have no choice but to come to us. We'll intensify our attacks, and as the Marchers attack, they can spread the word. The Raptor hunts. The more fearful the reivers are when they finally attack us, the better our chances of success."

20

FRUSTRATING LESSON

Sweat dripped down Kaylie's forehead, a weariness sinking deep within her bones. She felt much like she did when practicing the sword with Kael Bellilil, only exponentially more exhausted. She had learned quickly that the strength and energy required to do what she perceived to be the simplest of tasks with the Talent tired her quickly. Rya said that over time and as her skill improved, she would achieve a balance with the Talent. That she would be able to do more with the Talent at less cost to her body. But she hadn't reached that point yet. For now, learning how to grasp the Talent remained a struggle, but one she was more than willing to pursue.

"Again, girl. You can do this. You just need to concentrate."

Kaylie nodded, gritting her teeth. When Thomas had first shown her how to use the Talent, she had thought it a simple process. But with Rya's instruction, she had learned very quickly that she had barely touched the surface of what it meant to make use of the natural magic of the world.

Reaching out once more with her mind, Kaylie attempted to take hold of the Talent. The more often she reached for the Talent, the easier it became for her to sense, but that didn't mean she could easily turn it to the task given her by the demanding woman who had quickly become an important part of her life. Lifting the chest at the front of her bed should have been a fairly simple task, but for whatever reason, though she could touch the Talent, whenever she attempted to apply it, the power of the natural world slipped through her fingers.

She struggled for another few minutes, then screamed in frustration, her anger getting the better of her. It had been so easy before when Thomas had shown her how to search with the Talent. Why was it so difficult now?

"Temper, girl!"

The sharpness of Rya's tone jarred her. As the Princess of Fal Carrach, she was not used to such boldness. Kaylie felt like Rya was treating her as if she were an impetuous child rather than the heir to a Kingdom.

"You obviously can touch the Talent, but you're losing your concentration when it comes to doing something with it. You must focus. You cannot let your mind wander."

"I know, I know," Kaylie sighed miserably, a feeling of defeat winnowing its way within her. "I can feel it. All around me. The power feels so immense. But I don't know how to take in what I need. It's so vast, I just get lost in it."

Rya took a moment to consider what Kaylie had said. The girl worked hard, unwilling to give up. That was to her credit. Obviously she wanted to master this. So the fault wasn't with her effort, but rather her approach. She needed to be more precise. She needed to learn a more delicate touch. Perhaps there was a way to deal with that problem more effectively.

"It's a struggle, I know," agreed Rya. "A young man, a very difficult, stubborn young man, I used to train had much the same problem as you. I wasn't sure how to help him. But he figured out a way to get past this difficulty."

"What did he do?"

"He told me that when he reached for the Talent, he imagined a large door. If he wanted to actually make use of the Talent, in his mind he pretended to open the door, letting out just as much Talent as he needed to do whatever task I asked of him."

"And this worked?"

"It did. He said the visual was a way to trick himself. Then, as time went on and he grew more experienced in the use of the Talent, he no longer required the imagery. He had grown comfortable in the use of the Talent. But it proved useful in the beginning."

Kaylie nodded. "I'll give it a try."

Sweat dripping from her brow, Kaylie reached for the Talent once more. She smiled, sensing the tremendous amount of power flowing around her, simply waiting for her to take hold. Following Rya's advice, she imagined a large door, placing the natural magic of the world behind it. Satisfied, she then slowly nudged the door open just a tiny bit, letting out a small stream of the Talent, enough, at least in her estimation, to do as Rya asked.

She saw an immediate impact. The chest at the foot of her bed lifted a finger's breadth from the ground, hovering there for a second before settling back down on the floor.

Kaylie smiled, thrilled by her success after several previous hours of frustrating effort. She decided to open the door just a bit more, releasing more of the Talent. The chest rose quickly off the floor, faster than she expected, slamming into the ceiling and knocking off bits of plaster. Surprised by what she had accomplished, Kaylie lost her concentration, letting the chest drop toward the carpet.

Before it could slam onto the floor, Rya caught it with the Talent, setting the large chest gently back down at the foot of Kaylie's bed.

Kaylie smiled widely, exceedingly pleased with herself. Rya's stern expression wiped the pleasure from her face.

"Well done, at least for part of the task."

Rya sighed inwardly. Her grandson had done much the same thing when she had first trained him in the Talent using a chest as her object of instruction. Yet credit should be given where credit was due.

"Next time, complete the entire task before celebrating."

Kaylie nodded, chagrined. "So what's next?"

The girl's eagerness pleased Rya, reminding her once again of her grandson. It was getting late and there was another task that Rya needed to attend to, but she decided to humor Kaylie's request.

"I understand you know how to use a blade."

Kaylie's exhaustion began to melt away, her interest in the next lesson sparked. "Yes, I've been training with Fal Carrach's Swordmaster."

"Grab your blade."

Kaylie wanted to sprint across the room, instead settling for a fast walk as she tried to maintain the decorum appropriate for a Princess of Fal Carrach. Rya couldn't help but smile, understanding the girl's excitement. Kaylie pulled her sword from its scabbard, turning to face Rya, her eyes alight with anticipation.

"What I am about to show you is not a difficult thing to do with the Talent, but it does require concentration," said Rya. "I understand that you've come face to face with Ogren."

"Yes, in the Burren. Two Ogren attacked us and Thomas and this massive wolf appeared out of nowhere to help us. And then again when a pack of Fearhounds--"

"No need for stories, Kaylie. You've seen what it's like to fight Ogren, but have you ever come upon a Shade or some of the more deadly creatures that do the Shadow Lord's bidding?"

For a moment Kaylie didn't respond, wondering how Rya could possibly think that an Ogren was not as dangerous as some of these other creatures. "No, thankfully not."

Rya nodded. "We've talked a bit about how those practicing

Dark Magic came to be, how they've sold their soul for the power offered by the Shadow Lord. As a result, a different approach is required when defending yourself. For example, when facing a warlock, you must learn how to negate the compulsion and other nasty tricks they like to employ. But we will touch on that in greater depth when you're better versed in the use of the Talent. Instead, I will show you something that you can do when facing any dark creature, something that will improve your odds of surviving."

Kaylie jumped back in shock, almost dropping her sword when it burst into a blazing white light. Unable to stop herself, she reached down with her free hand, pushing gently for just a second against the blade. The light gave off no heat but sparked at her touch.

"The power of the Talent will not harm you," said Rya, coming to stand next to Kaylie. "But, it will burn through any defense offered by a dark creature, warlock or Fearhound or Ogren, it doesn't matter. When the blade is infused with the Talent, it will cut through anything, Dark Magic or steel armor, with equal ease. If at some point you face a Shade or some other minion of the Shadow Lord, this is something you can do to even the odds."

Kaylie was entranced by the white light that now illuminated her blade. "How do I ..."

The Talent disappeared from Kaylie's sword, leaving the cold, shiny steel in its place.

"Take hold of the Talent," Rya instructed.

Kaylie nodded. Reaching out for the Talent, once again it slipped through her fingers. Then again. And once more. She fought to control her rising irritation, taking a deep breath to settle herself. Remembering the advice Rya had just given her, Kaylie imagined a large, intricately carved wooden door, behind which she could sense the Talent. Slowly, with just her fingertips, she pushed on the door, allowing a tiny trickle of the

Talent to flow within her. Exulting in her success, she forced herself to maintain her concentration. She pushed on the door just a bit more, allowing the flow of the Talent to increase. Then, turning her attention to her sword, she opened a path for the Talent to flow into the steel. In an instant, her sword came to life, the Talent blazing brightly across its length.

"Well done," applauded Rya, smiling with pride. "Now release the Talent."

Kaylie did as Rya instructed.

"Good. Infuse the sword once more."

This time, in less than a second, the Talent coursed through the steel blade. Kaylie grinned in pleasure, finally having mastered one of the most important and basic tasks for working with the Talent.

"Well done, indeed, child. We'll continue the lesson tomorrow." Rya strode toward the balcony and the setting sun. "In the meantime, continue to practice what you have just learned until it becomes second nature and you barely have to give it a thought. We will build off your newfound skill during our next session."

"Where are you going?" asked the sweat-drenched, exhausted heir to the throne of Fal Carrach.

"Exploring."

The petite woman exited through the balcony doors, disappearing into the gloom of the evening. Kaylie watched her go, too tired to follow after and wondering if Rya liked to leave her in this manner for a reason other than the dramatic effect.

21

CALCULATED RISK

"It's been three days," said Seneca, voice tight, arms crossed against his chest. The grizzled Marcher was worried. "There have been no sightings of raiding parties by any of our scouts. Something's not right."

"Aye," agreed Nestor. The oldest and most experienced of Thomas' chiefs, he spoke the least but all listened to what he had to say. "Every raiding party Killeran has sent out in the last month we've either wiped out or sent back to him with their tails between their legs. My guess is that he's changing his tactics."

The other chiefs nodded their heads, agreeing with the assessment.

"We've heard tell that Killeran has pulled all his reivers into a central location in the lower Highlands, near the border with Dunmoor," continued Nestor. "That's likely the start of whatever he has planned."

Thomas grunted, acknowledging the soundness of Nestor's logic. He had used the Talent the last few days to scan the higher passes, searching for raiding parties to supplement the efforts of his scouts. Yet all that ever did was confirm Seneca and Nestor's findings. Thomas took hold of the Talent, allowing the power of nature to flow through him. Taking a moment to savor the energy surging within him, he began to search. The thrill of it, first experienced when training with his grandfather, never lessened. He started once again in the higher passes, close to the Crag, then expanded outward, his mind's eye soaring above the majestic Highland peaks, gradually extending his gaze as each second passed.

Thomas stretched his Talent beyond the Pinnacle, quickly expanding his senses to the very edges of the Highlands. As he had grown older and his strength and experience in the Talent increased, he could stretch his senses all the way to the western Kingdoms, even gazing down at the brilliant waters of the Western Ocean. But that wasn't necessary today. As he turned his attention to the southwest, he sensed the evil immediately, a blot of darkness on the land at the very edge of the Highlands, exactly where his scouts had reported Killeran had made his latest camp. But Killeran was on the move.

Thomas released his hold on the Talent, his anger brewing. "You're right, Nestor. Killeran has taken a different approach."

Killeran had formed the largest raiding party that Thomas had seen to date, essentially bringing together all his reivers. Moreover, he had acquired several hundred Ogren led by a handful of Shades. Warlocks, as well, shuffled along at the back of the long column. The vanguard of the raiding party was already several miles from Killeran's camp and well into the lower Highlands marching for the higher passes. If they continued on their route, Thomas guessed that they would reach one of the larger Highland villages in the western peaks in just a few days. With that large a raiding party, the village could not hold out for long. Killeran had, indeed, adopted a new strategy, but perhaps one that could play out to the gain of the Marchers.

Thomas had recognized the danger and the opportunity

immediately. This gave him the chance to destroy Killeran's Army of the Black Sword, to break their will, once and for all. But to fail with such an attack would be a crushing blow and most likely the death knell of the Highlanders. It would mean an end to the Marcher resurgence in its most nascent stage. Calculating the advantages and disadvantages, Thomas quickly concluded that the profit to be gained outweighed the potential risk.

His men could fight the reivers easily enough, and they didn't lack the courage and knowledge to take on Ogren and Shades, but the warlocks were a different matter. They had no way to defend against the warlocks' Dark Magic. That concern had faded when the Marchers saw the power that Thomas wielded through the Talent. He debated for just a moment longer the course to be taken, measuring whether he was strong enough to take on so many warlocks at one time. Because if he failed in that task, the entire enterprise was doomed, and his Marchers would be heading to their deaths or enslavement. Though some doubt and worry remained, he knew the decision that had to be made.

"Renn, find Oso and Coban," ordered Thomas. "Then gather the Marchers. I'll call in all the raiding parties and direct them where to go."

In addition to searching over great distances, Thomas had the ability to communicate with people from afar through the Talent as well. A useful skill when needing to coordinate the actions of so many Marcher squads functioning independently in such a rugged landscape.

"Why?" asked Seneca. "What do you see?"

"The reivers, all of them, heading for a village in the western Highlands that sits at the edge of a higher pass," explained Thomas. "Killeran's silent partner is coming to the fore as well. In addition to the expected warlocks, the raiding party contains Ogren and Shades."

The hoary Marcher spit in disgust, cursing under his breath.

"So the time has come more quickly than expected," said Nestor, the veteran Marcher conducting the same calculation Thomas had just completed regarding risks and rewards. "Victory or defeat."

"Yes, the time has come," said Thomas. "But in my mind there's only one possible outcome."

"And what would that be?" asked Nestor, having reached the same conclusion as Thomas after measuring and balancing all the different variables.

"Victory," said Thomas quietly. "And freedom for the Highlands. The time of the reivers has come to an end."

22

____

SUSPICION CONFIRMED

Rya stood silently in Dinnegan's office, the same room earlier in the day in which she and Kaylie had visited. Although guards patrolled the mansion and its grounds, which was located less than a league from the Rock, she had no trouble entering the estate and then the actual house unseen. One of the advantages of having mastered the Talent.

Before she began a more thorough search, she wanted to get a better feel for what was around her. During her initial visit she had focused so much attention on Dinnegan himself, she didn't have the time to scan her surroundings, other than to be repelled by Dinnegan's many trinkets that he had acquired in his drive for greater wealth. Rya huffed in disdain. If this was how he measured his success in life, a sad and lonely existence he must lead.

Reaching for the Talent, Rya let it flow within her. Smiling as she always did when she touched the natural magic of the world, she extended her senses. A mental map quickly formed in her mind. She noted the many rooms of the mansion, satisfied that she was alone. Two servants dallied in the kitchen, enjoying their privacy, as all the other residents slept except for the guards wandering around the mansion and the grounds. Dinnegan had the top floor to himself, alone and apparently asleep as well.

Not finding anything out of the ordinary, and certain that she would not be interrupted, Rya directed her senses toward the cellar. She found the hidden passage instantly. Most people used their cellars to keep their food fresh, but Dinnegan clearly had put it to another use as well. Something down there that appeared to be a black cloud had piqued her interest earlier in the day, and that same premonition of muted evil remained. Keeping the map of the mansion she had constructed in her mind, she stepped up to the fireplace behind Dinnegan's desk. Rya examined it for just a few seconds before finding the hidden latch.

Pulling back on the lever set just within the stone, a small door swung open to her left. Pitch-black darkness welcomed her. Rya crafted a small light with the Talent, just enough so that she could find her way without falling, then stepped onto a metal staircase that led deeper into the dark.

She took the staircase carefully, her progress impeded by two doors. One steel, the other oak. She knew the wooden door led to the cellar, so she focused her attention on the steel door. She wove the Talent into the lock, manipulating its mechanism. In seconds and with a barely audible click the door swung open on silent hinges.

Rya stood there for a moment, extending her senses into the inky murk. The feeling of wrongness increased tenfold. Dimming the light that danced just above her palm so that it was barely a glow, she walked on noiselessly down the dirt passageway. It wasn't long before she found what she was looking for.

The roughly cut passageway opened up into a large room dug out from the mansion's stone foundation. At the far end, she made out a gap, likely another way in and out of the rutted and pitted room. In the middle of the space, strewn out across the floor, irregular shapes lay covered by rough blankets. Black-clad men, swords, and daggers close to their hands, slumbered quietly.

Rya took it all in for a few moments then stepped back soundlessly. She made her way back through the passageway, locking the steel door behind her once again, then strode purposefully toward Dinnegan's office. The men felt wrong, tainted by darkness. That's what she had felt earlier in the day. But there was something else now, a stronger sense of evil. Something else had been there within the past day, something more powerful in Dark Magic. Something more dangerous. Thankfully, it had left, otherwise it would have sensed her. But the fact that she couldn't identify what it had been worried her. She didn't like not knowing what she faced.

Regardless, now she knew for certain, having confirmed her suspicions. Dinnegan had taken on a dangerous ally, and his play for Fal Carrach would come sooner rather than later.

23

LEADING THE PACK

Night had fallen. The massive wolf, a strip of white across its eyes the only break in its coat of thick black fur, stood patiently among the rocks, watching, waiting, hidden by the dark of the night and the shadows that played across the mountainside. All was quiet but for the rustle of the wind coming down off the Charnel Mountains far to the north and sweeping across the Northern Steppes into the northern Highlands. The large wolf scanned regularly from side to side, its sharp eyes picking up glints of light reflecting off the full moon above. Wolves lay in wait among the rocks and the trees, at least six packs. Under most circumstances the wolves maintained a good distance between the packs, respecting one another's territories. But the black wolf had called, and they had answered. They were there to hunt.

Thank you, Beluil, a voice whispered in the wolf's mind. *You have done better than I had hoped for.*

Beluil responded with a small growl of affection in his mind, pleased to be able to help his friend. With the Marchers concentrated around the Crag in order to better protect the Highlanders from the reivers, Thomas had agreed with Seneca and his other chiefs that help was needed if they were to begin the difficult process of reclaiming their homeland. They feared leaving the northern Highlands undefended against the constant encroachments of the Shadow Lord's dark creatures. Seeking a way to address this worry, Thomas had used the Talent to speak with Beluil. The large wolf had moved quickly to assist. In a matter of days, he had gathered all the wolf packs in the Highlands among the northern peaks. The wolves were more than happy to assist. They hated dark creatures with a vengeance, viewing them as sworn enemies and an affront to nature.

They come, Beluil. They're only minutes away. Fearhounds.

Beluil growled his acknowledgement, his attention fixed on the gully above which his hundreds of wolves lay in wait. Below a dry stream bed led up from the Northern Steppes, offering a ready-made path into the lower foothills.

Be careful, my friend. Good hunting.

With that, Thomas disappeared from Beluil's mind, leaving the wolf to his task. Beluil didn't have long to wait. He caught flashes of movement along the flanks of the stream bed, deep among the trees and boulders. Several packs had shifted silently from their perch above the gully so that their prey would have a harder time escaping once the attack began.

Beluil could sense the restlessness among the wolves. The restrained energy. They wanted to fight. They wanted to attack. They didn't have long to wait. Dozens of large shapes began to appear, barely distinct in the darkness, but easily picked out by the wolves' sharp vision. As the moon escaped the passing clouds once more, several Fearhounds were revealed by the bright light.

They represented just another one of the Shadow Lord's experiments, having been named because of their supposed ability to track their prey based on fear. The dark creatures appeared to be huge dogs, but that's where the resemblance ended. There was no mistaking their similarity to normal hounds in terms of the shape of their bodies, but actually they were the size of small ponies, their top two canine teeth extending beyond their lower jaw. Moreover, their thick, ridged hides made them a hard kill, providing only a few weak points to be exploited. But the wolves had fought these and other fearsome beasts for centuries. They knew what to do.

Beluil waited just a few seconds more, until the last of the Fearhounds had entered the gully, before leaping from his perch and digging his huge paws into the loose dirt and rock that led down to the dry streambed. He knew the wolves that had waited with him followed, barely making a sound, intent on the enemy below.

Only feet away from the lead Fearhound, Beluil let loose a howl that echoed off the surrounding peaks. His packs followed suit, surprising the Fearhounds, for they had failed to discern the trap.

Beluil slammed into the lead Fearhound, using his size to his advantage. Knocking the dark creature onto its back, Beluil leapt onto its belly and dug his sharp teeth into the Fearhound's throat, tearing it out with a twist of its massive head. The large black wolf immediately found its next opponent. A Fearhound charged toward him, its large craw opened as it hoped to use its blade-like teeth to slice into his flesh. Beluil waited until the very last second before jumping to the side, barely avoiding the creature's slavering jaws. As the dark creature skidded past, Beluil had reached out with its front paw, swiping across the beast's face and blinding it in one eye.

The Fearhound howled in fury from the pain as it struggled to stop its momentum and turn to attack once more. But Beluil never gave it the chance to do so. The large wolf rammed into the creature from its blind side and knocked it to the ground. Much as it did with the first Fearhound, before this one could scramble up, he tore into the dark creature's throat.

Beluil peered around the gully and smiled, his bloody maw visible under the brightly shining moon. All the Fearhounds were dead or soon would be. His packs had made quick work of the dark creatures, closing the trap quickly so that none could escape, then using their larger numbers to take down their bigger opponents much as they would a stag, one wolf attacking from one side, another wolf attacking from another side when the animal turned away, simply waiting for that one opportunity when the wolves could swarm the beast.

Beluil raised his head to the moon and howled, the echo traveling for leagues through the Highland peaks. The other wolves imitated their leader, the howls rising to a crescendo that traveled near and far, announcing their victory against their blood foes. The wolves had triumphed that night, but they knew more would be asked of them. And they welcomed it. The large black wolf led them, and they trusted that fighting by his side they would clear their lands of dark creatures.

24

TAKEN

The glowing green eyes had captured her. Unable to look away, she felt as if the strong gaze had seen into the very core of her being. He had appeared out of the forest gloom, leaping down from the intertwined branches above the waterfall to protect her from the two approaching Ogren. With the help of the large black wolf, the boy had dispatched the dark creatures swiftly, displaying a skill and intensity that had shocked her and thrilled her at the same time. She had seen him again with the great wolf on a knoll, calmly striking down Fearhounds as they charged up the hillside, each arrow slicing cleanly through the eye as the attacking dark creatures collapsed in the long grass.

Next she returned to the glade near Tinnakilly having learned his name. Thomas. He was giving her the first taste of the Talent, reveling in the experience of what she could see and what she could do with the natural magic of the world. Then she dreamed of flying, gazing down on the land as it transitioned from plains to forest to mountain, then back again. The feeling of freedom compared to nothing else that she had ever experienced before. Just as she turned toward the mountains her focus lapsed, the vision blurring then disappearing altogether. An incessant pounding at the door woke her from her dreams.

Raising her head groggily, Kaylie looked to the window, noting that the night still lay heavy on the land. She had slept for only a few hours since Rya had left, her exhaustion from training in the Talent still with her.

"Who is it?"

The soft but persistent knocking stopped. "Captain Garlan, Princess."

Kaylie reluctantly rose from her bed, pulling on a robe.

"I trust you understand that it's the middle of the night, Captain."

"I do, Princess. But I have news. While putting the measures in place as you instructed, we've come across two guardsmen who I suspect are involved in the plot."

That claim immediately woke up Kaylie as she strode to the door with a renewed purpose. Pulling the heavy wooden frame open, a feeling of darkness swept over her. She tried to reach for the Talent but her rising fear and her instinctual need to step back, to run, distracted her. She realized that in a matter of seconds, her body wouldn't respond to her commands. A cold fear settled into her heart. She tried to scream, but she couldn't. She could see all that occurred around her, but she had lost control of herself. It seemed like she had left her body, looking down upon it from above as it slowly slid along the doorframe to the carpet.

A tall, cadaverous man wearing a grey cloak stared at her. Bald, his features sharp and severe, his malevolent grin terrified her. His eyes appeared to be swirling pools of black that identified and played off of your greatest fear instantly.

"A pleasure to make your acquaintance, Kaylie, Princess of

Fal Carrach. I am Malachias." The tall man motioned to two black-clad soldiers standing behind him. "We have plans for you."

25

CALL TO WAR

The sun began to sink in the western horizon as late afternoon settled over the Highlands. With the shadows lengthening, Thomas approached the Pinnacle and began to climb the narrow steps carved into the massive stone. As he did so, he continued to relay instructions to his chiefs.

"Divide the Marchers into equally sized groups," said Thomas, capturing the eyes of Renn, Seneca, Nestor, Oso and Coban with his own before continuing. "You will each lead a war party. As we get closer to the village and I have a chance to survey the territory, we'll settle on the final plan."

His chiefs nodded their understanding, then stepped back. Reaching the top of the Pinnacle, the recent memory of standing on this same stone to be named the Lord of the Highlands flooded Thomas' senses. When Coban had declared him the rightful ruler of the Kingdom, he knew that they weren't alone. He had sensed the spirit of his grandfather, Talyn, standing with them. Thomas realized that in that moment his grandfather fully approved of his grandson finally assuming his rightful place as the heir to the Highland throne. But since then it had been one challenge after another, a constant stream of worries and fears that needed to be addressed if the Highlanders were to have any chance at reclaiming their homeland. And now their greatest challenge lay before them.

Thomas hoped that his grandfather's approval would continue based on his most recent decision, the risk he took, the danger he pushed the Marchers toward. A massive gamble, betting the future of the Highlands and its people on a single confrontation, but Thomas knew in his heart that he had chosen the right course.

Gazing out over the mass of Highlanders below the Pinnacle, his breath caught in his throat. Thousands of men and women stood before him. Many were Marchers, hardened fighters of the Highlands. Others were just boys and girls who had come to the Pinnacle, having heard that the Lost Kestrel had returned. And the older folk as well. The ones he could no longer ask to fight, but he could count on to handle other tasks. All staring up at him with faith in their eyes, believing that he would lead them to their greatest desire, to a time when the Highlands would once more be free. It took only a moment for silence to descend on the plateau that surrounded the Pinnacle when the assembled Highlanders saw their new Highland Lord step onto the stone.

"My friends," began Thomas. "In a matter of months the Highlands has changed. We have changed. We have begun forcing the reivers from our lands. Though at times we have struggled, we have risen to the challenge, freeing large portions of the Highlands from Killeran's grasp."

Cheers rang out from the Highlanders and Marchers, echoing off the surrounding peaks. Thomas waited for silence to return before he continued, his voice carrying easily across the plateau.

"Today, on this day, we have an opportunity to break the reivers once and for all. Killeran has massed his forces, his reivers and warlocks. And his hidden ally, recognizing the change in the Highlands, recognizing that now is the turning point and that the fate of the Highlands hangs in the balance, finally has shown his hand. Ogren and Shades march openly with the Army of the Black Sword, much as they did ten years ago when the Crag fell."

Boos and hisses traveled across the plateau at the news. Many in the crowd had experienced the Crag's fall, never forgetting that devastating night when one of their own had betrayed them, allowing their once unconquerable stronghold to fall and leading to the misery that had plagued them for almost a decade.

"Killeran heads for the village of Anselm on the southern edge of the Highlands," said Thomas in a strong voice, warming to his audience. "He will be there by first light. If the village falls, he can make directly for the Crag. But we can't allow that. Therefore, we must get there at first light as well."

Many in the crowd cheered once more, though just as many, particularly the younger ones, remained quiet.

"But how could we get there in time?" asked one Highlander. "Anselm is more than ten leagues from here. With night almost upon us, there is no way we can get there in time."

"I've heard the stories," said another Highlander. "About how the Marchers could march without tiring, always to a battle during the time of greatest need, always fresh to the field. But I always thought they were just stories, lore from hundreds of years ago. Just thinking about such a march is making my feet hurt, and we haven't even started."

Many of the Highlanders laughed at that, Thomas laughing as well, but only for a moment. His eyes burned fiercely, sweeping across his assembled people, capturing the gazes of many Highlanders and bringing quiet quickly to the plateau.

"Then we will run," said Thomas quietly.

Shouts of disbelief rose up among the gathered Highlanders, the uproar bouncing off the surrounding peaks. The hard stares of Coban, Oso, and the other veteran Marchers standing around the base of the Pinnacle finally gained silence once more.

"I have heard the stories as well," began Thomas in a voice barely above a whisper, yet a whisper that carried from the Pinnacle to the very edge of the gathered Highlanders. "My grandfather, Talyn Kestrel, told them to me before I fell asleep at night. He told me of the great deeds of the Marchers. How they could march fifteen leagues during the night then fight the entire next day, vanquishing the enemy. And then they would do the same the next night, marching fifteen leagues by moonlight to fall on their next enemy before the morning sun rose in the sky."

Thomas ran his ardent gaze across the thousands of Highlanders gathered before him, letting his fiery, green eyes capture theirs once more, trying to force belief into them.

"Yes, I have heard these and other stories. Whether you believe them or not doesn't matter."

Thomas bowed his head for several seconds, gathering his thoughts. The short period of silence added gravity as the time passed, the Highlanders beginning to discern just how important this moment was to them as a people. When he raised his bright, glowing eyes a few seconds later, his voice was louder, stronger, filled with a certainty that latched on to the hearts of the listening Highlanders.

"What matters is not what we believe, but what we do. For almost ten years, reivers have ruled our lands. Reivers have driven us from our homes, enslaved and killed our families. Reivers have tried to make the Highlands their own. That time ends now."

The surrounding Highlanders stared up at Thomas, the memories of the past decade strengthening their hearts and hardening their focus.

"A new time is beginning," continued Thomas. "Our time is

beginning. After tomorrow the other Kingdoms will know that once again the Highlands are free. They will know that if any trespass in the Highlands, they will face our wrath. They will be the ones to remember, to remember the glories of the Marchers. To remember our victories. To remember that to risk angering a Marcher means risking death."

The intensity in Thomas' voice increased as he bit off each word, which easily carried across the plateau. A palpable energy surged through the Marchers, as they too began to remember their past glories. They too began to remember the Highlands before the fall of the Crag.

"Just as you have, I too have heard the legends of the past. But those legends, they will remain in the past. For now, we must look not to the past but to our future. The future of the Highlands. Now is the time to make a new legend, our legend. Now is the time to march."

Cheers rose across the plateau as the Highlanders released their pent-up longing, caught in the energy and spirit Thomas had woven around them. Caught by the purpose the Highland Lord had imbued within them.

Thomas raised his arms, the Marchers quieting instantly. His shout sent a bolt of energy through them, electrifying them, sending their hearts surging. "It is time to wake the Highlands! The Marchers go to war!"

The roar of the Highlanders blasted off the peaks, creating a cacophony of noise. Coban, Oso and the other war chiefs immediately stepped forward, mixing with the Marchers and shouting instructions to gather their gear and form into their war parties.

On their own initiative, several of the older Highlanders stepped to the top of the Pinnacle, joining Thomas, bagpipes in hand. In just a few moments the haunting notes of the bagpipes began to travel across the Highlands, drifting among the mountain peaks to the very boundaries of the Kingdom and beyond.

The men in the raiding parties who had been summoned by the Highland Lord but had not yet reached the Pinnacle stopped to listen, then picked up their pace, determination driving them forward. They could hear the call, feel it in their blood and their bones. The Highland Lord called them to war.

26

THREAT REVEALED

Rya stepped quietly into Dinnegan's office, making sure to latch the hidden door behind her. The house still silent, she walked to the kitchen, the fires banked with the morning still hours away. She glided out through the servant's entrance to the grounds, having entered the same way, and was glad to see that nothing had changed. She caught a glimpse of two guards lazily patrolling along the property's wall far in the distance.

About to draw on the Talent so that she could return to Ballinasloe, Rya held off. Something didn't feel right. She stood there for a minute, not moving, taking in everything around her. Then she sensed it. A darkness approached, the same darkness she had felt in Dinnegan's cellar.

Hearing a commotion on the other side of the mansion, she moved unseen through the side garden until she had a good view of the front, remaining hidden from prying eyes. A carriage pulled by a team of horses skidded to a stop in the circular gravel path at the front of the mansion. Norin Dinnegan stood there waiting in anticipation.

Dinnegan's steward opened the door to the carriage,

allowing a tall, forbidding figure to step down to the stone gravel. The moonlight glanced off of his bald head and revealed his cadaverous features.

Rya hissed in anger. Malachias! She should have known. If the findings of her just-completed expedition were not confirmation enough, identifying a high-ranking minion of the Shadow Lord here removed any doubt. Dinnegan had sold himself to a power that he couldn't negotiate with and that he didn't fully understand. Eventually, he would realize his folly, but by then it would be too late for him.

Malachias reached back into the carriage and carefully extracted a still form draped in a robe. As he did so, several of the men she had seen sleeping beneath Dinnegan's mansion walked out the front door. Rya sensed the wrongness that enshrouded the black-clad soldiers. Their movements weren't as smooth or fluid as you would normally expect, as if their actions came in response to commands rather than natural instinct. Further, Rya could tell a small knot of resistance still remained within them, but with each passing day that internal conflict would lessen until the soldiers, once and for all, belonged to the shadow. She had seen this before and knew the cause. These men had doomed themselves as well, they just didn't know it yet. Trading your soul to the Shadow Lord guaranteed only one end.

Malachias handed what now appeared to be a girl to two of the men, who then turned back into the mansion, carrying her between them.

A glance of moonlight on the still form's face revealed her identity. Kaylie!

Rya's first instinct was to attack, to take in as much of the Talent as she could and rescue her pupil. But she stopped herself, though not without a difficult internal struggle. Rya didn't fear Malachias, but taking on that soul-cursed demon required all of her attention. She couldn't confront a dark creature of such power as Malachias and hope to rescue Kaylie at the same time.

Cursing silently, she stepped back into the garden and hurried toward the back of the massive property. Kaylie lived, but how much longer that would prove to be the case was anybody's guess. So time was of the essence. Kaylie's political instincts had proven correct. And a traitor in the Fal Carrachian Guard required their attention. But that could wait. First, Rya needed to get help.

Having reached the back wall and satisfied that Malachias would not sense what she was about to do, she took hold of the Talent. In a flash of bright, white light, she disappeared. In her place, a large hawk launched itself into the air, its powerful wings quickly gaining height. But rather than fly to Ballinasloe, the hawk banked to the west, following the road that led away from the capital of Fal Carrach.

27

THE PLAN

The Highlanders jogged through the night at a ground-eating pace, weapons tied across their backs and covered in cloth to prevent the clatter of steel from revealing their passage. A light snow fell, turning the world white and providing some small illumination since the clouds hid the moon. There were few sounds but the breathing of the Marchers and their light steps through the Highlands, that and the notes of the bagpipes that followed after them, which continued to float on the wind.

Highland scouts led the Marchers' advancing line, but few worried about detection by their enemies. Supporting the scouts, Thomas used his Talent to scan their immediate surroundings and get a lay of the land as they approached Anselm and Killeran's raiders.

During the early morning, the sky still slate grey, the snow stopped, leaving a light layer of powdery white on the ground. The clouds cleared, and the first dim rays of sunshine soon appeared on the eastern horizon. Thomas knew they were close, no more than a mile from the village. Calling a halt, he told his war chiefs, speaking to them with the Talent, to have their men rest for a few minutes, then prepare for battle.

Knowing that Renn, Seneca and Nestor would move quickly to obey, Thomas gestured for Coban and Oso to come with him. Together they pushed forward through the light snow over the last mile, stopping on a rise that offered an overlook on the walled village of Anselm. They stayed within the tree line, hidden in the early morning shadows, not wanting any errant eyes to notice them by chance.

Closing his eyes and concentrating, Thomas used the Talent to confirm his suspicions. The forest was clear of dark creatures and reivers, all of them with Killeran's raiding party. The scouts that he had expected would be there to protect Killeran's flanks were nowhere to be seen. Thinking perhaps that his dark creatures would deter any other Marchers from engaging, Killeran clearly wasn't worried about anything but taking the Highland village.

Set against the backdrop of a tall cliff that formed the edge of a towering Highland peak that rose into the clouds, to the west of Anselm the cliff dropped off to a precipice that ran along that side of the clearing. That precipice fell at least one thousand feet to a fast-moving river. A twenty-foot high wall made from stout timber with iron-bound gates surrounded the village. A good defense, but not one that would last long against dark creatures and warlocks.

Killeran had arrayed his forces in the large clearing in front of the village, his reivers to the fore, the warlocks behind them. He'd split his Ogren and Shades, putting them on the flanks, but behind the reivers. Apparently, the Dunmoorian Lord had decided to keep them from the initial assault.

Thomas, Coban and Oso remained hidden among the trees as they watched Killeran order the reivers forward. The Marchers thought the reivers obeyed reluctantly, probably wondering why the Ogren weren't made to serve as arrow fodder rather than them. The Highlanders manning the wall easily defended against the reivers' first attack. But clearly this initial assault was only a probe, an attempt to find any weaknesses in the village's defenses. Even the defenders knew that if Killeran's full force attacked, they wouldn't be able to hold them back for long.

Taking it all in, Thomas developed his battle plan quickly, knowing that every second counted. As soon as Killeran breached the wall, the fight would end. He'd flood the village with his warlocks, eliminating resistance, and then no one would escape because the Ogren and Shades would block their way, leaving the reivers to enslave those Highlanders able to work in the mines. For the too young or too old, the too sick or too weak, a worse fate waited at the hands of the dark creatures.

"Oso, bring your men up from the south. You're our left flank, and I want you on the very edge of the precipice. We're going to push in from the east, towards you, so you must hold that flank. You don't need to attack, but you must hold. If you break, we fail."

"Of course, Thomas. But there's a problem."

"What's the problem?" asked Coban.

"Anara came with us," said Oso, gesturing back a few hundred feet. The Marchers had taken a few minutes to rest and prepare for battle almost a mile from the village. But not Anara.

Leaning calmly against a tree, as if the all-night run through the Highlands had been no more than a short walk, stood a pretty, confident woman, short auburn hair highlighting her pixie-like face. She scraped a whetstone across her dagger, sharpening the long steel, though looking upon the blade Thomas judged that she did so more out of habit rather than need. She had followed Thomas, Coban and Oso, though not intruding on their strategy session. Thomas guessed at the cause but left it unsaid.

"So what if Anara came?" asked Thomas.

"It's just that ..." Oso tried to explain, but words failed him.

"Here we go," interrupted Coban, quickly understanding why the large Marcher was tongue-tied.

"Spit it out, Oso," demanded Thomas. "Time is wasting."

"Anara shouldn't be here," was all Oso could say, his face flushing red.

"Why not? She's a Marcher. She's a trained fighter. In fact, she's almost as good with a blade as you are."

"Yes, but ..." Oso tried to continue his protest, but it only came out in a weak sputter.

"The boy fears for her," sighed Coban. "He's in love with her but can't say it. He doesn't want her to get hurt."

"I'm not ..."

"Save it, boy," said Coban, not unkindly. "It's written all over your face. Whether you love her or not isn't relevant right now. That young lady is one of our best fighters. And she's tougher than anyone I know. Remember, she survived the Black Hole for almost six months. You can't keep her out of this. If you tried, she'd probably just stick you with that dagger of hers."

Oso looked back over his shoulder once more, Anara's strong gaze bearing down on him, challenging him, as if she knew what he had been talking about.

"You're right, Coban." Oso nodded reluctantly. "We'll hold. Don't worry for that. But I want Anara with me."

"I doubt you could get rid of her if you tried," chuckled Thomas. "Coban, you're with me in the center. We'll give Killeran and his forces something to focus on. We'll try to pin them in place."

"So that Renn, Seneca and Nestor can sweep through their left flank and push toward Oso and the precipice," said Coban, quickly putting together Thomas' strategy on his own. "A good plan. Let's get to it."

Thomas closed his eyes once again, concentrating, then relaying his instructions to Renn, Seneca and Nestor. The Marchers immediately began to move forward to their positions, making sure they stayed within the tree line to mask their arrival.

28

CHANCE MEETING

The sun had just broken over the eastern horizon, the giant eagle continuing to fly along the main road leading to Tinnakilly. The massive bird's sharp eyes scanned its surroundings dutifully, searching for something very specific, but with no luck for the past several hours. It had seen some early travelers on the road, but no one that captured its interest. So it carried on, tirelessly flying above the long-used road as it snaked its way through the Fal Carrachian countryside. The eagle didn't find what it was searching for until mid-morning.

Finally locating its quarry, the giant eagle landed in the road just ahead of a small party of soldiers riding toward Fal Carrach's capital. There was an instant of confusion, as the lead riders stared dumbstruck at the imposing bird that blocked their way. The lead horse having stopped no more than ten feet in front of the large eagle, silence enveloped the stand-off, the soldiers unsure of what to do, the eagle boldly staring back.

A broadly built man, his dark hair and beard sprinkled with grey, dismounted, giving the reins to the man next to him. Having never seen the like, he stepped forward gingerly, not wanting to spook the bird. The large predator examined him with piercing eyes. The man initially thought the creature might be a kestrel, one of the huge raptors of the Highlands. But though this eagle clearly dwarfed its smaller brethren, it did not match the size of the kestrels of old.

A flash of bright, white light forced the man to close his eyes as he spun away reflexively. When he turned back, a petite woman wearing a dark blue cloak stood before him. She had a presence about her that he had seen in very few people during his lifetime, her gaze strong and focused. As recognition dawned, this woman led him to think back to a time when things were different. To a time when his best friend had lived. To a time before a cloud had settled over the Kingdoms.

"My Lady Keldragan?"

The woman inclined her head in acknowledgement. "It has been a long time, King Gregory. Well met."

The identity of the woman before him confirmed, Gregory's thoughts drifted back to when he had met this petite but imposing woman for the first time. He had visited the Crag, spending time with his friend and fellow ruler, Talyn Kestrel, Lord of the Highlands. Talyn's son, Benlorin, had just married a mysterious girl who had lived somewhere in the deep Highlands. She was said to have the ability to do wondrous and, to many people, disturbing things. To do things that required a unique ability that most had thought had disappeared from the Kingdoms long before. A skill that Marya's mother had just demonstrated.

"I must say I'm surprised to meet you here," said Gregory, trying to keep his unsettled nerves under control. At least he was doing a better job of it than his men, many of whom still struggled to control their mounts, the quick flash of light having frightened them. "It's been what? A decade or more?"

"Close to it," confirmed Rya. "But I'm not here to exchange pleasantries."

Gregory smiled. Yes, indeed, this was the woman he

remembered. Straight to the point and blunt, and not one to waste time or mince words.

"Then may I ask your purpose for being here this morning? My men and I are just completing a circuit of Fal Carrach, and we'd like to get back to Ballinasloe by evening if possible."

"You will need to ride faster than that, Gregory."

Rya stepped forward, not one for ceremony and now no more than a few feet between them. Her sharp glance captured his own.

"Your daughter is in danger, and she needs your help."

"What! How do you know?"

Before the King of Fal Carrach could ask any more questions, Rya quickly explained all that had happened over the last few days as well as what she suspected, starting with Kaylie learning of the assassination attempt and ending with what she had discovered at Dinnegan's mansion. The more Gregory heard, the redder his face became, his anger boiling into a white hot rage.

"Dinnegan? That snake! I'll cut his head from his shoulders and ..."

"King Gregory, that is certainly the goal, but we don't have time for anger now. If what the lady says is true, we must focus on the danger to your daughter."

Kael Bellilil, a grey haired Highlander who served as Swordmaster of Fal Carrach, stood next to Gregory, having dropped down from his horse to hear what the woman who had appeared so unexpectedly before them had to say.

"You're correct, Kael. I shouldn't have allowed my anger to get the best of me." Gregory took several deep breaths, trying to regain some semblance of calm. Passion had no place in the moment. Only good, clear, rational reasoning.

"We are all angry, my lord."

Kael gestured back to the soldiers, all having finally regained control of their horses. They had heard everything as well. Their expressions stony, postures reflecting a cold, hard purpose, the men gripped their reins anxiously. They waited impatiently for the command to gallop to the city and eliminate the threat.

"I do not know the lady before us, King Gregory. So I simply ask you, do you trust what she has said?"

Gregory studied the diminutive woman before him, remembering how Talyn had grown to like her, to trust her. If his friend could do that, so could he.

"I do."

Kael nodded. "Then we must move quickly. If Dinnegan does have Kaylie hidden away on his estate, I doubt she will remain there for long. He will want her moved as quickly as possible to remove any suspicion."

"By this evening," said Gregory.

"Agreed. And if what the Lady Keldragan says is true, we will need more soldiers to rescue her. I have no doubt the men behind you will do all they can, but against a larger force, the odds, even for them, would be poor. We must be certain of success. Your daughter's life likely depends on it."

"What do you suggest, Kael?"

"We're less than a day from Ballinasloe. We have several outposts to the east and west of here. Send riders to gather those men and we meet on the road an hour south of Dinnegan's estate by late afternoon. We go forward from there. That way if, as Lady Keldragan suggests, we have a traitor in Ballinasloe, we can lessen the chance that Dinnegan hears of our approach."

Gregory nodded. "A good plan." He turned back to Rya. "And this Malachias? Can you manage him? If what you say about his abilities is true, we have no way to fight him."

Rya smiled, her gaze predatory. "Tell me, Gregory. After what you've seen this morning, do you still believe in the Sylvana?"

Gregory leaned back in surprise. First a meeting with someone he had not seen in years, and now reference to the legendary forest warriors charged with holding back the power and terror of the Shadow Lord. Remembering Rya's appearance before them just a short time ago, he couldn't deny his belief remained. In fact, her display had only served to strengthen it.

"I do, my lady."

"Then you can leave Malachias to me. You save your daughter, and I will take care of that dark-souled creature."

29

CONFIDENT START

"**O**clan, keep those men in line!" screamed Killeran. "I don't care if the Ogren make them nervous. They need to be ready."

"Yes, Lord Killeran," replied Oclan, the one-eyed reiver trotting off to do his best to keep his men calm and focused, or at least less anxious and agitated.

He could understand their hesitation, what with them being forced to stand so close to Ogren and Shades. The dark creatures made him nervous as well, the massive beasts towering over his reivers. Too often in the past these unwanted allies had made the mistake of attacking his men rather than the Highlanders. Yet that wasn't the worst of it. Every so often a Shade felt the need to feed, selecting the closest target. Several unfortunate reivers had met an untimely end in such a way, sucked dry by a Shade in search of sustenance. In the eyes of the dark creatures, Oclan assumed that he and his men appeared to be no more than an easy meal, a thought that kept the reiver captain continually on edge.

Killeran ignored the uneasiness in his ranks, sitting atop his horse, watching the warlocks continue their assault on the gates. The flames licked at the wood, catching along the edges, despite the Highlanders' frantic attempts to douse the fire with water. Perhaps their efforts would be rewarded if they struggled against natural fire. But not with the flames created by Dark Magic, which burned so long as the warlock maintained control of the corrupted energy. It was only a matter of time before his reivers would have an open path into the village.

But how long would it take? He shook his head in exasperation. He only had a handful of warlocks remaining with him now, compared to his attack on the Crag. Then, he had had several hundred warlocks, and working together they had blown huge holes through the stone walls of the fortress. But now, these dark creatures couldn't bring such power to bear. Thus, the much slower approach they took in order to break through the village's primary defense. Even combining their strength, these servants of the Shadow Lord didn't have the power to blow apart the village's gates as he had demanded when they had arrived on the plateau.

He struggled to control his irritation. Soon the gates would become a burning husk and he could implement the next part in his strategy.

Killeran smiled at the thought, his rat-like face twisted in glee. The first step in his plan to retake the Highlands was progressing exactly as he'd expected. Even though he had lost a large number of his warlocks during the destruction of his Highland fort, infamously named the Black Hole, and many of the remaining warlocks to the Marchers' ambushes, he no longer worried that this handful now working before him were all that he had left. The Ogren and Shades Lord Chertney had given him more than made up for his loss of those foolish souls skilled in the application of Dark Magic.

Yes, soon the Highlands would be his once more. They had

to be. Otherwise, he'd have to pay the price his benefactor had set for him. And that was a price he could not afford. A price that terrified him.

30

ARROGANCE OF POWER

Maddan Dinnegan sat in a centuries-old chair facing the bed. Handsome, confident, and born into a world of privilege and power, being the son of the richest man in the Kingdoms only added to the arrogance and conceit that seemed to seep from his pores. He could do what he wanted, when he wanted, to whom we wanted, usually with few, if any, consequences. And right now he wanted the young lady sleeping on the bed before him. He had wanted her for years. Desperately.

In his mind, Kaylie Carlomin, daughter of the King of Fal Carrach, belonged to him. The same age, he had met her when he went to the Rock for his education and training in weapons and the martial arts. Yes, she was beautiful, her long, black hair setting off her eyes. And her smile could break the coldest heart.

But it wasn't just her beauty that attracted him. No, he found her so intoxicating for a different reason altogether. She represented power. Real power. A power that only a few in all the Kingdoms could ever obtain. And as the son of the richest man in all the Kingdoms, he understood and appreciated power, believing it should belong solely to him. Therefore, the girl sleeping in front of him should belong to him as well. A tool. A trinket. Something to be used, however he so desired.

In fact, she would have been his by now if not for that incident in the Burren. He had schemed for weeks to convince her and their friends to picnic in Oakwood Forest. Once on their way it had been a simple matter to persuade them to risk the supposed danger of the Burren, a darker part of that forest with so many stories and legends swirling around it that most people kept well away from its borders. But he wanted to show her his courage, believing that such a display would win her heart, and with her heart everything else, including the power he so craved and deserved.

But the excursion had not gone as planned. The stories about the Burren unexpectedly had proven true, as two Ogren had attacked the group while they whiled away the afternoon at a small waterfall. Terrified, his first thought had been escape. His escape. The others in his group could fend for themselves.

His thoughts of Kaylie and proving his bravery had disappeared at the first roar of those terrifying beasts as they emerged from between the trees and charged forward. He never doubted that once he had gotten past that initial wave of fear, he would have acquitted himself well against the creatures that towered over him, their curled tusks dripping with strings of saliva, their roars setting his teeth chattering.

At least that's what he told himself, for he had never gotten the chance to prove himself. That infernal boy had dropped from the trees aided by that midnight black wolf. In seconds both Ogren were dead and Kaylie had become enthralled by an interloper who looked like he lived in the forest and had nothing to call his own but the clothes on his back and the weapons in his hands.

Pushing that bad memory from his mind, Maddan rose from his chair and sat on the side of the bed, stroking Kaylie's silky black hair gently. All that was in the past and no longer relevant. There was no one else to protect her now. Just him. The Princess of Fal Carrach was finally his.

"What am I doing here?" Kaylie asked groggily, lifting her head.

At Maddan's touch, she scrambled back from him clumsily, sliding off the bed and putting her back to the wall.

Startled from his reverie, Maddan smiled. "You're safe here, Kaylie. You have nothing to fear."

"Why am I here?" she demanded again, this time putting steel in her voice, her clouded mind beginning to clear.

"For your protection, of course."

Maddan started to walk around the bed toward her, but stopped when she moved away from him, sliding against the wall and keeping her distance.

"There was a man ..."

Maddan chuckled. "Yes, Malachias."

"You know him?" Kaylie asked in shock.

"I do. He's here with my father."

"But why would your father ..."

Despite having just broken free from the Dark Magic Malachias had used to whisk her out of the Rock with no one the wiser, Kaylie quickly regained her senses and put together the pieces of the puzzle. If Dinnegan worked with Malachias and she had been taken here, then her and Rya's suspicions were correct.

Dinnegan lay at the root of the assassination plot. Once her father was eliminated, Fal Carrach would fall to her. Or rather to Dinnegan once Dinnegan forced her to marry his son. Something that recent experience told her was well within the power of this Malachias. Even with her nascent skill in the Talent, she didn't have the knowledge or expertise to defend against the Dark Magic he would use against her.

Maddan shrugged, having watched the realization come to her, then walked toward the door.

"I see you've figured it out already. I should have expected no less." As he stepped through and began to pull the door shut, he called back over his shoulder, the smugness in his voice overpowering. "Just remember. Soon your life will depend on me. So I suggest you begin to accept the reality of your circumstances. One way or another, you will do what I require of you."

31

FINAL PREPARATIONS

Thomas waited for his Marchers to get into position, still hidden by the forest. He watched the battle progress in front of the stockade wall, the Highlanders fighting ferociously to hold back the reivers. His heart ached watching the boys and girls who stood on the walls with their mothers and fathers, brothers, and sisters, doing all they could to defend their village.

Coban appeared at his side, his men filing out behind them into a line of battle. Thomas knew that his Marchers were tired from the long march through the night, but many smiled or wore looks of grim determination, most of the men and women nodding in respect as they passed, a fiery gleam in their eyes. They could sense the opportunity and the risk just as well as he could. They knew what the day could bring, for good or bad.

"Aric, come forward," said Coban. "Open that package I gave you. You'll know what to do."

The tall Highlander, saved in the mines by Thomas, bent to his task. Thomas turned back toward the village, his attention focused once more on the current attack. Killeran had pulled his reivers back, sending his warlocks forward instead. Only a handful of the warlocks remained, but they still represented a major threat to the village as they hurled balls of fire at the gates. Though not strong enough to blow apart the steel-banded barrier, eventually the magical flames would win out.

Despite the best efforts of the Highlanders to douse the gates with water, it barely slowed down the inevitable as singe marks began to appear on the wood. Soon the fire from the Dark Magic would take hold, and then it would only be a matter of time before Killeran had his breach and the village fell.

Confirming that his fighters were in position, he took a deep breath to steady himself. It was time. Time for the Marchers, his Marchers, proud, strong, and hungering for revenge, to create their own legend.

Thomas turned back to Coban, ready to give the order to advance. Instead he stopped for a moment, surprised. Aric stood just a few feet behind him, Coban standing next to him. Both had huge smiles on their faces. He had forgotten about what Aric now held in his hands, though Coban clearly hadn't. He nodded his thanks to the Highland Swordmaster.

Well, grandfather, let's see if I can keep my promise to you, Thomas thought. He remembered vividly almost ten years before, escaping through the passageway beneath the Crag, his grandfather sealing him into darkness so that the Ogren and reivers that were overcoming the Marchers' furious defense of the Highland fortress could not pursue him. But before he did so Talyn had given him the Sword of the Highlands, the large two-handed sword with a double-edged blade, now strapped in the sheath across his back, and his mother's necklace. On the end of the slim, silver chain hung a finely carved talisman with the center showing the horn of a unicorn, the thick bottom of the horn spiraling up to a razor-sharp point. He had followed that necklace to safety and still wore it around his neck, along with the one he had earned when he had become a Sylvan

Warrior himself. He also remembered one of the charges that his grandfather had given him that night: "*You are Thomas Kestrel, Lord of the Highlands upon my death, and I charge you to remember that and to make sure others remember it as well.*"

Thomas was, indeed, the Lord of the Highlands. Now he would do as his grandfather required and make sure others remembered it.

"Aric, come with me," said Thomas. "Coban, I'll let you know when."

32

START OF THE SHOW

"Are you sure this is a good idea, King Gregory? There is no need for you to take this risk."

Gregory turned to the impressive, somewhat frightening woman standing beside him, understanding her point. Yes, she was right. Fal Carrach needed him. But his daughter more so.

"She's my daughter. I'm going."

Rya nodded, expecting nothing less. She looked behind her, satisfied with what she saw. Kael's riders had pulled from three garrisons stationed in the countryside around Ballinasloe. Several dozen soldiers hid in the forest just beyond the back wall of Dinnegan's estate. The remainder waited with Kael on the other side of the estate, closer to the gate.

"How do you propose to scale the wall without rope and hooks?" asked Gregory.

Rya grinned. "We'll be taking a different route. One that's designed to draw the attention of Malachias and his men. It will give Kael more time to advance through the main gate and hopefully take Dinnegan's men from behind as we discussed."

Gregory nodded, motioning for his men to prepare themselves. All gripped their daggers, swords, and axes, ready to attack. Several of the horses whinnied or stomped their hooves, feeding off their riders' anticipation.

Rya turned back to the wall. Several feet thick, the barricade rose thirty feet into the air. Her smile grew wider. This was going to be fun. Taking hold of the Talent, the power of nature streaming within her, she focused her attention on the stone blocking her path.

33

COMPULSION

"I won't do what you want," said Kaylie, her voice strong as she fought to control the fear that coursed through her.

Malachias chuckled, a terrifying sound that made Maddan think of claws skittering across stone.

Maddan sat against the back wall of the room, as far from the grey-cowled, emaciated figure as he could. Getting too close to his father's ally set his hands trembling, which prevented Maddan from projecting the image of strength and power he so desired.

Norin Dinnegan sat behind his desk, writing correspondence to many of the lords and ladies of Fal Carrach, ready to announce the untimely demise of the current king, something that would happen once Gregory returned from his circuit around the Kingdom. And then, after Dinnegan's assassin completed his work, he would be eliminated as well, removing any ties to Dinnegan and giving him a clear path to become the power behind the throne. A simple plan, as he preferred. Dinnegan had found over the years as a result of his many schemes and business dealings that simple plans were always best. Fewer possible complications meant fewer mistakes.

"That's the beauty of it, Princess," replied Malachias in his raspy whisper. "You will have no choice."

He walked closer to her, until she could see nothing but the swirling black pools in his eyes. She tried to maintain her composure, but she sensed the power he held and the evil that lurked within him. It terrified her, and she knew that even with her growing skill in the Talent she did not have the capacity to defend against his Dark Magic.

"You do remember what happened with that boy, don't you? The one who befriended you at the festival?"

"Thomas?" She had not meant to speak his name, but Malachias' hypnotizing gaze compelled her to reveal it.

"Yes, I assume that's the one. You didn't want to do that either, Princess. You didn't want to betray him. But you did."

The incident had devastated her and remained an open wound. She had been told that what she had done had been the work of others. Even Rya had confirmed it, explaining that she had no ability to resist the compulsion likely placed on her. But there had always been a nagging doubt, her remorse over the incident frequently getting the better of her.

"Yes, you see it now, don't you? Chertney compelled you to betray the boy. Just as I will compel you to do as I command once your father is dead." Malachias leaned down, his face just a finger's breadth from hers, his rancid breath making her feel ill. "You have no ..."

Malachias raised his head, listening to something that only he could hear. Then they all heard it. A great avalanche of stone crashed down, as if the side of a mountain had just collapsed.

Snarling, he strode through the door that led to the back of the property, followed by the black-clad soldiers that came streaming through the hidden door and the cellar beneath the mansion, summoned silently by their master.

"What are you doing?"

Dinnegan had ducked behind his desk, startled by the

resounding boom. Malachias responded to Dinnegan without breaking stride.

"We are under attack, you fool. Summon your guards. And make sure the girl doesn't wander off."

34

COMING TIDE

Crendall, reluctant leader of Anselm, stalked the walls of the village with a vengeance, cursing some of the Highlanders, exhorting others, doing whatever he could to keep them focused and on task. He never wanted the responsibility of leading the village during a time of crisis, but no one else would take on the role. The Marcher with the most experience, his friends had selected him. With no one else willing to step forward, he didn't have much of a choice. Now the fate of his village rested on his shoulders.

To describe the current attack as a crisis was an understatement, he thought to himself, as he yelled at his neighbors to keep up with their attempts to stop the fire on the gates from spreading. The flames had only caught in a few places because of their efforts, but Crendall knew their luck wouldn't last. The unnatural flames inexorably ate into the hardened timbers. The veteran Marcher understood that the warlocks' Dark Magic eventually would win that small, but all important skirmish.

No, this wasn't a crisis. It was going to be an all-out disaster. As soon as the reivers breached the gates the Ogren and Shades would storm through, force the defenders to one place within the village, then leave the warlocks to disable the Highlanders so that Killeran could enslave them once more and put them into the mines as laborers. What would happen to the weak or sick, the women and children unable to work, he didn't want to think about.

"Come on lads, keep at it," exhorted Crendall. "Leave the men above the gate to handle the flames. The rest of you ..."

"I'm not a lad," called out one of his fighters.

Crendall turned toward the soft voice with a smile on his face.

"Quite right, Margery. Quite right, my lass." Every able-bodied Highlander defended the walls.

"Keep your eyes open and your wits about you." Crendall continued his travels along the length of the parapet, repeating his instructions. "Stand strong. Watch each other's backs. The reivers will be back at us soon."

Crendall stopped in his tracks, about to upbraid one of his smallest fighters, a young boy named Hurlin, for getting distracted. Something far beyond the wall had caught the boy's attention. Crendall cursed once again. The boy shouldn't even be on the parapet. He was too young. He could barely lift the spear he held in his hands. But what choice did they have? He needed anyone who could carry a weapon.

"Hurlin, what in blazes ..."

Hurlin's squeaky words cut him off. "Look, Crendall. Look at the edge of the forest." Hope had worked its way into the boy's tinny voice.

Crendall followed Hurlin's gaze. And then he saw it. At the very edge of the forest, two men stood, one of them driving a flag into the ground. A flag he never thought he would see again. On a field of white, three mountain peaks served as a backdrop to a raptor streaking down from the sky, claws outstretched for the strike. He had heard rumors, but no one from Anselm had made it to the Pinnacle to confirm then. Then the threat of attack by the reivers required all their attention. Perhaps the rumors were true. The possibility energized him.

The flag now standing on its own, Marchers began to stream out of the wood, forming a battle line from the edge of the precipice all the way across the crest of the valley. The sight brought tears to Crendall's eyes. A Highlander had come to the village just a few days before, regaling everyone with tales of what had happened at the Pinnacle, tales of the Raptor actually being the Lost Kestrel. And last night he had heard the faint sounds of the bagpipes traveling on the wind. But he had been afraid to believe, not wanting to deal with the potential disappointment after almost ten years of struggle.

The reivers had yet to look behind them, seemingly more concerned by the dark creatures on their flanks, the bulk of their attention focused solely on breaching the gates. Crendall grinned wickedly. That bastard Killeran was about to receive the shock of a lifetime. Several Highlanders now stood by the flag, raising bagpipes to their lips. Crendall closed his eyes for just a moment, savoring the rich notes that blasted down into the valley. Momentarily the attack stopped as Killeran and his forces turned toward the forest, aghast at the Marchers aligned above them.

As if by some silent command, the Marchers as one stepped down into the valley. Swords, spears, and other wicked instruments of death held before them, they began at a walk, then moved to a trot. In absolute silence the Marchers advanced toward the reivers, the Ogren and the Shades, allowing the sharp notes of the bagpipes to drive them forward.

Crendall broke himself out of the spell that had kept his gaze transfixed on the Marchers and the flag that whipped violently in the now strongly gusting wind.

"Come on, my lads. Come on, my lasses. Continue your

efforts. Hold the walls." Crendall trotted across the parapet, a vicious smile on his face. "Now you're going to see what a real battle is like. Now you're going to see the Marchers in their full glory. Woe to any who stand in their way." He hadn't felt this good in years.

35

ENGAGEMENT

The Fal Carrachian soldiers formed a double wedge as they urged their horses across the rubble of the wall and moved swiftly across Dinnegan's property toward the mansion, Gregory at the point, Rya just behind. They dispatched briskly the few guards at the back of the estate, shifting their attack toward the black-clad men sprinting toward them in two perfectly formed lines.

"Remember, they are under a compulsion," shouted Rya. "They will never yield! They must be killed!"

Gregory nodded as he and his men urged their horses into a steady trot. It was then that he saw a tall, dark figure glide from the mansion and follow after the soldiers aligned against them.

"Hold your men here!" shouted Rya.

Gregory quickly gave the order, his men halting their advance. Rya walked her horse several yards in front of Gregory and his men, an unnatural calm settling over her. The Talent flowed through her with a purpose. Having used it to blow a hole in the back wall, she now applied it defensively, crafting a massive, glowing shield of white energy and placing it in front of her and Gregory and his soldiers.

The Fal Carrachians sat their horses bravely, seeking to calm their mounts, as bolts of black energy streamed toward them. They knew they had no defense against the Dark Magic sent against them, having no choice but to rely on the petite woman in their midst for their protection.

Their trust was rewarded. The black energy slammed into the shield, setting off a dazzling display of energy and sparks as the two sources of power struggled with one another, then merged, the momentarily grey shield returning to its brightly glowing white as Rya easily absorbed the Dark Magic Malachias had flung against her.

"Leave Malachias to me," Rya said grimly. "Kill his men and get to Kaylie."

36

DUEL

Leaving the black-clad soldiers to Gregory and his men, Rya dropped down from her horse and strode purposefully toward Malachias, the growing skirmish around her seemingly forgotten.

"It has been a long time, Lady Keldragan."

The gaunt man's scratchy whisper carried across the sculpted garden despite the rising noise of steel striking steel and the screams and shouts of fighting men.

"Not long enough, Malachias."

"I trust your husband is well. I am surprised that he is not here with you."

"He had other matters to attend to," replied Rya, who continued to advance on her adversary.

"A convenient excuse," said Malachias. "So I have no choice but to duel a woman. That hardly seems sporting."

"Yes, I know," said Rya. "I was hoping for a stronger opponent, but you'll have to do."

Rya's jibe struck home, Malachias spitting out his next words in a rage. "You believe you can challenge me? I stood at my master's side during the Great War. No one could defeat me then. No one can defeat me now."

"As I recall," said Rya, "you did indeed stand at your master's side, though the last time we met on the field of battle the last I saw of you was your backside as you fled with your master back into the Charnel Mountains."

"You disrespect me, woman!" hissed Malachias.

"I do indeed, Malachias. Now enough of this. It's time for you to be reminded of what a woman can do with the Talent."

Having no desire to engage in wasted conversation any longer, Rya grasped hold of the Talent, then released a stream of blinding white energy toward Malachias.

37

ANGER AND HATE

At hearing the sharp trill of the bagpipes behind him, Killeran wheeled his horse around, drawn by the haunting notes that smothered the small valley. The sight chilled him to the bone. The Marchers streaming quietly down into the Highland hollow would terrify any smart man. But even more frightening was the flag he had not seen for almost a decade and the boy who stood before it. The boy who had escaped his grasp in Tinnakilly. The boy who stood on the crest of the valley, eyes closed, hands raised to the sky. The wind whipped around him like a tornado, bolts of white energy twisting and turning, illuminating the source of all of Killeran's troubles of the last few years in a blinding glare.

A cheer rang out from the Highlanders defending the village, having seen the Marchers coming to their aid. Killeran violently turned his mount back toward the Highland village, not wanting to believe what he saw. Focused on their efforts, the half dozen warlocks attempting to burn through the gates failed to notice the Marchers approaching from behind. So intent on their task, they continued to hurl balls of black fire that began to eat deeply at the stout timbers, patiently waiting for their Dark Magic to burn through.

Yet the last three fireballs failed to reach the gates, stopped well short of the walls as if grasped by an invisible hand. Instead, the balls of black fire hung still for several seconds, then blinked out, much like a person putting out a candle flame between their thumb and forefinger. The warlocks stared dumbly at the smoldering gates. Black flames that had begun to burn suddenly winked out, scorch marks on the gates the only evidence of the warlocks' efforts. Stunned by what had just happened and not understanding the cause, they looked at one another in disbelief.

"Behind you, you fools!" screeched Killeran. "At the edge of the wood!"

The warlocks turned as one, quickly reclaiming the power of their Dark Magic, drawing on the gift given to them by the Shadow Lord as they found the source of their confusion. They released a burst of energy that darkened everything around it, the shadow streaking across the valley and striking the cause of their failure, covering the boy and the Highland flag in a swirling mass of biting blackness.

For a moment, an inky darkness reigned on the crest. Killeran cackled in glee, thinking the boy consumed, the root of his many failures finally eliminated. The Marchers even stopped their advance, fearful that their new Lord had not survived the attack. That their one chance to overthrow Killeran and his reivers had been taken from them in a single stroke.

Yet Killeran's pleasure was short-lived. Rays of pure white light began to spear through the blackness, more and more blinding rays blasting through like long, silver arrows tearing through the raging dark, until the boy appeared once more standing on the crest surrounded by a blazing pure white light.

Consuming the last of the warlocks' Dark Magic, Thomas opened his eyes, feeling the Talent flow within him. He took a moment to survey the battlefield, then turned his gaze to the warlocks who had attacked him.

Coban, Oso and the other Marchers let out a roar that echoed through the valley, exultant that the warlocks' assault had failed. Turning as one they began their advance once again, going from walk to trot to sprint in seconds. Brandishing their weapons, expressing their pent-up rage in screams of anger and hate, a decade of terror, loss and pain pushed them forward. And behind them stood the Highland Lord, their Highland Lord, looking up into the sky once more, hands upraised, white energy spinning faster and faster around him. The charging Marchers felt a prickle along the back of their necks as the air within the small valley became charged much as it did before a thunderstorm.

Drawing in as much of the Talent as he could, Thomas focused on the warlocks first. Pointing his right hand at the cluster of men who had sold their souls to the Shadow Lord for the power bestowed upon them, bolts of pure white light burst from his fingertips. The warlocks had no time to defend themselves. Sizzling through the air, the bolts struck true, blasting into them and turning their bodies to a grey ash.

Thomas fought to maintain his control, the tremendous power surging within him both exhilarating and seductive. He took a long moment to settle himself once again. Satisfied that he exercised control over the Talent once more, Thomas next focused on the Ogren and Shades. With flicks of his wrist he flung bolts of pure white light indiscriminately into the massed dark creatures. Bunched so tightly together, Thomas couldn't miss. Every bolt of energy struck home, killing Ogren and Shade instantly, their bodies burned beyond recognition, consumed by a heat that resembled that of the sun.

The reivers faltered as they saw the devastation occurring around them, not expecting such an immediate turn of events. Their initial confidence quickly turned to fear as the Marchers slammed into their wavering line, the Highlanders finally having the opportunity after almost a decade to unleash their repressed fury.

38

—————

DRIVING ANGER

"You cannot defeat me, woman. No matter what you try, I am too powerful for you."

Rya ignored Malachias' scratchy words. She continued to walk steadily toward him, halving the distance between them, then halving it again. A swirl of white energy surrounded her, and with each step she sent another bolt of white fire at her opponent. The inexorable assault forced the increasingly worried servant of the Shadow Lord to focus solely on defending himself.

"You shall feel my wrath, woman. You will beg for mercy before I kill you!"

Malachias' taunts barely registered with Rya. She knew that they were evenly matched. She didn't know if she had the strength to defeat Malachias, but she didn't care. He had taken her pupil, a young woman she had grown fond of, and likely someone important to her grandson. Normally controlled in her use of the Talent, for the first time in a very long time she allowed her anger to drive her. Narrowing her rage into a cold determination, she continued her advance.

As Rya drew ever closer to her opponent, Malachias began

to give ground and step back toward the mansion. He used a shield of black energy to block or deflect the bolts that sped toward him. He promised himself that she would pay the price for attacking her better, for having the gall to actually stand against him. Yet a quick glance to the side made him realize that having to concentrate on this insufferable woman had cost him in other ways. The bodies of his black-clad soldiers littered the battlefield. The Fal Carrachians had killed almost all of his men. Only a few continued to fight, forced to adhere to Malachias' compunction even with their lives at risk.

Malachias growled in frustration. Knowing that the tables had turned, Malachias reluctantly shifted his strategy. Pulling in more Dark Magic, he increased the size and density of his shield. When the next bolt struck, a massive explosion rocked the estate, the shield of black energy disintegrating as shards of black and white energy shot in all directions. Most disappeared harmlessly, though a few struck the mansion, shattering windows and blasting large holes in the brick walls and masonry.

Quiet settled over the grounds of the manor. When the dust and dirt finally cleared, Malachias had disappeared. Rya released her hold of the Talent. A crater several feet deep and wide around as a small house, blackened with ash, remained where Malachias had last stood. Scowling, Rya realized that to hope that the Shadow Lord's servant had died in that final explosion likely was a vain dream. She needed to see a body. She had defeated Malachias, but she didn't think that she had destroyed him.

39

NEW FRONT

"They barely defend the front, Swordmaster. They still haven't thought to close the gate."

Kael Bellilil nodded as he took in his scout's report. Not surprising. Dinnegan's men were not soldiers. Mercenaries and ruffians at best, and the events occurring at the back of the estate clearly had captured their attention. That was certainly something he could use to his advantage.

He trotted his horse forward a few paces, then spoke to the dozens of soldiers lined up behind him.

"Kill anyone who gets in our way. We ride to the princess."

Satisfied by the grim, expectant expressions of his men, he spun his horse back toward the mansion. He started at a walk, then moved quickly to a trot until he broke through the trees that surrounded the estate. Directing his mount toward the gate, he urged his horse to a gallop, his men streaming behind him in silence, intent on their mission.

No shouts. No screams. Just the sound of pounding hooves as the gate to Dinnegan's property drew closer by the second, the guards charged with defending it still distracted by what occurred behind them. By the time they realized the approaching danger, their fates had been sealed.

40

TO THE PRECIPICE

L ed by Coban, the Marchers drove into the Army of the Black Sword and pushed quickly through the center of Killeran's line. The reivers parted much like a ship's bow slicing through the water. More Marchers streamed forward to widen the gap, keeping the reivers between them and the Ogren and Shades on the flanks so that the dark creatures could not advance unless they charged through their reluctant allies.

Following Thomas' instructions, Oso kept his fighters in check. He maintained a slow, steady advance, guaranteeing that his Marchers kept their shape and the left flank remained a solid, unbroken line. Anara stood next to the large Highlander, dagger in one hand, sword in the other, lunging and slashing at the reivers seeking to break through, a determined glint in her eye.

Now pressed on two sides, Killeran tried to turn his forces as best he could. Yet he struggled to bring his Ogren and Shades to bear. He knew that these dark creatures were his only chance to shift the tide of battle now that the boy had incinerated his warlocks. Screeching at the top of his lungs, he strove desperately to regain control, ordering his men to reform their lines. But the Marchers would have none of it, inexorably pressing forward, compressing Killeran's reivers into a tighter and tighter space, pushing what was left of Killeran's Army of the Black Sword closer to the walls of the fortress and the left flank protected by Oso and his Marchers.

Soon the Marchers' efforts brought them into contact with the remaining dark creatures. The Marchers had a harder time against the Ogren and Shades, but they knew how to fight the minions of the Shadow Lord. For them, their strategy came down to basic math. Knowing that a single Marcher stood little chance against either adversary, they always sought to have three or four Marchers fight against one Ogren or Shade, using their superior numbers to overwhelm their foes.

Thomas joined the fight after destroying the warlocks and continuing his attack on the Ogren and Shades until his Marchers began to engage the dark creatures, forcing him to stop his assault with the Talent so that he did not inadvertently harm his own fighters. Energized and focused, barely hearing the clash of steel on steel, the cries of agony and the other sounds of battle swirling around him, he had eyes only for Killeran. He ran down the crest into the valley and entered the melee. Infusing the Sword of the Highlands with the Talent, the blade gifted to him by his grandfather glowed brightly, energy sparking along the steel. Leaving the reivers to his Marchers, he cut through the Ogren and Shades with ease. With the Ogren, he targeted their legs, slicing hamstrings or thighs to get them to the ground, knowing that the Marchers following after him would dispatch the dark creatures quickly. With the Shades, he was more precise, striking for the neck or head with a killing blow, not wanting to risk an injured Shade still killing one of his Marchers.

The Highland Lord was almost through the mass of dark creatures, no more than thirty feet from Killeran, when the Dunmoorian lord finally saw him. Killeran pulled his horse back in fear, terrified of the burning anger he recognized in the boy's blazing green eyes. With a final slash with his sword, Thomas took the leg off an Ogren at the knee and stepped clear of the dark creatures, his Marchers pouncing on the injured beast.

Nothing stood between Thomas and his prey as he stalked forward with a determined stride. He raised his sword to strike, Killeran simply sitting his horse dumbly, frozen by the sight of this relentless boy advancing toward him, when two Shades stepped in Thomas' way.

The two dark creatures moved sinuously, like snakes gliding around him, always ready to attack once a weakness was found. Swords at the ready, they jabbed, trying to catch Thomas off balance. Thomas brought his sword up quickly, defending against a strike from the front, then twisting inhumanly fast to block the expected stab to his back from the second Shade. Under normal circumstances, Thomas would have approached this fight cautiously, knowing that a single touch by the poisoned blade of a Shade would lead to a terrible death. But he didn't have the time, seeing that his main quarry was slinking back through his reivers in search of a path to escape.

Not wanting to lose his target, Thomas drove forward in a furious attack, forcing both Shades back in a whirlwind assault of slashes and stabs that left the two servants of the Shadow Lord dripping black blood from a half dozen wounds each. Moving forward lightning fast, Thomas lunged for one Shade's stomach, knowing his opponent would escape the blow and the second Shade would swing down for his exposed neck.

Thomas stopped the lunge midway through, then sliced upward, taking off the head of the Shade bringing his sword down. The Shade collapsed, his head dropping to the bloody grass. Thomas continued the movement of his blade, turning it at an angle to bring it down on the back of the other Shade's neck as the dark creature lunged forward in an attempt to catch

Thomas in the gut. The Highlander proved faster, as the second Shade's head fell to the ground to rest next to that of its companion.

Thomas surveyed the battlefield, Killeran no longer in sight. His enemies were finding their mettle as the action became more desperate for them. Driven back by the Marcher attack but not broken, Thomas sensed that it was time to strike the decisive blow.

"Marchers!" he shouted, his voice carrying across the valley through the aid of the Talent. "To me! For the Highlands!"

The cry stiffened the resolve of the already engaged Marchers. And it finally released those Marchers who had waited impatiently for their chance to fight for their homeland. Renn, Seneca and Nestor led their men out of the forest on the eastern side of the valley. Sprinting across the long grass, their rage driving them on, they slammed into Killeran's left flank. The Marchers' surprise complete, the reivers and remaining dark creatures almost broke as the Marchers pushed them inexorably to the edge of the precipice.

Taking the attack of the Marchers on the west as their cue, Oso and Coban exhorted their fighters to push forward as well, catching the reivers, Ogren and Shades in a vice that continued to tighten slowly but surely. It was then that an unexpected gift was given to the Highland Lord.

With the reivers' attention focused on the Marchers they had already engaged, Crendall opened the smoking gates of Anselm. A phalanx of Marchers sallied forth, driving the reivers who had been attacking the walls before them and cursing with every step they took. Crendall had recognized Thomas' plan immediately and fully approved, exhorting his Highlanders to link up with the Marchers that had come to their aid and continue to push their opponents toward the cusp of the escarpment.

41

A NEW SKILL

"Take her," commanded Dinnegan. "We must go!"

A guard from the front of the manor had sprinted into Dinnegan's office with the dire news that Fal Carrachian soldiers had broken through the gate with barely any resistance. They had almost reached the mansion. Dinnegan looked out the window to the back of the property and saw that Gregory himself stood there leading his men against Malachias' soldiers.

At first he thought it an even fight, but the black-clad men faltered when their master engaged the woman who now stood calmly while surrounded by a swirling mass of white energy, releasing bolt after bolt at Malachias. She walked toward him step by step, gradually closing the distance between them, seemingly unperturbed as Malachias did all he could to fend off her constant attack. He knew it! It was the same woman who had visited with the Princess, the one who had unnerved him. He had discerned that there was something about her that wasn't quite right, and now he knew why.

He could have waited to find out if Malachias defeated the woman and turned the tide of the fight, but his well-tuned survival instinct told him something else. It was time to leave. He walked through the hidden door from which the black-clad men had first appeared, carrying several bundles of documents, not bothering to look back at his son.

Maddan stood there for a long moment, frozen, shocked by the sudden turn of events. All their plans had been moving forward as expected and were well on their way to completion, yet in a matter of minutes it had all fallen apart.

"Stop!" he shouted, a ripple of fear making his voice waver.

With his father's disappearance into the tunnel and the guard gone, Kaylie had begun inching toward the open door that led to the front of the mansion.

"You're coming with me."

Maddan walked toward her, pulling the dagger at his belt. Kaylie scanned around her in desperation, seeking anything with which she could defend herself. Kael had trained her in the blade, but there was nothing within easy reach. And though she had begun to learn how to defend herself with only her hands, she doubted she had the ability or strength to take on the larger and slightly crazed Maddan.

With no other options coming to mind, Kaylie returned to her training with Rya. She immediately felt more confident. Despite the fast-approaching threat presented by Maddan, she took hold of the Talent in an instant. Unsure of what to do, as she had had limited instruction, she fell back to her most recent lesson, though refining it just a bit.

Much to her delight, it worked. A small chest that sat on Dinnegan's desk began to hover a finger's breadth above its surface. With a flick of her wrist the chest flew through the air toward Maddan's head.

He almost saw it too late, but he ducked at the last second, uncertain of what had just happened. He didn't have time to think on it.

Pleased with her first attempt and now confident in her

newfound ability, Kaylie used the Talent to fling a crystal bowl through the air aimed at her attacker, followed by a pair of candlesticks and then several books from the stacks behind her.

Maddan defended himself as best as he could, the dagger useless in his hand. But it was the last object that rose from his father's desk and shot toward his chest that was the final straw. Dropping to the ground, he scrambled on hands and knees to the hidden door, lunging through and slamming it shut behind him just as the letter opener dug into the wood, quivering from the force of the strike.

Kaylie smiled and took a deep breath, relieved.

"A new skill, Princess?"

Kael Bellilil stood in the doorway to the office, his sword, covered with streaks of blood, in hand. So focused on defending herself, she had not heard the Fal Carrachians break into the mansion.

"Yes." She had no other reply, her pride obvious.

"Seems quite useful," he said with a grin. "Now if you're finished, it's time to go."

42

STATEMENT MADE

The two Shades dispatched, Thomas sought to continue his advance toward Killeran, but a new opponent appeared before him.

"So you're the boy causing all the trouble," muttered a scarred reiver missing his right eye. "I'm going to end everything right now, as I should have long ago."

Thomas remembered the reiver from ten years before as if it were yesterday. Oclan. The man had tracked him through the Highlands when he made his escape from the Crag at his grandfather's behest. Thomas had survived the pursuit by hiding in the Southern River, breathing through a reed as he waited for the reivers to move on unaware of how close they had come to finding their quarry.

The reiver leapt toward Thomas, his war cry preceding him. Thomas stood there calmly. If the reiver thought that his demonstration would force Thomas into doing something foolish, he was mistaken. As the reiver slashed his blade toward Thomas' neck, he ducked and rolled, shifting his grip on his sword and stabbing backward, his blade sliding into Oclan's back, its point emerging from his chest. Red blood welled up on

Oclan's shirt, saturating his leather armor. Thomas stood there for a few seconds, not even turning back to the reiver, as the battle-scarred warrior slid off his blade and fell to a heap on the ground, his lifeless eyes staring up at the grey sky. Thomas took no satisfaction in his victory, knowing only that it was necessary.

Thomas jumped back into the battle, but much to his dismay, he saw Killeran riding hard to the east, Renn and Seneca unable to close a gap between their two war parties before Killeran slipped through protected by a handful of Ogren. Aggravated by his bad luck, Thomas turned his thoughts away from pursuit and retribution. Instead, he focused on the larger task at hand as his Marchers drove into the enemy host with a vengeance.

The Marchers continued to push, tightening the vise, forcing their enemies closer and closer to the precipice. His prize having escaped him, Thomas concentrated on the last Shade standing. Thomas suspected that this Shade differed from the others. Therefore, he approached the dark creature warily, oblivious to everything else around him. Not wanting to give Thomas the advantage of an attack, the Shade released a shard of darkness, followed by another, and then another.

Momentarily taken aback, never having come across a Shade with Dark Magic, Thomas used his Talent to call the wind, which became a swirling mass in front of him and deflected the deadly bolts, knowing that if the Dark Magic struck him it would destroy him in seconds. Tamping down his surprise, ready for anything now, Thomas continued his approach, walking slowly, gracefully, toward the Shade, blazing sword held at the ready, a look of grim determination on his face.

Thomas attacked first, his blade a whirl of steel, the Shade barely able to keep up with him. A small space had opened up around them, as the reivers, driven close to the edge of the precipice, began surrendering. The Marchers killed the remaining Ogren with no mercy, oftentimes just forcing them off the edge. Some of the reivers were caught up in it, shoved off as well, but that didn't bother the Marchers in the least. These men had murdered and tortured their families and friends. A fall to their death was a better ending than many deserved.

Thomas reached the precipice, the Shade trying to gain room to maneuver by jumping up onto a sliver of stone that rose up above the ground and hung out over the thousand-foot drop. Thomas refused to allow the creature to disengage, following him out on the stone, his blade a steel blur as he continued to push the creature back toward the edge, much like a pirate forcing an unlucky captive to walk the plank.

The Shade had nowhere to go. Every time their blades met, sparks flew around them. Thomas began to break through the Shade's defenses with regularity, slicing the creature in a dozen places, the strange black goo that was its blood leaking out and staining the stone upon which it stood. Desperate, the Shade tried one more time with its Dark Magic. In a flash of black light, a dark creature almost twice as tall as Thomas appeared in front of him on the stone. Thomas had never seen its like before.

Resembling a Nightstalker, but with no wings, the beast attacked Thomas with razor-sharp claws and a tail that resembled a whip as thick as a man's forearm. The creature snapped its tail continually at Thomas, forcing him back across the stone. Several times Thomas brought his shining blade up just in time, deflecting the creature's tail and taking a chunk of hardened flesh from it. But the wounds had no impact on the dark creature called by the Shade. Despite its exertions, the beast never seemed to tire or feel pain, fueled by a berserker rage. Each time its tail missed Thomas, the scorpion-like point at the end chipped into the stone, sending small rocks flying off into the abyss. Thomas concentrated on defending himself, staying out of reach of the tail and catching the creature's claws on his glowing blade before they could cut through his defenses.

The duel fully consumed Thomas as he knew that this last fight must be won for the Highlanders to declare victory. The reivers having surrendered, all the other Ogren and Shades driven off the precipice, the Marchers stood there silently, watching, mesmerized by the speed of the combat, barely able to track the lightning fast movement with their eyes. Losing patience and tired of the onslaught, Thomas drew on a hidden reserve of resolve.

As the creature's tail came down, its claws coming forward, Thomas used the Talent to throw a bolt of light between them, momentarily blinding the beast and giving Thomas the second he needed. He brought his sword up in a blindingly fast stroke and sliced off the demon's tail.

Then, calling on more of the Talent, he infused his glowing sword with even more of nature's power, to the point where it burned so brightly the Marchers watching could see nothing but the dazzling light and no sign of the steel beneath it. The raging energy blinded the creature, and Thomas used its momentary hesitation to slide the infused steel through the demon's attacks and into its heart. In an explosion of blackened ash, the demon disintegrated before his eyes, the strong wind whipping across the sliver of stone and scouring clean the corrupted cinders, which drifted down to the gorge below.

Sword still filled with the Talent and burning brightly, Thomas turned his merciless gaze, fiery green eyes glowing brightly, to the Shade. Thomas attacked with a controlled fury. He lost himself in the fighting. His body and mind were one with the blade, the steel simply an extension of his arm. He felt no emotion, only purpose. It was over in less than a minute. Unable to withstand Thomas' assault, the glowing blade sliced cleanly through the Shade's neck. The dark creature tottered on the edge of the stone for a moment before gravity pulled it down toward the river raging far below.

Thomas breathed deeply as he stood on the sliver of stone, somewhat elevated above his Marchers. He closed his eyes to center himself, then turned slowly, sword in his hand, the energy of the natural world still pulsing across the blade. Thomas surveyed the battlefield, the eyes of the men and women who believed in him, who had trusted him, turned toward him. Unexpectedly, he felt a pull much like he had when he became a member of the Sylvana, like a binding to the land, knowing that he truly was the Lord of the Highlands now, that the Highlands were his to rule and protect, that the Marchers were his to lead.

Lord of the Highlands and truly the defender of the Highlands as a Sylvan Warrior. He was of the Highlands and the Highlands were a part of him. He closed his eyes, taking in everything around him, just like a raptor flying across the land peering down at the valleys, the trees, the peaks, watching the fish swim in the rivers. He soared among the highest peaks, swooping over the cliffs, feeling the rush of the water in the streams, the breeze sweeping across the long grass. For a moment, this new awareness threatened to overwhelm him.

The screech of a massive raptor, circling above him, awakened him from his trance. The bird was defiant, proud. The raptor swooped down over Thomas then settled on the wall of Anselm, staring at Thomas with what he imagined to be pride. He had no doubt that he knew the raptor. It was the same one he had come across when he visited the Roost just a few short weeks ago.

Smiling broadly, he looked down once again, surveying his fighters, acknowledging their determination and pride, their tension finally released by having accomplished something that just months before they never thought possible. Thomas raised the pulsing Sword of the Highlands above his head. He glanced at the inscription running the length of the blade on both sides: "Strength and courage lead to freedom."

Thomas had always thought those words applied to what he had to do. He didn't realize until that very instant that the words applied to him as well. Thomas finally understood that those words, so long a part of his Kestrel family legacy, could also help relieve him of his own burdens, his own responsibilities.

"We are the Highlanders!" yelled Thomas, his voice carrying well beyond the small valley. "The Highlands are ours once more! The Highlands are free! We are free!"

A mighty cheer erupted from the Marchers, his Marchers. And then the chant began: "For the Highlands! For the Highlands! For the Highlands!"

The chant echoed off the surrounding peaks, traveling for leagues throughout the Highlands.

Then ever so subtly the chant changed: "For the Highland Lord! For the Highland Lord! For the Highland Lord!"

The Lost Kestrel had returned. And he had made the Highlands and the Marchers his own.

43

WORTHY PRIDE

"**W**ell done, girl." Having confirmed much to her frustration that Malachias had escaped, Rya had walked to the front of the estate and embraced Kaylie in a warm hug. "I'm proud of you."

Kaylie beamed with pleasure at the compliment. Kael stood protectively behind her as her father conversed with his soldiers and gave orders for a search of the estate. Gregory doubted he would catch Dinnegan and his son, but it was worth the attempt. If they failed to bring him and his son back, he promised himself that eventually he would catch up to Dinnegan. When he did the traitor would pay the ultimate penalty for his greed and treachery.

"Lady Keldragan, my thanks." Finished issuing orders, Gregory joined them. Now that his daughter was safe, he could breathe easier.

"It was nothing, King Gregory. Besides, I have a special interest in this one."

Gregory glanced at his daughter. She seemed to be trying to appear unobtrusive, which was an uncommon undertaking for Kaylie.

"Oh. How so?"

"She's one of my better pupils."

"Pupil?"

Gregory saw Kael grin, but that quickly disappeared when his daughter scowled at the Swordmaster.

"I'm sure your daughter will fill you in," said Rya, her pride in the Princess of Fal Carrach still evident. "Kaylie, you will need to continue on your own for a time. I expect you to have mastered your lessons by the time I return."

"But why?" asked Kaylie. "Where are you going?"

"I have things to do that simply can't wait any longer. And my friends need to know about Malachias and what's been occurring here in Fal Carrach."

Kaylie was flustered for a moment. She actually found Rya's prickly demeanor comforting. Rya was sharp with her words and demanding. But she had quickly grown on the young woman who had never had a strong female presence in her life.

"But does the threat …"

"Kaylie, remember what we have talked about. Remember what you have learned. There is much you can do. You need only think and apply yourself."

She nodded, saddened to lose Rya if only for a time, but heartened by her words.

The petite woman stepped forward and gave Kaylie another hug. She then whispered into her ear, "You will know what to do when the time comes. Stay strong. Stay sharp."

44

THREAT ELIMINATED

Captain Garlan knelt on the hard stone floor of the Rock's great hall, his hands chained behind him.

"Enough, Garlan. Your lies will do you no good. You betrayed my daughter. Who aided you?"

Taken from his room during the night, Kael Bellilil and his men had been less than gentle, having little patience for traitors. At first Garlan offered one falsehood after another for his actions, yet none believable. Finally, after Kael and his men worked to convince him to tell the truth, the story started to come out. Garlan's anger at never being considered for Swordmaster was well known within the Rock, but usually ignored by the Fal Carrachian soldiers stationed there, believing that based on his competence Garlan had already risen higher within the ranks than he deserved. Garlan had revealed much of his thinking beyond the Rock during his frequent visits to the harbor's many taverns, so it didn't take long for Dinnegan to identify him as a possible accomplice and then apply the screws needed to gain his willing engagement in the plot.

Kaylie stood beside her father, forcing herself to watch the interrogation, knowing it was important to do so. She had no doubt that Garlan had participated of his own free will and had not been compelled by Malachias. The large bag of gold found in his room, likely provided by Dinnegan, suggested his real motivation. Yet Kaylie knew the puzzle still missed a piece. Garlan was a conspirator, but he was not the assassin.

As she allowed her mind to wander and follow that loose thread, she sensed a disturbance above them. Without even thinking she took hold of the Talent. A crossbow bolt shot straight toward her father, and with a deft control she used the Talent to stop the steel shaft, holding the missile in midair, just feet from striking home.

Her father watched in amazement, completely taken aback. Before Kael could even pull his sword from his scabbard to defend his king with a flick of her wrist Kaylie sent the bolt back in the direction from which it had come.

A groan echoed through the chamber, followed by a clatter as a hooded man, dressed in black and grey to better hide in the shadows, fell from the rafters that crisscrossed the great hall.

For just a moment, silence reigned. That was quickly broken as Kael and the guards at the back of the hall drew their blades and approached the body, confirming that the curly-haired assassin was dead.

Kaylie did not experience any guilt at what she had just done. She had never killed a man before, so she did feel queasy, her stomach beginning to voice its displeasure at watching the assassin's blood spread across the floor. But she felt pride and relief as well at having protected her father. She tried to avoid her father's stare, but found the task impossible. When finally she turned, she saw a knowing expression on his face. She assumed that he understood now what type of instruction Rya had been talking about after the skirmish at Dinnegan's estate.

"I guess I forgot to mention a few of the things that happened while you were away," she said sheepishly.

"Yes, you did."

45

BAGPIPES

The stars had just appeared in the night sky, a cold wind buffeting King Gregory as he walked the battlements of the Rock. He wanted some time alone and this was how he often obtained it. He had felt anxious the past few days following the rescue of his daughter and the quashing of the assassination plot. Moreover, he was still coming to terms with his daughter's newfound ability. Though a bit disconcerting at first, her growing skill in the Talent certainly had come in handy. Moreover, in just the few weeks he had been gone, Kaylie appeared to have acquired a new level of maturity, likely due in part to the guidance of Lady Keldragan. As these and other thoughts flitted through his mind, a grave expression never left his face as he walked the parapet. His wandering had more to do with reminiscing than checking on the guards and his defenses. He liked to meander when he wanted to think and remember his wife.

Sadness always threatened to overwhelm him when reminiscing about Laura, what she had missed since her passing, not seeing Kaylie grow into a beautiful and strong young woman, the years they didn't have together. Yet his responsibilities to Fal Carrach continued to intrude on his personal thoughts.

His worries multiplied as he prepared to travel to Eamhain Mhacha for the Council of the Kingdoms. Rodric could take the Highlands once and for all with the ten-year regency expiring. That would be a terrible result for all the Kingdoms, but particularly for Fal Carrach, as he saw such an occurrence as triggering several other immediate challenges, much like a falling domino. In his mind, the Highlands functioned as the linchpin. If that Kingdom came under Rodric's sway permanently, he had no doubt that the scheming High King would fix his attention next on Fal Carrach with Benewyn to follow.

As he approached the northern battlements, which faced the Highlands, he could just barely make out the outline of the higher peaks through the dark. He began to hear the lilting song of the bagpipes, drifting down from the southern Highlands. He stopped for a moment, surprised, thinking it might be something else. But then the gusting wind confirmed his initial belief. He hadn't heard the bagpipes in a long time, almost ten years in fact.

A soldier walking the parapet stopped for a moment, staring at Gregory in concern, the king of Fal Carrach apparently caught in a daze.

"Are you all right, King Gregory?" asked the soldier with some worry. "Is there anything I can do?"

Gregory came back to himself upon hearing the soldier's voice.

"I'm fine, thank you, Derric. I was just listening."

"The bagpipes?" asked the soldier. "I wasn't too sure myself, but I've been catching snatches on the wind for the past few hours."

Gregory wished Derric a good night, then continued along the wall. He quickly became lost in thought once again, pondering why the bagpipes were being played after such a long time. He stopped once more, peering at the Highland peaks, an image of Thomas popping into his mind.

The last he'd seen of the boy, he was jumping off the parapet of Tinnakilly's fortress in an attempt to escape the High King. He owed more than he could ever repay to that boy, appreciating that he'd saved his daughter's life and his own and that of many of his soldiers. The image of Thomas bravely standing on the hill, calmly firing arrows down at the charging Fearhounds, played through his mind, never to be forgotten.

Yet Gregory had failed the boy in Tinnakilly, unable to keep Rodric from his plans of torture and an eventual slow death. This boy who brought the memory of Talyn Kestrel to his mind, only at a much younger age. The last Lord of the Highlands had been his best friend, yet then as well Gregory had not been able to prevent Talyn's death, much as with this boy. He should have seen the resemblance between the two in Tinnakilly, but he had been concentrating on other things. Could the boy have been the Lost Kestrel? Gregory shook his head in frustration. Now he likely would never know.

When Thomas took that fateful step off the Tinnakilly parapet, his daughter had changed. Kaylie was always serious, but the loss of her friend made her almost severe in some respects. She threw herself into her training with Fal Carrach's Swordmaster, Kael Bellilil, with a vengeance, to the point where she had become a better sword fighter than many of his soldiers.

She blamed herself for Thomas' death, believing that she was responsible for his capture. And now the training she had received from Lady Keldragan had given her another point of focus, a way to center herself on the present rather than the past. Learning that his daughter could use the Talent, the natural magic of the world, still unsettled him. But he was proud of her as well.

Nevertheless, though all evidence suggested that Thomas

had perished from the fall, he still couldn't believe it. There was something about the boy that made him stand out, a quiet power or strength that he didn't think anyone could silence easily. Yes, the boy leapt from the battlements, but no one had ever found his body. Gregory just couldn't shake the feeling that the boy still lived, no matter how unrealistic that thought might be. Perhaps it was the bagpipes, the notes becoming stronger, more insistent as the wind picked up. He'd heard this rhythm before, a long time ago when he and his friend Talyn Kestrel had rode out together against brigands who had sought to make the Burren their base of operations. If he wasn't mistaken, it was the Highland call to war.

Perhaps there was hope after all with the Council of the Kingdoms fast approaching, slim though the chance may be of an outcome that didn't leave Rodric strengthened and a greater threat to Fal Carrach and the other Kingdoms. Gregory stood on the wall for quite awhile, finally returning to the memories of an easier time, when his wife Laura was still with him. The cold finally seeping through his cloak and into his bones, Gregory made his way to the steps leading down to the court-yard in search of Kael. Maybe his Highland born friend could confirm what the bagpipes meant.

46

RECLAIMING THEIR HOMELAND

The Marcher chiefs sat around a fire just inside the walls of Anselm. Crendall had taken a squad of Marchers from the village into the valley to burn the bodies of the reivers, Ogren and Shades that littered the landscape, several bonfires already illuminating the night. They also established a stockade for the captured reivers. Nestor had disagreed, suggesting instead that pushing them off the precipice as they did the Ogren offered the easiest and best solution.

Many of the Highlanders likely agreed with him, and took a great deal of pleasure in discussing it in front of the defeated reivers. Thomas refused to sanction the plan, noting that no matter how deserving of such a fate the reivers might be, the Marchers would hold to their code of not killing prisoners. Nestor expected as much, but he didn't see any harm in having a little fun at the reivers' expense.

Thomas looked up, gazing at the flag of the Highland Lord flying above the village's scorched gates. His grandfather Talyn would be proud, but just for a few minutes, as the previous Lord of the Highlands already would have turned his focus to all the work that still needed to be done. The Marchers had routed the reivers, but they had not completely driven them out of the Highlands.

Moreover, the hardest task remained. Rodric wanted the Highlands, and he'd do anything to take the rugged land. Even if Thomas successfully declared himself the Highland Lord and the other rulers acknowledged his claim, the threat of an Armaghian invasion only would increase. He had no doubt that Rodric would find some excuse to press his claim. The High King's strategy for conquering all the Kingdoms depended on first assuming control of the Highlands. Thomas viewed it as a game within a game. Time was running out for him to reclaim the Highlands and end Killeran's regency, but something also needed to be done about the larger concern of Rodric's expanding power throughout all the Kingdoms.

As Thomas ate his stew, Coban explained to the other chiefs the need to rebuild the Crag. Knowing that Rodric would attack eventually, the Crag could once again serve as their primary fortress and staging ground for the Highland response to any invasion.

Oso glanced at his friend, who didn't seem to be paying much attention. Thomas ate mechanically, his thoughts apparently elsewhere.

"Thomas," said Oso. "What's on your mind?"

"That it doesn't work," he replied, setting his bowl down on the ground. "It's a good thought, but it won't work this time."

The other chiefs stopped their conversation, considering Thomas' words.

"What are you thinking?" asked Coban.

"I was thinking that we're focused on reacting, defending."

"That's not true," responded Renn. "We're planning how to drive out the reivers."

"Yes, Renn, I was listening. But that's not enough. We can drive them out. We will drive out the few who remain within our borders. But they'll just come back in larger numbers with

Rodric offering some other excuse for the attack so that we remain isolated. And the Ogren and Shades we just faced here are likely only the beginning. The dark creatures are still crossing the Northern Steppes and trying to raid the northern Highlands. That won't stop. In fact, I expect those incursions will increase in frequency."

"Did you have something else in mind, Thomas?" asked Seneca.

"All the Kingdoms know that we've never had a large army, and our numbers have dwindled during the last decade. But they've always feared us because we can fight."

Thomas rose from his seat and began to pace around the fire, his energy infectious.

"Then what do you propose?" asked Coban.

"We have many concerns that need to be addressed," began Thomas. "But let's focus on the three big ones. The threat from Rodric, the declaration, and the Shadow Lord."

"The Shadow Lord?" asked Seneca, jumping up from his seat on a log. "You can't be serious."

"I am serious. Deadly serious."

Seneca caught the look in Thomas' eye and promptly sat back down.

"Thomas is right," said Coban. "The Ogren and Shades we just fought prove his intentions. They offer proof of his return, even if the bastard is still hiding behind the High King."

"The Shadow Lord is a threat," stated Thomas. "For more reasons than you know."

"But he hasn't attacked for centuries," protested Seneca, not yet ready to acknowledge such a troublesome and frightening reality.

"Not only am I the Highland Lord," said Thomas. "But remember, I'm also a Sylvan Warrior. We have not forgotten our struggle with the Shadow Lord. Other members of the Sylvana have confirmed that the dark creatures hiding in the Charnel

Mountains stir. That can mean only one thing. Besides, we all know that our northern border has faced more forays by dark creatures in the last year than in the previous twenty combined. That is not happenstance. The Shadow Lord tests us. And as we've just confirmed, he's allied to the High King."

"Thomas is right," said Coban. "Rodric is in league with the Shadow Lord. And Killeran has been his lackey ever since the Crag fell. I don't think it was just Rodric who wanted the Kestrels murdered that night. I believe the Shadow Lord ordered the attack on the Crag. Rodric was more than happy to become involved because it served his purposes as well. But Thomas threw an unwanted twist into his plans by surviving that cursed night."

"I agree with Thomas as well," said Nestor. "We don't have as many fighters compared to the other Kingdoms. Rodric wants to follow in the footsteps of the first High King, Ollav Fola, and create a single Kingdom. But he's spread thin at the moment and can't devote the necessary resources to the Highlands, not with Gregory of Fal Carrach and a few other rulers watching him closely and continuing to resist his entreaties. But we must focus on the most immediate concern. If Thomas doesn't appear at the Council, Rodric takes the Highlands by law and he moves forward with his plans. Then the Shadow Lord has a staging ground much closer to the Kingdoms and no longer has to worry about forcing the Dark Host beyond the Breaker. I doubt that fool High King even recognizes the likely result of whatever bargain he's made with the Shadow Lord. His rule will last for only so long as the Shadow Lord allows."

"Nestor speaks sense as well," said Renn. "Why have we never eliminated Killeran and his reivers before? Obviously the warlocks made it difficult. But there have always been times when there weren't enough warlocks to do Rodric, or Killeran's, bidding. Whenever we gathered a large group of Marchers, dark creatures always seemed to threaten our northern border, requiring us to split our forces. It was a good strategy and helped to keep us weak and disconnected."

"I can see where you're going with this," said Coban. "By allying with the Shadow Lord, Rodric has effectively tied us down, forcing us to defend on two fronts against two enemies we aren't strong enough to fight at the same time."

"Correct," said Thomas. "But no longer. Now we're going to do something about it."

"What do you suggest?" asked Nestor.

Thomas glanced at Nestor, giving him an appraising look and happy to build off of the grizzled Marcher's gentle prod. Nestor had figured all this out before anyone else, but he didn't share his thoughts until he assumed everyone else had reached the same conclusion on their own. Thomas would have to remember that approach and how beneficial it could be in the future.

"First, we eliminate our vulnerabilities," began Thomas, pacing around the fire once more. "We don't have many villages along our northern border. The Shadow Lord usually sends a few hundred of his dark creatures at a time across the Northern Steppes. My guess is that he doesn't like to be without too many of his Ogren and Shades because he's still building up his strength. But those raiding parties could easily devastate any of the villages located there."

"So we pull them together," said Coban, reaching the same conclusion Thomas had.

"Yes, we pull all the small northern villages together for a time. That many Highlanders in one place can defend themselves against anything the Shadow Lord may send across. Then we set up more signal towers along the very edge of the border peaks. We also send one war party of Marchers to the north. If any large group of dark creatures tries to cross our northern border, we'll know, we'll be ready, and we'll defend ourselves."

"I like it," said Nestor. "In fact, I have family in the north. It'd be an honor to take on this assignment."

"Done," said Thomas, grateful for the offer. "Second, we rebuild the Crag. We don't want to be tied to a fortress, as our ability to move quickly is more important. But just making the effort to rebuild the Crag will send a strong message to our people and to the other Kingdoms. We need the Crag as much for a defensive stronghold as for a symbol."

"It also might centralize any outside attacks," said Coban. "In most wars, the attacking force usually wants to capture the other side's capital, even if it holds no military value. That could work to our advantage. When Rodric or Killeran attack again, if they come for the Crag, we'll have multiple opportunities to ambush them and whittle away at their strength."

"Quite so, Coban. Will you take on that responsibility?"

"It would be an honor, Thomas," replied the old Swordmaster.

"Thank you, my friend." Thomas stopped pacing and looked at his other chiefs, the two who had been required by law to try to kill him when he sought to become the Lord of the Highlands. "Renn, Seneca, I would ask that you take your war parties to the south and west, respectively. Prepare the signal towers, rebuilding those that once stood along the edge of the Highlands and adding any more that you deem necessary. But we will not defend. Again, the towers are a method of communication and a symbol more than anything else."

"And once that's complete?" asked Seneca.

"We attack," answered Thomas simply. "We defend no more. We will not wait for reivers or Rodric's soldiers to enter the Highlands. If any enemy decides to encroach on the Highland borders, eliminate them. Let our enemies remember the price they will pay if they try to enter the Highlands without our permission."

"With pleasure," said Renn, the aggressive strategy playing perfectly to his personality.

"What about me, Thomas?" asked Oso.

"Oso, I ask that you lead the reserve of Marchers at the Crag," said Thomas. "Renn, Seneca, Nestor, if more men are needed send word to Oso and expect an immediate response. Remember, we will not be tied to any one village or location. Our defense will be our offense, which will extend to the very edges of the Highland borders. Rather than waiting to be attacked, we will do the attacking."

"I like the way your mind works," said Nestor.

"I had a good teacher," replied Thomas, his chiefs acknowledging the truth of that statement.

"And the declaration?" asked Coban. "What of that? The deadline approaches. The Kingdoms will gather in only a few months, and according to the law Rodric will get the Highlands if you don't appear."

"Over my dead body," said Thomas. "I'll be taking thirty men. Coban, I ask that you join me. Oso, you as well if that's all right."

"What do you mean?" asked the large Highlander. "Why wouldn't it be?"

"I just think you should speak with Anara first. You saw how well she fought today. I'd like to stay in her good graces if at all possible."

The Highland chiefs laughed heartily at Thomas' humor. Oso attempted a chuckle, then grimaced. How would Anara react to his leaving? Should he speak with her? Despite the fact that they had almost a month before they'd have to set off for Eamhain Mhacha, his increasing worry set his heart racing.

"While we're away, I'll ask Anara to manage things here at the Crag. Send any requests for fighters or supplies to her.

Renn, Seneca, Nestor, protection of the Highlands falls to you until we return. Once the Council is over and our claim legitimized, we will put our larger plan into action."

The Highland chiefs nodded their understanding.

"But won't they try to kill you, Thomas?" asked Seneca. "If Rodric suspects that you're coming, he'll try to take you on the road where he can bring a bigger force to bear. Besides, you maimed his son, which will add oil to the fire. He has multiple reasons for wanting you dead."

"True," answered Thomas, his green eyes burning brightly in the firelight, his voice strong and commanding. "But wanting and getting are two different things. The other Kingdoms have ignored our plight for almost a decade. It's time to remind them of who we are. It's time to remind them of what we can do. It's time to show them the price they will pay if they attempt to tread on us once more."

47

———

A FAVOR

Thomas enjoyed the brisk wind that buffeted him as he walked on a narrow path toward one of the many small clearings that dotted the rough countryside surrounding the Crag. He knew all the secret glades situated around the Highland citadel, having spent many happy hours exploring them when he was younger. Work on the Highland stronghold had stopped for the day. They had made remarkable progress in just the last few weeks, all thanks to Coban. The moss, creeping vines and underbrush that had covered the massive keep had been cleared. Masons and stonecutters now worked to close the many massive holes that dotted the outer wall and had been used by the Ogren to enter the fortress almost a decade before. Once they repaired the outer curtain, they would turn their attention to rebuilding the towers.

A smaller group of Marchers, thirty in all including Coban and Oso, made last-minute preparations for their journey. They planned on traveling lightly so that they could move fast, but they also knew that Rodric or the Shadow Lord would watch for them, waiting and hoping for the opportunity to stop them from reaching their objective, the Council of the Kingdoms at

Eamhain Mhacha. Thus, the necessity to be prepared for anything.

Thomas found a space on a large rock that jutted out over the valley encircling the Crag, presenting him with a view of the western Highlands. The sun sat at the very edge of the horizon, darkness about to fall across the land. He caught a glimpse of a large hawk winging its way toward the clearing. He closed his eyes for a moment so that the flash of blinding white light that he expected to his left wouldn't affect his vision.

"I'm glad to see you, Rynlin," said Thomas. "I've missed you. I've had no one around to look over my shoulder to the point where I didn't know what to do with myself."

"You know very well, Thomas, that I never ..."

Rynlin Keldragan, Thomas' grandfather and member of the Sylvana, stopped in his tracks and stared at his grandson, seeing the smile playing across his face. He smiled as well, enjoying the fact that even though so much had changed in just a short time – Thomas becoming a Sylvan Warrior, then Lord of the Highlands, and all his associated travels and travails – some things, like his grandson's constant teasing of him, had not.

To Thomas' eyes Rynlin hadn't changed much in the months that had passed since they had last seen each other. The same dark hair and beard powdered with grey, the blue eyes similar to his own burning brightly in the rapidly descending darkness. That and his grandfather's height, giving him a tall and imposing appearance, led most to describe his countenance as threatening, and at times frightening, something that Rynlin viewed as a compliment and took great pride in maintaining.

"Congratulations on becoming the Highland Lord. Your grandmother and I are both very proud of you."

Rynlin settled on to the stone next to Thomas, patting his grandson on the knee with pride.

"Thank you." Thomas flushed from the praise. Rynlin rarely gave compliments. "But that's not why you came here."

"How did you know?" asked Rynlin.

"I felt you coming through my necklace," replied Thomas, fingering the silver chain and amulet, which depicted the horn of a unicorn. "I could tell there was more on your mind, that it wasn't just a visit to catch up."

Rynlin sighed, not surprised that his grandson could sense his concern.

"When do you leave for Eamhain Mhacha?"

"Tomorrow."

"You'll be careful?"

"Of course, Rynlin. I don't want Rya to get angry with me."

Rynlin chuckled, knowing the truth of Thomas' words. When Thomas was growing up, any injury he obtained made his grandmother angry. That anger was, to a certain extent, directed toward Thomas, yet she also reserved a portion of it for Rynlin, as if he could protect Thomas from himself every second of the day. Though barely five feet tall, his wife carried herself like a queen, her inner fire dominating the space around her. That was one of the reasons why even after all the years they had been together, he loved her as much, if not more, than when he first set eyes on her.

"A sensible concern," said Rynlin.

"What did you really want to talk to me about?"

"I just wanted to share a story."

Thomas settled on the stone, finding a comfortable position. Rynlin's stories could go on for a long time. His grandfather always sought to teach a lesson through each one, and then if he believed it necessary he would repeat himself just to make sure that you remembered the moral of the story. Thomas had no doubt such would be the case now.

"Have I ever told you the story of Icarus?" asked Rynlin. He didn't give Thomas time to answer, knowing that he probably had but not caring and continuing anyway. "As a boy he spent all of his time staring up at the sky, looking at the sun, believing it was a god traveling across the heavens in his chariot every day. He wanted to do the same, to be the sun god. But he had no godly power and no flying chariot. So what was he to do?"

Thomas would have answered, remembering the story and exactly where he had been when Rynlin first told it to him. They had been sitting on the sand at Shark Cove, a small inlet at the Isle of Mist, watching the huge fins of the Great Sharks cut through the waves where the sea floor dropped away into the quiet, dark abyss of the ocean. Thomas recognized that the story was as much for his grandfather as it was for him. So he kept his mouth shut, wanting to give his grandfather his moment.

"A smart boy, very industrious, Icarus built himself wings and soon he flew the skies much like the sun god. But Icarus didn't realize that the arrogance of youth can often lead to mistakes, which sometimes turn deadly. He flew too close to the sun god as it moved across the sky, and the wax holding his wings together began to melt. It was only a matter of time before Icarus plummeted to his death."

"And you're worried that I'm about to do the same?" asked Thomas. "When have you ever known me to get a big head and allow arrogance to get in the way of what needs to be done?"

"Never," replied Rynlin. "I just want to make sure you don't have your head in the clouds. That you understand the challenges of the situation and the consequences of failure."

"Don't worry," said Thomas, grateful for his grandfather's concern. "I'm well aware of how things will turn out if we don't succeed."

"I figured you did. But as your grandfather I'm allowed to worry. And to help alleviate my worry, I told you that story, so I guess it was more for me than for you. Now that I feel better, I'll be heading off. Rya's expecting me in the Northern Steppes."

"Before you go, can I beg a favor?"

"Of course, Thomas. Anything."

"I've reorganized the Marchers so that we can fight not only against the reivers, but also the dark creatures that keep trying to sneak into the northern Highlands. Since you, Rya, and I'm assuming several other Sylvan Warriors are watching the passes coming out of the Charnel Mountains on to the Northern Steppes, I was hoping that when you locate any dark creatures, you'll warn the Marchers protecting the northern border. Nestor has responsibility for the north, and Beluil and his wolfpacks are helping as well, but I'm sure they would appreciate any assistance you and any other Sylvan Warriors with you could provide."

"We'd be happy to, Thomas."

"Thank you, Rynlin. And thank you for coming here. I do appreciate it."

Thomas rose from the stone and hugged his grandfather, who was somewhat taken aback by his grandson's display of affection but also was pleased by it. Traditionally, a stoic approach was expected in the family, but Rynlin gladly hugged him back.

"Beware, Thomas. You have a great many enemies now who would like nothing more than a chance to stick a blade in your back."

"I'm aware, Rynlin. Thank you for the warning. But as Rya likes to say, 'You must do what you must do.'" Thomas sighed, kicking at a rock, needing some kind of release from the stress that had been building up within him. "This is something that I must do. The fate of the Highlands depends on it. So I expect treachery. And I'll be ready. In fact, I might even have a few of my own surprises ready."

Rynlin smiled wickedly as he stepped farther to the edge of the rock.

"That's good to hear, Thomas. Though I would expect nothing less."

In a flash of blinding white light, Rynlin disappeared. Thomas made out in the darkness a large hawk pulling itself higher into the sky heading north toward the Steppes and the Charnel Mountains. He watched his grandfather until he was no more than a speck in the sky, then he turned and walked briskly back down the path. He still had things to do, and he wanted to speak with Coban and Oso one more time about the route they'd selected.

If everything went well, they would reach the walls of Eamhain Mhacha with none of their enemies the wiser. But he knew from experience that even the best laid plans never matched reality.

48

A PROPOSITION

The sun dipped toward the western horizon, turning the calm waters of the Heartland Lake a bright gold. A gentle breeze swept in, cooling the warmth of the day as the moon began its ascent.

Maddan Dinnegan stood on the terrace of the small house in Mooralyn, a town just to the northwest of Eamhain Mhacha and close to where the Crescent River began its long journey to the Winter Sea. The son of the richest man in the Kingdoms was oblivious to the beauty of the evening. His world had been turned upside down, he and his father's plans destroyed. At this very moment, he should have sat on the throne of Fal Carrach. Yet here he stood, living on a small farm at the edge of the backwater village, he and his father the supposed guests of the High King. Maddan scoffed at the thought. The soldiers tasked with protecting them from any retribution by the King of Fal Carrach actually seemed more intent on keeping them where they were more than anything else.

All because of that cursed woman and Kaylie Carlomin. He had grown up with the princess of Fal Carrach by design, his father wanting to ensure that their family had a clear path to political power to match their untold riches. But now it was all gone. He had seen Kaylie as pliable, someone he could turn to his purposes. But he had failed. Her streak of independence had somehow given her the wherewithal to sniff out the assassination plot his father had so carefully orchestrated.

Where had she learned to use magic? That unexpected and unwanted discovery had almost cost him his life. She had almost gutted him with a flying letter opener. And who was that blasted woman? He had never laid eyes on her before, yet there was a power in her that he had never sensed in anyone else. Not just in her bearing, but she had fought Malachias and his Dark Magic to a stalemate, forcing him to flee. The thought of that cadaverous warlock sent a shiver down Maddan's spine. There was something so unsettling about that man, so terrifying, almost inhuman, that secretly he was pleased to be out of that creature's presence. But if gaining the throne of Fal Carrach meant tying himself to that spiteful, frightening ghoul, he would do so gladly.

Maddan shook his head in frustration, wanting to scream in rage. All for naught. King Gregory lived, declaring him and his father traitors and sentencing them to death. Their holdings in Fal Carrach – their lands, their businesses, their industries, their sources of income – all had been taken by the crown. Leaving them here, on a small farm in a different Kingdom with few allies and limited resources.

True, his father had squirreled away some of their wealth, protecting against a day such as this. But it didn't compare to all that they had lost. And now his father, once the richest man in the Kingdoms, a man who had almost gained control of the legendary wealth of the Highlands, had been reduced to a beggar. In fact, his father had left earlier in the day, hat in hand, to meet with the High King and seek his indulgence for their continued stay here. Maddan had never been so humiliated. Grabbing a small branch that had fallen from the tree above him, he swung it viciously again and again at the shrubs by the terrace, needing to release some of the anger that boiled up within him.

The sight of an arriving coach drawn by eight horses, black to match the falling night, stopped his attack on the bushes and pulled him from his depressing, unbalanced thoughts. But it did not give him the energy to leave his place on the terrace, a malaise having settled within him after his and his father's failure. Instead, he simply waited, curious about who had the ability to get by their supposed protectors so easily but unwilling to exert the energy to find out.

He didn't have long to wait. Corelia Tessaril, Princess of Armagh, daughter of the High King, swept out the doors opening on to the terrace. Her long, blonde hair caught the very last glimmers of light before night settled over them completely. She stood there for a moment in silence, the fire in the small house's kitchen shining through the windows and giving them just enough illumination to see each other dimly.

Maddan simply stared, once again taken by Corelia's beauty. Perhaps Kaylie had been the wrong match, the wrong path to power. Perhaps ... He let the thought burn to ashes before he pursued it further. Yes, the Princess of Armagh was beautiful. But also cunning, determined, untrustworthy and dangerous. Definitely not characteristics he was looking for in a bride. Besides, the wealth he could have offered her no longer existed. And if he for some strange reason did marry Corelia, he knew in his heart that she would overshadow and potentially dominate him, something that could never be permitted.

"How are you enjoying your new surroundings, Maddan? Comparable to your other homes?"

Corelia smirked, clearly seeking to irritate him. Much to his dismay, it was working. The anger that always seemed to be just below the surface because of all that had happened during the last few weeks bubbled up once again. The Princess of Armagh had a unique ability to know exactly what to say or do to get under someone's skin.

"Princess." He bit back the sharp retort that passed through his mind, knowing that he needed to stay within her good graces if he and his father were to extricate themselves from this current predicament. "A pleasure to see you this evening."

Corelia's expression changed to a pout, which in Maddan's opinion made her all the more attractive. She was disappointed at not being able to incite the reaction she sought.

"I see you're not going to be any fun tonight, Maddan."

"You can speak of fun at a time like this?" asked Maddan. He tried to speak in a strong, confident voice, but the words came out more like a whine, his simmering anger threatening to overtake him.

"Then let me be direct. I assume you still have dreams of ruling Fal Carrach?"

Maddan stared at her in shock, not expecting her candor or the topic of discussion. But for some reason, he couldn't lie.

"I do, Princess."

Corelia nodded. "I expected as much. Your father is speaking with mine right now, seeking some accommodation. Some other way to gain control of Fal Carrach."

"I know. But what could we possibly do now? Gregory lives and is likely wary of another assassination attempt."

"I would expect nothing less," replied Corelia, watching Maddan intently. "But there are always multiple paths to achieve a goal."

She had assessed him the second she had stepped out onto the terrace. Arrogant. Conceited. Spoiled. Soft. And someone desperately craving power. Something she understood quite intimately and could use to her advantage.

"Of course, Princess, but what other paths might there be?"

"What do you truly want, Maddan?" asked Corelia, ignoring his question.

Maddan stared at Corelia, thinking, wondering if he should reveal what was truly going through his mind. He decided he had nothing to lose.

"I want Kaylie Carlomin," replied Maddan, his voice strident and his eyes burning with a feverish light. "I've wanted her since we were children. She belongs to me. She should be mine."

"And what if that could still be arranged, Maddan? What if you could still have Fal Carrach and Kaylie Carlomin?" Why he would be so obsessed by the somewhat skittish daughter of Fal Carrach's king, Corelia didn't know. Kaylie clearly didn't compare to her. But so be it. There was no explanation for some people's tastes.

Maddan stared at Corelia sharply, knowing that there was more to this conversation than met the eye.

"What do you want, Corelia?"

"So you do have some of your father in you after all," Corelia chuckled. "What I want is none of your concern. Now a final time. What if I could give you Fal Carrach and Kaylie Carlomin?"

Maddan tried to resist the offer, knowing the danger of accepting, knowing that there would be hidden strings attached that could strangle him at some point in the future. But he couldn't resist.

"Then I would do whatever you wanted."

Corelia smiled. She expected that this was going to be easy, but she never thought it would be this easy.

"I thought as much. Maddan, I have a proposition for you."

49

IRRITATION

Lord Chertney, wearing his traditional black silk that barely stirred with the breeze, cursed under his breath as he surveyed the Inland Sea, a large body of water that separated Dunmoor from Fal Carrach and was shaped like a funnel in which the southern section tightened near Tinnakilly before opening up again as it flowed down to Stormy Bay. The Shadow Lord knew that the Highland upstart still lived, telling Chertney that he could feel the boy like a splinter under his skin. The Shadow Lord also made clear that he tired of that prickly feeling and wanted the splinter removed once and for all.

Chertney desperately wanted to comply. He craved returning to the good graces of his master, but how he could do that positioned just a few miles north of Tinnakilly, across from the Pool, a small body of stagnant water that curled off the Inland Sea, he didn't know. The Shadow Lord enjoyed the competition between him and Malachias, as they both strove for more power at the other's expense, power that only the Shadow Lord could bestow. Yet, how was he to compete in this latest task with the Shadow Lord having given his nemesis all the advantages?

If that impudent boy still lived, and there was no reason to doubt his master, as doing so often led to a premature death, then the boy who had caused so many problems in recent years needed to get to the Council of the Kingdoms before the gathering came to an end. The boy clearly would assume that there were those seeking to keep him from Eamhain Mhacha. So his most likely route involved slipping out of the western Highlands and sticking to the forests that bordered both Dunmoor and the Clanwar Desert before following the Corazon River to the capital of Armagh. It was the easiest route and the fastest. And then, much to Chertney's irritation, the boy would fall right into Malachias' hands, who had been charged with patrolling the area north of the Corazon River.

Blasted fools! He surveyed the Ogren who stood dutifully behind him hidden among the trees, then he stalked away from the river and back to his small camp. He had done nothing wrong that he could tell, yet the Shadow Lord seemed to hold him responsible for Killeran's failures in the Highlands and Rodric's in Tinnakilly, when that fool High King actually had the boy in his grasp but allowed him to escape. Chertney had captured the boy during the Eastern Festival, serving him trussed up like a pig for the spit as his master had demanded. Rodric should have killed the boy then and there. But no. The half-witted High King had wanted to demonstrate his power in front of the other rulers, so Rodric had tried to make an example out of the boy. In the end, it had all gone terribly wrong. True, Chertney had witnessed much of it, but he was never in a position to do anything about the High King's stupidity. All he could do was watch and grow more frustrated as his carefully laid trap achieved its purpose, yet proved to be wasted effort in the end.

And now because of his master he had no choice but to wait

here, hoping that the boy would seek to avoid the dangers and traps set for him farther north. He had considered moving farther north himself to be closer to the southern bank of the Corazon River, but he feared disobeying the Shadow Lord. He had seen the price that others paid for taking the initiative and failing. Nevertheless, he was responsible for all the territory south of the Corazon River, so why not shift his forces a little closer? He would adhere to the charge his master had given him, even if that meant Malachias had the chance to seize the glory. But if for some reason the boy traveled too far south, he would be ready.

50

DANGER APPROACHES

Thomas sat quietly by the bank of the Corazon River, watching the swiftly flowing water run to the east. The sun had just set, the sky still a pinkish red to the west. His Marchers rested among the small copse of trees lining the bank, caring for their horses, cleaning their gear, and preparing dinner. Coban already had set the pickets for the night, Oso readying his bow for some quick hunting.

At present, it seemed like it would be a peaceful evening. The Marchers had made good time, slipping out of the south-western Highlands on their way to Eamhain Mhacha. After entering Dunmoor, they had taken the longer route around the northern shore of the Inland Sea, but then cut across the Corazon River to the southern bank.

Thomas expected Rodric would try to prevent him from reaching the Council of the Kingdoms. He just hadn't expected the High King would make the trip so difficult. The Marchers had yet to engage in battle, slipping around or between various Ogren war parties on the northern side of the river, wanting to keep their presence hidden from those searching for them. But there had been too many close calls for his taste, and he had every expectation that before they reached Eamhain Mhacha it would come to a fight.

Munching on an apple, Thomas enjoyed the brief respite. The thirty Marchers had traveled hard since leaving the Highlands, the deadline pressing on them. Perhaps this evening they could gain some much-needed rest. Throwing the core into the bushes, Thomas used his Talent as he had every few hours during the day to extend his senses, reaching out in all directions to determine if any danger lurked. Thomas abruptly jumped to his feet.

"Coban! Get everyone on their horses. We have three Ogren war parties moving this way."

The Marchers immediately went to work, stopping what they had been doing, and saddling their horses.

"Oso, take five of our best bowmen to the southwest. The three groups of Ogren will converge here. They're trying to hem us in against the river. You'll be free of them in a league. I'll take the larger group to the west. Stay parallel with us but keep your distance. I have no doubt the Ogren will adjust once they realize their prey has escaped so do what you can to slow them down."

"Consider it done, Thomas," replied the big, shaggy haired Marcher. He strode off to select his men, quickly understanding his friend's plan.

Thomas trotted off to prepare his own horse for travel, hoping he and his fighters would have time to slip the noose before it tightened around them.

51

AMBUSH

The Ogren raiding party led by a handful of Shades tromped across the grassland bordering the southern shore of the Corazon River. They paid little attention to the copses of trees that dotted the landscape, intent on their quarry just a few miles ahead.

Oso was thankful for that. He watched impatiently from just within the trees, staying hidden within the shadows to avoid being seen. He and his Marchers remained on their horses, bows at the ready. Just a few more seconds and he could put his plan into action.

"Ready," he called quietly. Six bows were pulled back, aiming for the back of the Ogren column. "Remember, two quick shots, a third on the string, then we circle around to the west."

Oso waited just a few seconds longer, wanting a bit more distance in order to provide a larger buffer for the Marchers' attempted escape.

"Release!"

Six arrows streaked through the air, followed by a second flight right behind. The steel-tipped bolts slammed into the backs of the Ogren, a few driving through their hearts from behind. Those dark creatures that didn't fall dead in the grass roared in agony, reaching their huge claw-like hands behind them trying to pull the arrows free from their flesh. The Ogren closest to the unlucky beasts turned at the cries, only to feel the impact of the second wave of arrows, all finding their target, whether in the chest or the neck.

The Marchers didn't wait to examine the results of their ambush, driving their horses from between the trees, their mounts quickly galloping beyond the raiding party. Several Ogren roaring with rage sprinted after them, gaining ground, able to reach speeds almost as fast as a horse over a short distance. But the extra seconds Oso had waited before attacking gave the Marchers the additional space they needed to avoid the dark creatures. It also gave them a final opportunity to strike.

The Marchers turned in their saddles as the pursuing Ogren closed on them, releasing their last arrows at no more than twenty paces in some cases. The proximity proved deadly as all the Marchers' arrows struck their quarry. The dark creatures crumpled in the long grass, the long shafts sprouting from their necks or heads.

Oso smiled grimly. A good result for just a few minutes work. But it would be harder next time. The dark creatures would be expecting an ambush. And the Marchers were running dangerously low on arrows. He estimated that he and his fighters had one more good attack left in them before they had to return to Thomas and the main group of Marchers. So be it. Oso would make it count.

52

POOR ODDS

The going had been difficult the last two days. The Marchers had gotten little sleep after escaping through a small gap between two of the Ogren war parties that had tried to herd them against the Corazon River. Thomas had considered cutting south, away from the river, to gain more space to maneuver. But every time he searched with the Talent, he was always presented with the same picture. Several other Ogren war parties paralleled his own course. Therefore, he led the Marchers west at a steady clip, pushing hard for Eamhain Mhacha and trying to put some distance between them and their pursuers.

Eventually, their luck gave out. One of the war parties had picked up the scent, followed by two more. Now several hundred Ogren tracked the Marchers, and the dark creatures were gaining on them. Oso and his archers had eliminated several dozen from afar, poaching at the Ogren whenever they could. But when they had run out of arrows, Oso and his small band had rejoined Thomas and the other Marchers, knowing that their continued survival would depend on their ability to work together as a fighting unit.

Their odds of reaching Eamhain Mhacha continued to worsen as the Ogren drew closer. But Thomas still held out hope for an escape. Using the Talent, he realized that the Ogren had almost encircled them. He also identified something else that might prove useful, if he and his fighters could reach it before the trap closed. Letting go of the Talent, Thomas scanned the shoreline to the west, finding what he had seen using the Talent just a short distance farther down the river.

The Corazon River curled just ahead, forming a bight, before straightening out once again. He led his Marchers into that curl, allowing the river to protect them on three sides. Leaving the horses behind them, his Marchers formed a defensive line several ranks deep along the small opening of grass, no more than twenty feet across from one riverbank to the next. The Ogren could attack, but only a few at a time. The river was too deep and flowed too swiftly for the dark creatures to attempt an assault on their flanks or from behind.

Thomas would have preferred to keep running, but he had not seen a better defensible position within leagues. Now he would have to trust in the strength of his Marchers' sword arms, and perhaps a few tricks he had up his sleeve.

53

MISCALCULATION

For almost an hour the Ogren stood a short distance from the Marchers, massing behind one another as the three war parties finally converged. The Marchers had observed in muted surprise. Based on their past experience with dark creatures, they had expected an immediate attack, the Ogrens' hunger normally driving them on. But the Marchers didn't mind the respite. The Highlanders stood calmly, watching the Ogren, ready for the assault they expected at any second, yet also knowing the defensibility of their position, having confidence in their own skills and experience, and believing in the Highland Lord.

"You have afflicted me for far too long, boy. No more. You die here and now."

The scratchy voice carried over the sounds of the milling Ogren, the dark creatures parting to allow a tall figure dressed in black silk to step to the front. A shadow seemed to cover the man, despite the bright sunlight of the day.

Thomas stepped forward as well, finally understanding the reason for the Ogrens' remarkable display of control and their ability to track the Marchers. Lord Chertney commanded these war parties, and he wanted to be there for the final kill.

"Tasked with finding me?" asked Thomas, the derision in his voice clear. "I would have expected that by now you were licking the feet of your master. No? Perhaps someone else has taken your place because of your many previous failures?"

Thomas' goading had its desired effect. Chertney had wanted to savor this moment before releasing his Ogren to overwhelm the Marchers and eliminate the Highland whelp once and for all. But Thomas' words hit too close to home.

"Words will do you little good, boy," rasped Chertney. "Your short reign as Lord of the Highlands ends today."

Chertney seized his Dark Magic, releasing a blast of darkness that surged toward Thomas.

The Marchers gasped in shock at the demonstration of power, ducking involuntarily as the Dark Magic sped toward them. They were even more surprised when Thomas simply reached out a hand and grasped the Dark Magic, holding the spinning mass of pitch black in his palm. Even Chertney was taken aback by the Highland Lord's action, a lump of fear settling in his stomach.

Thomas focused his attention on the inky black, staring into the churning mass, studying it for a few long seconds. Then he placed his other palm above it. Bolts of white light began to spin with the dark, fighting it, consuming it, changing it, until the swirling mass of black became a swirling mass of white light that spun faster and faster, gradually expanding between Thomas' hands.

"The last time we met, Chertney, I didn't have the strength to do what I wanted to do," said Thomas calmly, pedantically, referring to his unpleasant experience in Tinnakilly with the High King seeking to parade him in front of the attending potentates and nobles. "But circumstances have changed. For as you can see I have the strength now."

Chertney's face, normally a mask of contempt, became one of horror as he realized he had seriously underestimated his prey. He had never considered the possibility that this boy had control of the Talent, but now he sensed the power within him. Even worse, Chertney understood much too late that he didn't have the strength to fight the boy and win. The Shadow Lord's servant began to inch backward, seeking some means to escape. But the solid mass of Ogren that had formed up behind him prevented it.

Lord Chertney watched in horrified fascination as Thomas opened up his palms, the ball of swirling white energy spinning in a blur before him. With a flick of his wrist, the ball of energy surged towards Chertney and the Ogren, the surging white light breaking into smaller balls of energy that slammed into the first few rows of dark creatures. The fiery energy Thomas had released burned through the chests of the massive beasts, leaving nothing but charred and smoking husks in its wake.

54

NEW FRIEND

Kael Bellilil sat on his horse easily, spending as much time in the saddle as on his own two feet. His men and the Marchers wandered slowly among the corpses, making sure that no Ogren or Shades survived. When necessary, they helped the beasts that had not yet expired along the way.

"So what are Highlanders doing in the middle of Dunmoor?" he asked.

Kael had stayed behind in Fal Carrach for a few extra days, promising Gregory that he would catch up to him in Eamhain Mhacha before the Council of the Kingdoms began. There were rumors of dark creatures near Fal Carrach's southern border that he wanted to confirm. After verifying the reports and eliminating some of the dark creatures, he and his soldiers followed the Ogren war parties to the west into Dunmoor. Having connected with the Highlanders at the tail end of the battle, the mystery of why these bands of dark creatures had emerged from the Highlands and into the open had been solved.

Thomas had sensed the Fal Carrachians following behind them. Thus, his decision to form the Marchers in line for battle, hoping to buy some time for his potential allies to catch up before the skirmish became too much for his Marchers. When Chertney stepped forward, though, Thomas had found it too difficult to contain himself, unable to resist the challenge and not caring if his use of the Talent marked him for every dark creature from there to Eamhain Mhacha. Nevertheless, despite his best efforts, the Shadow Lord's minion had escaped. Somehow the bastard who had tortured him in Tinnakilly had managed to slither free again. That fact continued to nag at him. Next time, Thomas would pay Chertney what he was owed.

Thomas stepped forward, sword still in his hand. He bent down, using the dirty garments worn by one of the Ogren to wipe the blood off the blade.

"I doubt I could come up with a lie that you would believe," answered Thomas with a smile. "Thank you for your help."

"Aye, thank you, Kael. Who knows how it would have played out if you had not arrived."

Kael turned at the voice, remembering it from his youth in the Highlands.

"Coban?"

"It's been a long time, Kael. You've moved up in the world."

Kael hopped off his horse and clasped hands with Coban, who had trained him as a Marcher before he had journeyed to Fal Carrach and decided to stay there as Swordmaster.

"Coban, it's good to see you. But that doesn't explain why Marchers travel well outside the Highlands."

"We make for Eamhain Mhacha and the Council of the Kingdoms," said Thomas.

Kael stared at Thomas for a moment, the stories of his homeland coming back to him. This was the boy who had defied the High King in Tinnakilly. Who had wounded Ragin. Who had leapt from the battlements of the keep before Rodric could kill him. His body had never been found broken against the rocks below or floating in the Pool, and now he stood before him. This was the boy around which many rumors and insinuations revolved. Upon taking in the dark creatures that littered the long grass, and realizing how they had died, Kael concluded quickly that the majority of those rumors and insinuations likely were true.

"And you came this way to avoid dark creatures and perhaps others wishing you harm. Yet it didn't work."

"No, it didn't," confirmed Coban.

"Tell me, Swordmaster." Thomas stepped closer to Kael, his brightly glowing green eyes capturing the soldier's gaze. "Though you're loyal to Gregory of Fal Carrach, you're obviously of the Highlands, and you've had the pleasure of Coban's teachings."

"Yes, I was born in the Highlands, but my mother came from Fal Carrach. When my father died, I traveled with her back to Ballinasloe."

"Then you recognize these."

Thomas held out his sword. The mark of the Kestrels flashed on the pommel, the distinctive script "Strength and courage lead to freedom" running along the blade. Placing the blade in the scabbard across his back, Thomas moved the wrist guard so that Kael could see the mark of the Kestrel clearly.

"And now you know where we're headed and why. We have three days to reach the Council. Can you help?"

Kael bowed his head slightly, bringing his blade to his forehead, a sign of respect in the Highlands.

"Yes, Lord Kestrel. I can and I will."

55

GROWING CONCERN

Rodric sat upon his uncomfortable throne brooding, his left leg bouncing incessantly to release the nervous energy that danced behind his eyes. Those black eyes that every so often displayed a touch of insanity, and which now bore into Killeran. The Lord of Dunmoor stood there, head down, staring at the worn stone tiles.

"It was him, my lord," finished Lord Johin Killeran, reluctant to make this report but knowing he couldn't avoid it. "With thousands upon thousands of Marchers. They outnumbered us at least five to one. Even with the dark creatures we didn't stand a chance. And the flag, the same as that of Talyn Kestrel."

"I find that hard to believe," replied Rodric Tessaril, his left leg now still, his eyes burning. He pounded his palms against the arms of his throne, the angry slap echoing in the deserted throne room. "You had ten years to eliminate the Marchers, and now you tell me thousands appeared out of the woods with you completely unaware of their existence. Where have these thousands of Marchers been for the last decade? Besides, Talyn Kestrel is dead!"

"My lord, you know how difficult it's been ..."

"Enough! How could it be that scoundrel?" demanded Rodric, spittle flying in his rage. "He jumped from the battlements. No one could have survived!"

"I don't know, my lord," answered Killeran meekly, cowed by Rodric's rage. "I don't know how anyone could survive a fall from that height."

Rodric stewed, his anger boiling, the blood vessel in his forehead pulsing rhythmically as he tried and failed to control his rage.

"We will deal with this later, Killeran," whispered Rodric, his thoughts obviously elsewhere. "Whether or not you speak the truth, nothing can be done right now. Not with a decade's labor hanging in the balance. We must focus on that now. Despite your repeated failures, the Highlands can still be mine within the week."

56

POLITICAL IMPLICATIONS

The Council of the Kingdoms occurred every two years, dating back to the time when Ollav Fola, the first High King, ruled all the Kingdoms as one. The monarchs of every Kingdom, or at least their representative, always attended, for the Council provided the perfect opportunity for the far-flung sovereign nations to manage trade and other issues. Moreover, during the Council at no time could a person raise a hand against another, no matter the cause, at least within Eamhain Mhacha itself. Thus, the environment proved more conducive to negotiation rather than conflict, something that the various kings and queens appreciated as they sought to address matters more directly rather than relying on time-consuming diplomatic negotiations. Of course, beyond the borders of the city proper, it was a different story, as some disputes inevitably were handled in a bloodier fashion. Duels hidden by the copses of trees that sprung up in the countryside surrounding Eamhain Mhacha were all too common.

The rulers of the Kingdoms met in a massive circular chamber, the chairs set out in a semicircle, lords and ladies and lackeys standing around the room to assist if required, but more often than not they were there to watch and wait for the inevitable entertainment of the verbal clashes and histrionics that sometimes broke out between the participants. A chair on the end of the semicircle had sat open for almost ten years, representing the place of the lost Lord of the Highlands. But that would change after this Council, as one of two things would occur. Either a claimant would take the open chair or the chair would be removed, signifying that the High King officially assumed responsibility for the Highlands because there was no living, confirmed heir to the Kestrel line.

Gregory, broad-shouldered King of Fal Carrach, stood talking with Sarelle, Queen of Benewyn, and Rendael, King of Kenmare. His black hair peppered with grey belied Gregory's vigor, and there remained a glimmer of youth in his eye. The cause for that was likely Sarelle, thought Kaylie, who stood near her father listening to their conversation. Sarelle had made her intentions known to Gregory several times in the last few years, though for various reasons he had either been oblivious or unsure. Kaylie suspected that perhaps her father was beginning to understand. At the moment Sarelle stood almost on top of Gregory, but that didn't seem to bother him at all. In fact, he appeared to enjoy the closeness.

Kaylie attended the Council of the Kingdoms at her father's request, as he hoped that watching and listening would help prepare her for when she needed to assume the throne of Fal Carrach. In the past, she would have viewed her participation in the event with boredom and disinterest, finding the often long and inconclusive discussions tedious. Her perspective had changed after having spoken with Thomas in Tinnakilly and spending so much time with Rya. Her experience with that mysterious woman and her own efforts to thwart the assassination attempt on her father's life had changed her standpoint. She had begun to better understand the burdens and challenges her father juggled daily and deftly, and that she would need to do the same eventually or her Kingdom and her people would suffer.

Nevertheless, despite her best efforts to concentrate and learn, thoughts of Thomas continually played through her mind. She had met him at the Eastern Festival, entranced by his skill with a bow, mesmerized by his brightly glowing green eyes and serious, calm demeanor. He seemed equally taken with her. Yes, she had been told she was beautiful many times, her long black hair and twinkling blue eyes capturing the attention of several suitors. Many a young man, particularly those similar to the privileged, grasping, and conniving Maddan Dinnegan and Ragin Tessaril, sought the pleasure of her company, and perhaps something more.

Yet these boys appeared preoccupied by what she could offer them as heir to the throne of Fal Carrach more than anything else. Something that Maddan had just made abundantly clear, as he and his father had attempted to steal her Kingdom for themselves by eliminating her father and trying to push themselves into the Carlomin line through her forced marriage to Maddan. The thought of that recent incident infuriated her. She wanted justice but knew it would have to wait. Nevertheless, she had to acknowledge that she had benefited from the experience. It had given her greater confidence in herself and the belief that if a challenge or threat arose she would step forward rather than step back.

Her thoughts returned to the green-eyed archer. Thomas had shown no interest in anything like that. He seemed focused solely on her and not on what she represented. In the short time they had spent together, she connected with him in a way she had not connected with anyone else before. He had explained what he saw as the value of learning to rule, the importance of observing both the words and actions of her father and the other monarchs, so that she could become more educated in governance and leadership from both the good and the bad decisions.

So she came to the Council with a new perspective, hoping to glean as much from the happenings as she could so that she could use what she learned in the future. Yet despite doing her best to listen to all the conversation around her, her eyes inexorably drifted to the open seat that belonged rightfully to the Lord of the Highlands.

Her father had pondered the destruction of the Crag and the loss of Talyn Kestrel, his best friend, ever since that formerly indestructible keep fell. Rodric claimed that a group of renegade Highlanders murdered Talyn and his son, Benlorin. Gregory, Sarelle and a handful of other rulers didn't believe him, guessing that Rodric had authorized the attack because his larger plans required control of the Highlands.

Thus, when the grandson disappeared, as required by law Rodric appointed a regent to serve for ten years, until such time as the heir of the Highlands appeared. If, at the end of that time period a legitimate successor did not step forward, the High King would assume formal control of the Highlands.

Gregory had met Thomas several times, noting the similarity to Talyn Kestrel. Rodric's efforts to ensure the boy's death when he put the boy on Trial during the Eastern Festival strengthened his belief that there may be more to the boy than met the eye. No matter what the boy did to survive the dangers and false charges Rodric set against him, the High King threw up another obstacle or offered another lie as he pursued the boy's death. In the end, Thomas had leapt from the Tinnakilly battlements and Gregory had no way to confirm his suspicion that the boy was Talyn's grandson.

The additional burden his daughter carried as a result of that experience weighed heavily on Gregory in part because as a father he wanted to fix the problem, but he had no way to do so. However, despite an exhaustive search, Thomas' body had never been found. So Gregory still carried some hope that the boy had survived and a claimant for the Highland throne would emerge before the Council ended, for Rodric had placed the most important business of this Council, the decision regarding the Highlands, on the last day.

"How much longer do you think we'll have to wait?" asked Gregory, shifting from side to side, his natural instincts as a warrior chafing at having to spend the bulk of the next few days stuck inside a stifling chamber with his peers.

"You know how Rodric is, Gregory," responded Sarelle, touching his arm and keeping her hand there, something he noticed immediately and secretly enjoyed. "He'll want to make a grand entrance. He only has so many opportunities to impress us, so he has to make the most of them."

"I'd find a bear walking on his hind legs more impressive than Rodric," muttered Gregory.

"Quite so," laughed Rendael gaily. "Have you noticed that no one stands for Inishmore?"

All the other Kingdoms were represented except for the chiefs of the Clanwar Desert. At the beginning of the Councils a millennium in the past, these nomadic rulers had been invited to attend, though even Ollav Fola had failed to bring the Clanwar Desert under his control. In part because of the ferociousness of the desert tribes, but even more so the realization that conquering a desert wasted his resources and offered no real benefit. Since the chiefs of the desert clans never attended, the High King no longer sent invitations.

Inishmore remained a regular concern for Rendael, as it shared a border with Kenmare. A king had once ruled Inishmore, yet his murder led to years of plotting and scheming by that Kingdom's many lords and ladies seeking the throne, as there was no heir and no noble house was strong enough to hold the crown. To date, no one had held that cursed throne for more than a few months before another claimant, usually because of an unfortunate, suspicious, deadly accident, took control for a brief time. The instability in the Kingdom worried Rendael, forcing his soldiers to pay close attention to that shared border so that the murder and mayhem so common to Inishmore did not carry over into his own Kingdom.

"The latest round of attempts for the throne have proven particularly deadly," continued Rendael. "It appears that there are now two primary factions, one supporting a Lord Eshel, who my spies tell me is in Rodric's pocket, and a Lady Colasa."

"That's worrisome," said Sarelle, who had a mind for intrigues and alliances. "But not unexpected. Rodric will seek to take advantage of any unrest or opportunity that comes his way."

"True, true," said Rendael.

"What worries me the most are the ones over there," said Gregory, nodding across the chamber where Killeran, a Lord of Dunmoor but someone openly in Rodric's service, spoke with Malachias, supposedly one of Rodric's advisors.

Both he and his daughter had cause to arrest Malachias, their memories and emotions still raw from the failed kidnapping Malachias had helped Dinnegan engineer. But nothing could be done about it now during the Council. It would have to wait until the Council's close, but it would not be forgotten or forgiven. Gregory had sworn to himself that Malachias would pay for what he had done, but he also knew there was more to Malachias than met the eye. A darkness surrounded him, and it had nothing to do with his black cloak and garments. In watching the conversation for a moment, despite Killeran talking and gesturing vehemently, Gregory could tell that Malachias actually was the one in charge, but for whatever reason allowed Killeran to think he was an equal in the relationship. At least for now.

"So what's going on in the Highlands?" asked Rendael. "I've heard rumors of some kind of uprising. Perhaps that's the cause of the little tiff that seems to have sprouted up between our two favorite people."

Rendael gestured to Malachias, who had decided he had had enough of Killeran's haranguing and now dominated the conversation. His gestures and voice appeared controlled, yet his intensity was also evident, which left Killeran leaning away from him, almost cowering in fear, perhaps realizing it was never smart to poke a snake. Do it once too often and they tended to bite.

Kaylie's ears perked up at Rendael's question, finally finding the conversation turning in a direction of immediate interest to her.

"I don't know for sure," answered Gregory. "Rumors of the Lost Kestrel, of course. Some are saying that the Lost Kestrel and this Raptor, whomever he is, are one and the same."

Gregory suspected that Thomas may have been the Raptor. He had saved him and his daughter from Fearhounds, and his ability with a bow mirrored the stories of what this Raptor could do. But Gregory had no proof, so there was no cause for conjecture.

"I do know there has been some fighting in the Highlands, though," continued Gregory. "More than usual. And now signal fires dot the peaks of the Highlands and the sound of bagpipes drifts on the wind. A few of my scouts have tried to enter the Highlands in the last few weeks just to see if they can find out what's going on. But every time they've tried to go across the border, a party of Marchers has met them, telling them to turn back. One scout told me that the Marchers he met even offered a message: 'Tell the other Kingdoms to beware. The Highlands wake.'"

"I take that as a positive sign," said Sarelle. "In the past the only fighters in the Highlands were Killeran's raiders. If the Marchers are attempting to reassert themselves and reclaim what is theirs, perhaps there's hope for the Highlands after all."

"Perhaps," said Rendael. "Though the sands pass through the hourglass, as they say. If the Marchers are going to do anything, they have only a few days left to do it. Rodric still has Killeran there as his regent?"

"Not for much longer, most likely," answered Sarelle. "The ten-year regency ends at this Council. If there isn't a legitimate claimant for the Highland throne, Rodric can take it for himself. He won't have a need for Killeran any longer."

"Well, he's ruled the Highlands for the past ten years through Killeran," said Rendael. "It's just a change of appearances."

"Yes, but once he has the Highlands for his own, I think we will be in for even more difficult times," said Gregory, his hand twisting around the pommel of his sword out of habit. "Fal Carrach in particular, as I assume that once Rodric has the Highlands, Loris of Dunmoor will increase his raids across the border we share. From that you can easily guess at Rodric's next steps."

Sarelle and Rendael both nodded. Kaylie as well recognized the potential danger. They had all had to deal with Rodric's increasing demands. Small at first, in some respects perhaps even inconsequential, but all designed to increase Armagh's power at the other Kingdom's expense.

And after the injury sustained by his son, Ragin, Rodric had become more demanding and authoritarian, essentially playing at Ollav Fola yet not wanting to recognize that each of the Kingdoms still remained independent. The stress of his son's near death and permanent marking had eliminated what little patience the High King had had to begin with. Clearly, though over the centuries the position of the High King had lost much of its power and was now primarily viewed as a cere-monial position, Rodric had other ideas as he attempted to expand his reach whenever and wherever he could.

If Rodric took the Highlands as permitted by the law, he

could expand his power much more easily. He would charge Highlanders who failed to acknowledge him as their rightful ruler as criminals, and he could do whatever he deemed necessary to quell any resistance, while at the same time making use of the Highland mines to fill his treasury and use those riches to weaken or gain a foothold in the other Kingdoms.

"What of this Lost Kestrel?" asked Rendael. "Gregory, you had mentioned him just a few minutes ago."

"Likely a myth," said Sarelle. "Not too long ago, Gregory, Kaylie and I met someone who resembled the legend, but he's gone now."

"Yes," said Gregory with a heavy sigh, still angry at his inability to save the boy. "But there is something going on in the Highlands, more than just Marchers appearing at the border. I just don't know for sure what might be happening."

"What do you mean?" asked Sarelle.

"The bagpipes."

"Bagpipes?" Sarelle repeated, not understanding.

"Yes, the bagpipes. As I mentioned, I've heard the sound of bagpipes drifting down from the Highlands to Ballinasloe. I haven't heard the bagpipes since the time of Talyn Kestrel."

"What do you mean?" asked Rendael, who also had known and admired the former Lord of the Highlands. "Why would that be relevant?"

"The call to war," explained Gregory. "At least that's what I interpret the notes to be. The Highlander call to war."

"Interesting. Interesting, indeed. Well, the declaration won't take place until the end of the Council. Perhaps something will occur before then with respect to the Highlands. I'd love to see one of Rodric's famous fits if the dice don't fall as he expects they will."

"As would we all," agreed Gregory.

Rendael smiled at the thought of Rodric getting his

knickers in a twist. "Until then we've got plenty of other issues to worry about."

"Yes, we do," agreed Sarelle.

Their conversation quickly came to an end as a handful of trumpeters walked into the chamber, blasting away as Rodric Tessaril entered behind them with his retinue.

57

LAW AND CUSTOM

High King Rodric Tessaril walked into the chamber believing he was about to bring back the glory days of the first High King, Ollav Fola. Almost ten years before he had helped to engineer the death of Talyn Kestrel, Lord of the Highlands. After the success of that secret play, as well as the murder of Talyn's son, Benlorin, Rodric would have gained the first piece to the puzzle he was trying to piece together.

But Chertney and Killeran had failed him by not confirming the death of the grandson, Thomas Kestrel. Thus, the placement of Killeran as regent so that he could begin to take advantage of the riches hidden in the Highlands, even if he couldn't exploit them to the fullest extent until the decade-long time limit passed because of the continued obstinance and forbearance of the Highlanders.

Now, with the Council of the Kingdoms finally upon him, he expected to take the Highlands for his own once and for all. Then he could begin to play the other pieces he had accumulated over the years. Loris of Dunmoor had his uses. But there could only be one true High King. Once Rodric had the Highlands under his control, he could turn his attention to

Dunmoor and put his plan in place for taking that Kingdom. With Armagh, Dunmoor and the Highlands under his thumb, and having gained control of the Corazon River and the Inland Sea, he could apply greater pressure on Benewyn by choking the trade down through the Gullet to Stormy Bay whenever he deemed it necessary.

Sarelle Makarin, proud though she may be, then could not ignore the threat that Rodric posed to her Kingdom, as he could easily strangle the commerce upon which Benewyn depended. Rodric could remove Sarelle if he so desired. Or, perhaps, he would consider a closer, more personal alliance with her if she were willing. Either way, he would bring Benewyn into the fold.

From there, Fal Carrach would be isolated, and as a result it would be just a matter of time before Rodric gained all the Eastern Kingdoms. Then the west would follow, as he either subverted the rulers of those lands to his own purposes, as he had already done with Eshel of Inishmore, or eliminated them. Eventually, he could drop the façade hiding his actions. With his secret ally behind him, no one could stop him. But the Highlands first, and thus the importance of this Council of the Kingdoms.

Yet, even with his grand plans, Rodric's appearance within the throne room failed to put forward the image he wished to present as he walked into the chamber. The purple cloak dragged across the stone floor, much too big for his frame. The same could be said for his gold crown, which perched precariously on his brow, a couple sizes too large for his head. His dark, swarthy complexion and lank, greasy hair didn't help matters.

Rodric thought the stares were for him as he made his way toward the semicircle of thrones, not realizing that his daughter, Corelia, entering on his arm, had attracted the gaze of almost all the men, and quite a few women, as she passed. The beautiful Princess of Armagh knew how to command attention by her mere appearance.

So much so that in addition to putting her father in her shadow, only a few noticed the absence of her brother, Ragin. Once handsome, arrogant, and gregarious, only the arrogance remained. His ill-fated decision had left a scar on the right side of his face that destroyed his once good looks and left him in a perpetually foul mood. Moreover, Ragin's stricken vanity kept him in his rooms, unwilling to risk the stares of those saddened by, or more likely pleased by, his misfortune.

Rodric stopped before the throne, Corelia moving to stand behind the chair. The other monarchs soon stood before their own chairs, their family and retainers standing behind them as well. Killeran and Malachias remained in the shadows of the chamber, not wishing to step forward and announce their presence or their well-known allegiance to the High King.

From her position behind her father's chair, Kaylie glanced over at Corelia, noting the knowing smirk that rarely left her lips. The princess of Armagh was beautiful, true, something she admitted reluctantly, yet her ambition was plain. She would use anyone she could if it suited her plans and purposes. In that way, at least, she was very much like her father.

"My lords and ladies, welcome to the Council of the Kingdoms," intoned Rodric, attempting to sound kingly despite his less than regal appearance as he recited the well-known introduction. "As we have done since the first Council, our actions here will be decided by words, not blades. Let every ruler approach every issue with an open mind, striving for harmony among the Kingdoms rather than discord. For we are the descendants of Ollav Fola, who taught that law and custom should take precedence over all else."

With that Rodric sat on his throne, ignoring the irony of the words he had just spoken, though several other rulers shook their heads with chagrin or amusement as they assumed their places.

Settled on his uncomfortable chair, Rodric opened the Council: "Let us begin."

Immediately, Lord Dorgas of Ferranagh stood and stated his claim for a small tract of land that now belonged to Kashel, but had once been a part of Ferranagh several hundred years before. Kashel's representative took issue with the claim and a shouting match erupted.

Expecting nothing less, Gregory sighed as the two lords began throwing insults at one another. This was the first of five days in this chamber. How was he going to survive? Well, maybe Kaylie would learn something, he hoped. Yet his daughter's mind had already turned to other things as she took the chair placed behind her father's throne. She barely paid attention to Ferranagh's claim. Rather, she kept peeking at Corelia and thinking of Thomas. Corelia had shown an inordinate amount of interest in the green-eyed boy when he had appeared before them in Tinnakilly.

Kaylie fought to keep her ever-present guilt from consuming her. Thomas was the only person who had treated her as an equal. Yet she had been the cause of Thomas' capture in Tinnakilly. He was likely dead, and that grief stayed with her every minute. But in a hidden part of her heart she hoped that he still lived, remote though that chance may be, and that she would have just one more chance to see him again.

58

AN OFFER

Gregory entered Rodric's personal quarters with a guard at his back. He noticed immediately the soldiers standing to either side of the door he had just entered, as well as the two stationed outside the private office Rodric just exited as he walked into the room. Gregory had been on edge as soon as he received Rodric's request for a private meeting. He was even more so now, instantly aware of the dark shadow hidden deep within the High King's office. Clearly, this was not meant to be a private meeting after all.

"We have never been on the best of terms, Gregory," acknowledged Rodric, twirling his finger in a glass of blood red wine after having taken a seat in the only chair in the room. Apparently the expected niceties between peers weren't needed for this conversation. "I'd like to change that."

"I doubt we'll ever be on the best of terms, Rodric."

Gregory stood stiffly in front of Rodric, dwarfing the High King. During the long period of time he had been forced to interact with Rodric, Gregory had grown accustomed to his mercurial moods, volatility, and instability. But what he saw now worried him even more. There was a glint in Rodric's eyes. The glint of madness.

"One can always hope," said Rodric. "This is only the first day of the Council, four more to go. Little of the business will interest us until we reach the last day and the final item on the agenda."

Gregory smiled briefly, having to give Sarelle credit. He had spoken with her before coming to meet with Rodric, not knowing why the High King would want to talk with him considering their long, troubled history of having opposing perspectives on almost every issue raised between them. Sarelle had guessed immediately why Rodric had requested his presence.

"He's nervous," she had explained. "We keep hearing more and more rumors of this Lost Kestrel, which is to be expected with the deadline for deciding the fate of the Highlands fast approaching. Consider, as well, the growing unrest. As you said, the Marchers apparently have reawakened, staking claim to a large swath of their territory, and we know from your scouts that reivers are leaving the Highlands as quickly as they can, so obviously Killeran has experienced a major setback, if not more than one. Rodric desperately needs the Highlands, so he's going to try to hedge his bets with you just in case."

Rodric quickly brought him back to the present. "I don't want to waste your time, Gregory. We are both men of action. Men of deeds."

Gregory found it difficult to contain the smirk that threatened to escape him, not expecting such amusement so early in this conversation. Men of deeds, indeed.

"Let's cut to the chase, Rodric. What do you want?"

"Never one to engage in conversation if it's unnecessary. As I said, Gregory, men of action."

Rodric placed the wine glass on a small table, turning his full attention to the King of Fal Carrach. He tried to gather himself in a way that added to his less than regal appearance. Yet despite his best efforts, it was not to be.

"Allow me to make this plain. In a few days, as prescribed by the law, I will rule the Highlands, to do with as I think best. Perhaps you should think about how we could work together, to keep both our Kingdoms strong during this time of transition. If we were partners, we could accomplish much to the benefit of both. I have a son. You have a daughter. It would be easy to arrange the match."

Gregory stared at Rodric as if he were a fool. Did the High King really believe he would be so stupid as to agree to such a pairing? Fal Carrach would be severely weakened and his daughter would disown him.

"And if I don't accept this offer? What then?"

"Then Armagh gets stronger with the Highlands and Fal Carrach weaker, Gregory. As I said, I will rule the Highlands and do what I think is best. If you want to continue to rule Fal Carrach as you think best, it would be wise for you to do what I think is best as well."

"A hard offer to refuse," chuckled Gregory.

To think that he would ever consider such a thing, knowing that the man standing before him likely ordered the murder of his friend Talyn Kestrel. To say nothing of the barbarity he had demonstrated in Tinnakilly in how he treated the boy. Moreover, how could Rodric think that he would put his daughter and his Kingdom at risk, particularly considering who Rodric's silent partner likely was based on his involvement with Chertney and Malachias? Truly, Rodric's arrogance and ignorance astounded him.

"You find this amusing, Gregory? Will you find it so amusing with Armagh's soldiers to your north and Dunmoor's to your west? Will you go running to your precious Sarelle in Benewyn when you realize the untenability of your position? I assure you, Gregory, Benewyn can offer you nothing, except perhaps a romp in the hay, which even I would find hard to turn down. In just a few days you will have few, if any, options. I suggest you take advantage of the opportunity you have now. An alliance between Armagh and Fal Carrach would aid us both."

Gregory's face turned a bright red as Rodric spoke. His reference to Sarelle sent his hand to his right hip, but he restrained his desire to free his sword because of the restrictions of the Council. He sought an outlet for his fury, but saw no purpose in fighting four Armaghian soldiers and not knowing but suspecting who hid in Rodric's office. Instead, he refocused his mind, working to ensure he didn't allow his temper to get the better of him.

"Your threats are growing tiresome, Rodric. Tell me, oh grand High King, even if this Lost Kestrel does not appear, how do you expect to actually rule in the Highlands? From what I hear, the Marchers have won some victories, and some say that the reivers, led by your loyal Lord Killeran, are fleeing the Highlands in droves. So yes, by all means, best of luck in trying to lay claim to the Highlands. You've failed to conquer that Kingdom for the past decade. Why you think you could do so now is beyond me."

Rodric's rage almost boiled over, his face becoming a mottled red.

"You cannot speak to me this way," screeched Rodric. "I am the High King! I am ..."

"You are the High King, I'll grant you that," said Gregory, his smile thin, veiled, as if he sought to further antagonize Rodric. "But High King in name only. And that will never change. You made an offer at the beginning of this conversation. Now allow me to offer you a certainty. There will be no bargain between Fal Carrach and Armagh. Law or no, Fal Carrach is ready to assist the Highlands. If the Marchers choose to stand against you after this Council, then Fal Carrach will stand with them."

Gregory turned on his heel, striding purposefully for the door. The soldier standing there quickly opened it, allowing him to pass, not wanting to get in the way of the formidable King of Fal Carrach. Gregory scowled as he walked back toward his chambers, thinking that he would have Kael increase the number of guards tonight, then remembering that Kael had not yet arrived at the Council. He would do it himself, then. Tweaking the nose of the High King had proven fun, almost refreshing, but better to protect against any unforeseen consequences here in Eamhain Mhacha just in case, not trusting the truce of the Council to be obeyed.

59

REMINISCING

"I never thought we'd reach this point," said Coban. He sat against his saddle in front of the small fire, enjoying the breeze of the early evening. "I remember that night in the Crag so clearly."

Coban replayed the events of that cursed night from almost a decade ago, sharing the story with Oso. He had watched Thomas escape, then ran into the Hall of the Highland Lord to fight to the death with Talyn. When Talyn fell, before he died, the Highland Lord told Coban and his surviving Marchers to follow his grandson. He and a few others escaped reluctantly, then went in search of Thomas. They followed him through the passage, tracked him through the Highlands, found the glade, and there the trail ended. They searched for months, but to no avail. The whole time reivers and Ogren were at their heels, pressing them, as they too seemed to be in search of the heir to the Highland throne. In the end, the trail cold and having no other options, he and his Marchers had assumed the worst and made for the safer, higher passes.

Oso simply listened, never having heard the full story of the events that occurred after the fall of the Crag. Coban then focused on the importance of Thomas declaring himself.

"As I said, once the time has passed, if there is no legitimate claimant, then the High King could do what he wants with the Highlands," explained Coban. "And it would give Rodric a power that previous High Kings have not enjoyed for centuries."

"How so?" asked Oso.

"Over time the High King has become a figurehead," answered Coban. "The first High King, Ollav Fola, united the Kingdoms into a single entity. Though he allowed each Kingdom's ruler a level of independence, all remained subservient to him. Ollav Fola began the great gatherings, what became the Council of the Kingdoms, that continue to take place in which the major lords and ladies of the land gather at Eamhain Mhacha to enact laws, settle disputes and successions, essentially conduct any business needed to keep the united but somewhat distinct Kingdoms functioning as a whole, with a good bit of feasting thrown into the mix as well. During the gathering, all enmities had to be set aside, and no man could lift a hand against another."

Coban shifted against his saddle, his old bones protesting at having to rest against the hardened ground.

"It was inevitable, I guess. There was no ruler like Ollav Fola, and once he died, over time, due to wars and poor judgment, the power of the High King waned and the individual Kingdoms once again gained dominance. Armagh is now simply another Kingdom, rather than *the* Kingdom. Rodric wants to change that. He wants to make Armagh *the* Kingdom once again. And if he took the Highlands that would be an important first step in that direction."

The Swordmaster chuckled softly. "Rodric wasn't even supposed to become the ruler of Armagh, and thereby the honorary High King. His cousin was in line for the throne, yet within a few weeks of his uncle dying, Rodric's cousin died mysteriously as well. Some said it was an illness that came on quickly, sapping his strength and attacking his heart. Others expected poison."

"What do you think happened?" asked Oso, intrigued by a history he had never heard.

"Need I even answer?"

"Are you done reliving the past?" asked Thomas, who stepped noiselessly out of the shadows.

"Thomas, you must stop doing that!" protested Coban, startled by his sudden, silent appearance. "It might be fun for you, but it's not fun for me."

"It's fun for me, too," said Oso, laughing and enjoying Coban's discomfiture. "You should have seen the look on your face. It was like you saw a ghost."

"Careful, lad," replied Coban. "I'm still better than you in a fight. If it's a ghost you want to see, it'll be you."

"Enough," said Thomas, settling before the fire. "I didn't mean to frighten you, Coban. My apologies."

"You didn't frighten me," responded Coban. "I was simply startled because I was ..."

Coban would have continued his argument, but seeing Thomas and Oso's grins, knew it was useless.

"You two are insufferable," huffed Coban. Thomas and Oso broke out into laughter, and it wasn't long before Coban joined in. Allowing Thomas and Oso to have their fun for a brief moment, Coban sought to shift their focus to more pressing matters. "Anything to worry about?"

"No," said Thomas. "Nothing around us for leagues, and right now there's nothing in the way to stop us from reaching our goal."

"Finally some good news," said Oso.

"For now, yes," agreed Thomas. "But that could change. Let's talk to the Marchers and the Fal Carrachians tomorrow morning. They need to prepare for what's going to happen next."

60

QUITE A PERFORMANCE

Rodric threw the glass he had placed on the table against the wall, watching it shatter and the wine drip slowly down the stones to stain the lush carpet. His rage knew no bounds, yet he had no outlet. He looked quickly around the room, seeking more things to break, when he felt a cold shiver run down his spine.

His rage dissipated, replaced by an unsettling fear as Malachias stepped out of Rodric's private office. Even the guards, hardened fighters, found Malachias' presence unsettling. He held a power that none of them could even imagine. For the guards, that made them afraid. Yet for Rodric, his fear barely outweighed his jealousy, hating anyone who had more power than he did.

"Quite a performance, Rodric," hissed Malachias in a raspy voice, his thin lips, almost hidden by his beard, barely moving.

"I did think I handled that quite ..."

"Not you, Rodric. King Gregory. Quite a performance, indeed. If ever there was a candidate for High King ..."

"Enough!" shouted Rodric, his rage returning ten-fold at the slight. "I am the High King! And the Kingdoms will acknowledge that as they should, Malachias. In less than a year, many of the Kingdoms will be mine."

The shadowy figure stared at the High King, his black eyes boring into him. He felt the urge to crush the little man, but knew that his master wouldn't approve. Not yet, at least. And there was never any good reason to antagonize his master.

"Let's hope so, Rodric. I would hate for you to disappoint our master. He has little patience for those who fail to meet his objectives."

"I have nothing to fear in that regard, Malachias. I will do as I have promised. Now do as you have promised. You were sent here to do what I needed done."

"Be careful, Rodric. I serve you only because our master requires it. If the time comes when you are no longer of use..." Malachias didn't see the need to complete the threat. Yet it was wasted effort, as Rodric's rage continued to get the better of him.

"Your threats be damned. I have a simple task for you, Malachias. Ensure that Gregory never makes it back to Fal Carrach."

"And his daughter?"

"Take her," replied Rodric, weighing his options. As the heir to Fal Carrach, she could still be put to use, whether she wanted to be or not.

61

ENTERING THE FRAY

Malachias sat in the second semicircle of chairs in Eamhain Mhacha's throne room, just behind Rodric. Every now and then Kaylie Carlomin glanced his way, as did her father. They wanted his head for her kidnapping. Malachias smiled evilly, making sure they saw his contempt. Their hopes would never become reality. They could do nothing here at the Council. And once the gathering ended tomorrow? Well, gaining revenge would be a long-lost memory and the furthest thing from their minds. They would have more important things to worry about. In a matter of days the girl would once more be his and the father eliminated.

He turned his attention back to the murmurings and movements in the throne room. The High King wished to ignore what had been happening in the Highlands for the last few months, believing the Marchers' last gasp effort to maintain control of their Kingdom would end in failure. Malachias knew better following word of Chertney's most recent disastrous encounter, information he had chosen to keep to himself. He hoped that the dark creatures he had left in wait on the northern side of the river had more success than that fool did. But he didn't hold out much hope.

Whether there was any truth to the claim that a Highland Lord once more stood on high was just one concern. The Marchers had proven, much like the long grass so common to the Highlands that was flattened to the soil when tread upon and then after a time sprang back up, that though beaten regularly during the last decade, the men and women of the Highlands were not yet defeated. A strange, disturbing feeling had wormed its way into Malachias' stomach since the start of the Council, and it had increased as each day passed. Now, with the final day of the Council upon them, this unwanted sensation felt as if it were going to explode in his gut. A feeling that he had not experienced in quite some time. Fear. It annoyed him to no end, but he could not escape it. Thoughts of the green-eyed boy who had wriggled free in Tinnakilly, in large part due to Rodric's stupidity, continued to plague him. With all the continuing problems in the Highlands, who would his master hold responsible? Who would pay the price for failure?

Yet Rodric, sitting on his throne, remained oblivious to Malachias' concerns. On this, the final day of the Council of the Kingdoms, the High King had concluded that the Lost Kestrel was indeed lost, never to be found. For days, his scouts swept every inch of land for ten leagues around Eamhain Mhacha, with not one Highlander located.

Because of that, the High King's smile threatened to blind anyone looking at him. Normally impatient, he sought to savor what would be his greatest and most sought after victory. After a decade, the Highlands finally would be his. And with the Highlands in his grasp, he could play the next few pieces on the board to solidify his dominance of the eastern Kingdoms.

"My lords," began Rodric, the chamber settling into a reluctant silence. "As you know, ten years ago unknown attackers brutally murdered the Highland Lord and his family with many suspecting rebels to be the cause of this tragedy. Survivors of the Kestrel line have never been found, despite our best efforts since that tragic day. As a result, for the last ten years I have looked after the Highlands as if it were my own Kingdom."

BOOM!

Rodric lost his train of thought for a moment, startled by the slam. The hallway leading to this chamber stretched out for several hundred feet, segregated by five massive double doors spaced along the way. At each doorway, just to ensure no disruptions occurred on this day of all days, Rodric had placed soldiers at each entranceway. Yet it had sounded like a set of doors had banged open. He regained his focus and continued.

"Therefore, as required by the law, I named the trusted Lord Killeran of Dunmoor regent."

BOOM!

It sounded like another set of double doors, weighing well over one thousand pounds each, had just slammed open. Many in the chamber now turned toward the muted cacophony coming from the hallway, what sounded like shouts and scuffles drifting through the closed doors into the chamber.

Rodric had begun to sweat, his fear growing. What could be happening? Not wanting to stop, he ignored the growing unrest within the throne room.

"During his time as regent, Lord Killeran has done his best to protect the Highlands and its people, hoping that someone, perhaps this Lost Kestrel, would return to make a legitimate claim so that the people of the Highlands could rule themselves once more. Unfortunately, we have had no such luck."

Murmurs began among those in the chamber, mostly from those who suspected that Rodric had masterminded the attack on the Crag and the murder of the Kestrels. Gregory's stony face stated clearly where his thoughts on the subject lay.

BOOM!

The latest crash startled Rodric, the murmurs in the crowd growing louder, their attention wavering. Whatever was taking place in the hallway threatened to overshadow the High King's moment. Recognizing this, Rodric quickly pressed on.

"Since we have not found a surviving Kestrel, according to the law the Kingdom reverts to the High King."

BOOM!

The penultimate set of double doors slammed open, the murmurs in the crowd shifting to raised voices and shouts. Many in the throne room, like Rodric, strained to look over the heads of their peers to see what all the commotion out in the hallway was about despite the fact that the last set of double doors that led into the room remained closed. Several of the monarchs, including Gregory and Sarelle, stood up to get a better view.

"Therefore ..."

BOOM!

The final crash reverberated throughout the chamber. Shouts followed with the sounds of a struggle just beyond the doorway drifting into the throne room. Even with all the commotion going on around him, not to be deterred, and not knowing what else to do, Rodric continued in a squeaky shout.

"Therefore, according to the law, I must ask the question: Who stands for the Highlands?"

Silence fell within the chamber as well as beyond as a result of the High King's question. Rodric's initial consternation from the distractions dissipated. His goal was almost within his grasp. After a decade, he would finally have what he so desperately wanted. He could barely control his rising excitement as he sought to conclude the day's business.

"With no ..."

"I stand for the Highlands."

The strong voice shot into the throne room like an unexpected lightning bolt.

Rodric stood transfixed, shocked at the interruption. Malachias, seated behind him, rose, trying to get a better view.

Every pair of eyes in the chamber turned to stare at the entranceway as a brown-haired young man wearing forest garb and trailed by a troop of Highlanders pushed their way through the crowd to stand in front of the semicircle of rulers.

Kael Bellilil and the soldiers of Fal Carrach followed behind the Highlanders. Kael took his men through the crowd to stand next to Kaylie, who had risen from her chair behind her father with a lump in her throat. Thomas stood before her, his green eyes blazing, boring into those of the shocked High King. He was alive.

62

____

CLAIMING THE HIGHLANDS

Thomas stood defiantly in front of the High King, a dozen hard-faced Highlanders standing with him. Corelia Tessaril, long blonde hair capturing the rays of sun that streamed through the chamber's windows, looked appraisingly at Thomas. Her cold and calculating eyes did not match the smile she gave him. Though Thomas ignored it, Kaylie saw it clearly, and that suggestive glance sent a stab of jealousy through her.

"You!" exclaimed Rodric, pointing at Thomas as if he could defend himself with his finger.

"Yes, me."

"You dare to show your face here after what you did to my son?" demanded Rodric. "After the crimes you committed in Tinnakilly? You have no right to be here. Absolutely no right!'

"I have every right," Thomas replied sharply. "As some of the people in this room can attest, Ragin brought his injury upon himself. I'm sure many of these people also remember what you did to me without justification. Something that I have not forgotten, but we will deal with that another time."

Rodric took the cold certainty with which Thomas bit off his last sentence as a threat, as was intended.

"We Highlanders pay our debts," continued Thomas. "And the debt I owe you will be paid, that I can assure you."

The faces of the Highlanders standing behind Thomas turned to stone. Their intentions were clear though left unsaid. The debt to their Highland Lord would be paid. The debt to the Highlands would be paid. One way or another.

"But it will have to wait. At a Council of the Kingdoms, the past has no meaning."

"The young man is right," said Gregory, stepping forward to stand just a few feet in front of Thomas, that simple movement essentially giving the King of Fal Carrach control of the proceedings.

"During the Council there is an amnesty for any crimes or transgressions committed previously." Gregory smiled a bit as he considered the position Rodric had placed himself in with the Highlanders. The High King would not like the reckoning that would be coming his way. "Any charges to be made, or debts paid, will have to wait until tomorrow, after the Council. At that time, the past may be remembered and acted upon."

"That is the law," said Sarelle Makarin, Queen of Benewyn.

"So it is," confirmed Rendael, King of Kenmare.

Several of the other monarchs murmured their assent. Having lost control of the ceremony, Rodric slumped back into his throne, his hands covering his face as his years of planning slowly and inexorably unraveled around him.

"I believe we have a claimant before us," said Gregory. "Who stands for the Highlands?"

"I stand for the Highlands." Thomas stepped forward proudly.

"Your name?"

"Thomas Kestrel."

Gasps of surprise burst out within the throne room, exclamations of shock rising to a crescendo of noisy disbelief and excitement. The clamor quickly dissipated to a low murmur when Gregory raised his hands for silence.

Rodric tried one last time to regain control of the situation. "Say what you want, boy, claim to be whomever you wish to be. The grandson died in the attack on the Crag. As I was saying before I was so rudely interrupted, according to the law of the Kingdoms, I will decide the fate of the Highlands!"

Thomas smiled at the High King, much like a predator about to strike. The room sensed the increasing tension, the Highlanders themselves seeming to want that tension to explode, their anger at the last ten years plain on their faces and in their stances.

"That won't be necessary, Rodric."

"And before I have you thrown into the dungeon, boy, why is that?"

"Because I am the Highland Lord. I am the grandson of Talyn Kestrel."

Total silence fell across the chamber, many of those in the room stunned by Thomas' announcement, even catching Rodric off guard, who found himself speechless. Once again, Gregory took control of the proceedings.

"Can you prove it?" asked the King of Fal Carrach.

Thomas stepped toward Gregory, pulling his sword free from the scabbard on his back, then holding the blade in two hands to allow Gregory to get a closer look at the weapon. As Gregory examined the blade, his smile grew. He knew this sword. He would never forget it, having fought beside Talyn Kestrel too many times to not have the shining blade burned into his memory. And he would never forget the words that ran the length of both sides of the sharp steel: "Strength and courage lead to freedom."

"I see before me the blade of the Kestrels, the Sword of the Highlands," confirmed Gregory.

Shouts of surprise ran through the chamber.

"That proves nothing!" shouted Rodric, trying to be heard over the commotion. "It may be the blade of the Kestrels but that does not mean that this charlatan is a Kestrel."

Thomas deftly slid the blade back into its scabbard. He rolled up his right sleeve, then pushed his wrist guard to the side. He raised his arm up so that it captured the light streaming in through the windows.

Gregory's smile grew even bigger. Sarelle Makarin stepped up next to him, grinning as well. The mark on Thomas' wrist, the claw of a kestrel, was unmistakable and well known throughout the Kingdoms. Several in the crowd gasped or shouted confirmation at what they saw, never expecting to view the mark again. For they all knew what it meant.

"I see before me the Highland Lord," intoned Gregory, who inclined his head slightly toward Thomas as a show of respect between peers.

Thomas returned the nod. Many of the other rulers did so as well as Rodric sat flabbergasted, unable to speak.

"I see before me Thomas Kestrel, grandson of Talyn Kestrel, long lost Lord of the Highlands."

A massive cheer erupted throughout the chamber, many caught up in the excitement of the moment, many pleased that Rodric had been thwarted. Yet the Highlanders stood behind Thomas calmly, Coban and Oso surveying the throng, focusing their attention on those few unhappy with the surprising turn of events. Just in case.

"Lord Kestrel," asked Gregory in a strong, clear voice. "Would you like to take the chair that once belonged to your grandfather?"

Thomas hesitated for a moment, the emotion of the moment catching up to him. As he looked at the chair, he thought he could see the spirit of his grandfather rising from it and gesturing him toward it, a large smile on his face. Thomas stepped up to the throne and turned, scanning the room, seeing the pleasure and joy on so many faces, smiling even more at the anger openly displayed by Rodric and Malachias and anyone else who had stood to profit from Rodric taking the Highlands.

As he sat on the chair, a roar erupted throughout the chamber. The Lord of the Highlands had returned.

63

THE PULL

Ragin Tessaril had remained hidden away in his room for months, preferring the darkness and solitude of his chambers and refusing to leave once he saw the gruesome scar that trailed down his face. He adjusted his eyepatch for the hundredth time that day, scratching where his right eye should have been. Itching. Always itching. No matter what he tried. The itch drove him to distraction, especially at night, when his dreams always returned to that fateful night in Tinnakilly.

The boy on the battlements, wounded and exhausted, should have been an easy kill. An easy victory for Ragin and a way to enhance his standing in the eyes not only of his father, but also the other rulers of the various Kingdoms. But events had not played out as he expected. Night after night the images played through his mind. Night after night he reached the same conclusion. The boy had gotten lucky, the quick slash of his sword catching Ragin across his face. Moreover, the wound had done more than mar his appearance. It had changed him deeply.

No longer did he seek to assume his father's place as the High King. That didn't matter to him anymore. The power, the wealth, held little meaning for him. No, he wanted only one thing in life now. A simple thing. He wanted revenge on the boy who had taken so much from him. His father had said the boy was dead, not understanding how he could have survived his jump from the battlements. But Ragin knew. He knew in his heart that somehow the boy still lived, mocking him.

It was that feeling that made him turn from the window he stared out of, just a small slit between the drapes allowing his good eye to peek out on the world he no longer felt a part of. Ragin frowned, trying to make sense of what tugged at him. Today was the last afternoon of the Council of the Kingdoms. He had no desire to attend, not wanting to deal with the smirks of triumph or the looks of empathy for what had happened to him. He had wanted to stay here in this one place where he believed he could still exert some control over his life. But even that seemed to be slipping from his grasp. The tug grew stronger, becoming an insistent pull, almost a need that had to be fulfilled.

Taking hold of his sword and scabbard for the first time in months, Ragin pushed the door to his chambers open and stepped out into the deserted hall. He turned left, then left once more, allowing the pull to guide him. Several maids and servants stepped out of his way, bowing their heads as he passed, whether out of respect or not wanting to see his wound, he didn't know and he didn't care.

Ragin guessed at where the pull was leading him. The throne room of Eamhain Mhacha. He didn't want to go there. But he couldn't stop himself. The pull was too strong, too demanding. He continued on, at first trudging reluctantly, and then picking up the pace as the pull within him became a nagging need until he jogged through the halls. As he drew closer, the jog became a sprint until he burst into the throne room. The throng of participants in the Council apparently were in an uproar, all talking and moving at the same time, shouts of surprise and hurrahs echoing throughout the chamber.

He ignored the gasps around him, trying to figure out why he had been pulled here. And then he knew. On the other side of the chamber he caught a glimpse through a squad of Marchers of a boy in a green shirt and brown breeks making his way toward the doors that led to the entrance of the keep. The boy from the battlements. The boy who plagued his dreams night after night.

Ragin tried to push his way through the crowd, his frustration increasing as the various Kingdom representatives unknowingly blocked his path. With a snarl of rage Ragin grasped the hilt of his sword, but he was only able to pull a few inches of the blade free before a strong, skeletal hand enclosed his own, locking it into place. Struggle though he might, he could not dislodge the crushing grip.

"Release me, Malachias," Ragin hissed. "I have business to complete."

The tall man ignored Ragin's demand, holding the Prince of Armagh firmly in place with his long, skeletal fingers. He leaned down so that his words could only be heard by Ragin, who attempted to move backwards when Malachias' malevolent eyes caught his own. Yet the Prince of Armagh could do nothing but stand there, still as a mouse bewitched by a snake awaiting its fate.

"If you pull your blade and attack the new Lord of the Highlands, your life is forfeit."

"The Lord of the Highlands? That whelp! I'll ..."

"Think, fool. You are the heir to Armagh. You have had the best in martial training. You failed to kill him in Tinnakilly when he was at his weakest. Why would you expect to defeat him now?"

"That was no more than luck," Ragin hissed.

Malachias pulled Ragin closer, his foul breath resembling

the decaying stench of an open grave, wafting over him and making his eyes water. "That was skill, you imbecile. Besides, he has a power, an ability, that is beyond you. To do what you want to do now would make your certain death meaningless."

"I don't care if I die," Ragin snarled. "I want revenge. That's all that matters to me."

Malachias smiled, seemingly having heard exactly what he had expected. "I understand. And I can give you your revenge."

"You? How?"

"In time, boy, I will show you. But not now. Now you must be patient. You must be willing to learn. You must be willing to risk all for you can only attain all by risking all."

"I'll do whatever's necessary," replied Ragin, finding Malachias' choice of words strange. "I'm not afraid to die."

"That's good, my young prince. For you may very well die if you persist. But then again, Ragin, there are worse things to fear than death. Much worse."

64

STRONG WORDS

Kaylie Carlomin stood behind her father's chair, scarcely able to believe what had just occurred. Thomas was alive! And more than that, he was whom he originally seemed to be. As the kings, queens, and their many courtiers and servants burst into applause upon her father naming Thomas the Lord of the Highlands, she sought to push her way through the excited crowd and speak with Thomas, offering him an apology and perhaps ... beyond that, she didn't know. She only knew that she had to speak with him.

Finally having slipped through the throng, she was about to sprint down the long hallway, glimpsing the backs of the Marchers as they made their way out of the palace. But before she could, a figure stepped in front of her, blocking her path.

"Quite exciting, was it not, Kaylie? Certainly unexpected."

Corelia Tessaril, daughter of the High King, stood before her.

"I don't have time for this, Corelia," replied Kaylie, an angry glint in her eyes.

Kaylie stepped to the side, seeking to get past the High

King's daughter. But Corelia moved with her, preventing her from pursuing Thomas.

"After all that has happened between you two, do you really believe that the dashing Lord of the Highlands will want to speak with you?"

Corelia's words struck Kaylie to the core. Kaylie pondered the question as she watched the backs of the Marchers disappear from view. Could she be right? Kaylie shook off Corelia's comments, knowing that her words could just as easily ensnare someone as her looks.

"This has nothing to do with you, Corelia. Thomas will or will not speak to me. That is his choice. But I will speak to him."

Corelia chuckled, clearly amused. "Strong words, Kaylie. But do you really believe them?" Corelia began to walk around Kaylie, the Princess of Fal Carrach finding herself rooted in place as every one of Corelia's words hit home. "Tell me, Kaylie. Why would the new Lord of the Highlands be interested in you? Were you not the cause for all he was forced to endure in Tinnakilly?"

Corelia continued her pacing, circling round and round, much like a shark before it launched itself at its prey. "I would think that of all the people who have wronged the new Lord of the Highlands, you have hurt him the most."

"I had no idea ..."

Corelia stopped in front of Kaylie, her voice hard as she cut her off. "You had no idea what? That such harm would befall him? That he would almost die? Do you think that really matters? I would think that the young Lord of the Highlands would not forget the cause of all that he suffered. I would think that as a result his eye could be turned by someone else."

"What are you suggesting, Corelia?" asked Kaylie, her anger rising. The words of the Armaghian Princess had played on her guilt, hitting home in a way that she refused to reveal. But that challenge she noted in Corelia's last comment had pulled her out of her rapidly growing remorse and given her a renewed focus.

"I'm not suggesting anything, Kaylie. I'm stating a fact. With the weight of all that has occurred between you and the Lord of the Highlands, I doubt he'll have any desire to see you again. But he is a young man, and you know where the thoughts of young men tend to wander. If you could catch his eye so easily, I have no doubt that someone else could."

Kaylie's eyes narrowed as she struggled to control her growing fury. "You? You think that the Lord of the Highlands will be interested in you?"

Corelia's knowing smile disappeared, replaced by a predatory smirk. "I'm absolutely certain. I have much to offer him, Kaylie. Much indeed. More, in fact, than you."

The knowing smile returned as Corelia stepped away from Kaylie and lost herself among the assemblage. Kaylie remained where she was, her gaze fixed on the now empty hallway, wondering if the Princess of Armagh was right.

65

——————

CHALLENGES

It was late afternoon, but it appeared to be dusk. Most men refused to enter the Charnel Mountains, and those who did rarely returned. Any who traveled within three leagues of the forbidding peaks could sense the evil lurking there, hidden away from the sight of man, but always there. Watching, waiting, until it was too late.

Some said the Charnel Mountains were an abomination, caused by a tremendous magical battle between the forces of good and evil. Those who followed the light had won, but they could not destroy the dark. It was too strong, too powerful, too sinister. So instead they imprisoned their enemies in the mountains, sealing them away for eternity, or so they thought. Dark grey stone formed the mountains, the very tips of the monstrous peaks a sooty black.

The tallest of the mountains could not be seen completely, as fully a third of its mass stretched into the clouds. Known as Blackstone, that single peak had an even older name. Shadow's Reach. On certain winter days, when the sun was just right, the shadow of Blackstone reached out across much of the Northern

Steppes, turning day into night and, for those lone travelers caught in that desolate land, life into a nightmare.

But today was different. A strange event was occurring once more. An incident that had only begun to happen during the last few years but with increasing frequency. A single ray of sunshine had fought its way through the thick clouds, shining down on Blackstone, illuminating the abandoned city. The sunlight flickered, struggling against the murky shadow. But it was getting easier now, the light forcing its way through the gloom and murk. The shadow fought hard, but the light refused to yield, building in intensity with each passing second. The ray of light shone down through a glass dome situated on top of the largest building in the city, a massive structure that resembled a castle, yet in the place of crenellations stood gargoyles and other hideous creatures in gruesome poses. As the darkness dissipated in response to the growing strength of the light, the room revealed its secrets. Massive marble columns stationed around its perimeter appeared. Black and white tiles as wide as a tall man covered the floor. If there were any doors, they remained hidden in the darkness.

The beam of sunshine settled on the room's most unique characteristic, a stone disk with an intricate design set in the very center of the floor. Two figures emerged from the cuts in the block, done with such excellent workmanship that they appeared lifelike. The first resembled a young man with a blazing sword of light. Opposing him was a tall man with a cruel face wielding a sword that swallowed the light. They were locked blade to blade, their faces no more than a finger's breadth apart. The boy wore a look of determination, the man a grin of arrogance and sure victory. As the sun touched the stone it grew warm. A rumble began in the room, drifting out to the very edges of Blackstone. It was not an earthquake, for that was something of an end. Instead, it was a beginning. An awakening, perhaps?

The Shadow Lord stood on a large black tile, avoiding the sunlight, his gaze fixed on the disk. The rumbling grew louder as the ray of sunlight blazed with increasing intensity, illuminating more and more of the chamber.

"Enough!"

The Shadow Lord's shout reverberated throughout the room. His hands, twisted and scarred, slipped from his robes as he raised them toward the dome of glass above him. A black mist began to form, coalescing into a circular shape. With a flick of his wrist, the swirling black mist sped to the top of the chamber, seeking to block out the sunlight. But the sunlight fought back, pushing against the circular shield of inky blackness, trying to fight its way through.

With a growl of anger, the Shadow Lord increased the vigor of his effort until the disk moved slowly but relentlessly to the top of the chamber, finally settling in place on the glass dome and blocking out the blazing ray of light.

Much to the Shadow Lord's relief, the chamber returned to its normal murky grey. He remained standing in place, staring at the disk before him, having no trouble picking out the intricate carvings as his blood-red eyes blazed brightly.

He had thought that with his carefully laid plans he could have avoided the prophecy, nipped it in the bud. Eliminating the boy as a child should have been an easy task, yet his minions had failed. Since then many more attempts had been made yet they all had failed. Time and time again the boy escaped.

The Shadow Lord felt a tinge of worry. The boy was proving more resilient, more of a challenge, than expected. He had a knack for creating problems. For getting in the way without even knowing it. In an instant, his rage rose within him like a long smoldering fire reigniting. Why was it so difficult to kill a boy?

This time the Shadow Lord allowed his anger to surge

through him, relishing the experience, enjoying the rage as it energized him. Perhaps this was the way it was supposed to be, he thought, his burning eyes still fixed on the disk before him, taking in every detail of the carving. Perhaps no matter his best efforts the terms of the prophecy would need to be met.

So be it. His plans would continue as they should. And if this boy continued to be a thorn in his side, no matter. Eventually he would have the opportunity to remove that thorn once and for all.

This new Lord of the Highlands could savor his victory for now. He would meet the same fate as his father and his grandfather. It was simply a matter of time. One way or another, whether by his hand when the final combat came or by the hand of one of his minions before that, the boy would die.

The End.

~

Keep reading for the first three chapters of Book 7, *The Claiming of the Highlands.*

BONUS MATERIAL

If you really enjoyed this story, I need you to do me a HUGE favor – please follow me on Amazon and BookBub.

And if you have a few minutes, consider writing a review.

Keep reading for the first three chapters of Book 7 of *The Sylvan Chronicles, The Claiming of the Highlands.*

PETER WACHT

THE CLAIMING OF THE HIGHLANDS

7

THE SYLVAN CHRONICLES

Published in the United States by Kestrel Media Group LLC.

ISBN: 978-1-950236-12-1

eBook ISBN: 978-1-950236-13-8

Library of Congress Control Number: 2020912186

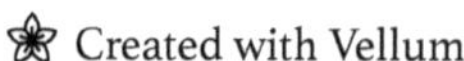 Created with Vellum

1. AMBUSH

"Steady, lads. Steady, lasses. Steady."

Nestor, a grizzled Highlander with a white beard trailing halfway down his chest, whispered his instructions to the men and women hidden among the trees, Marchers all. Trained as the warriors of the Highlands beginning at the age of ten, they were a hard people. But such a practice proved necessary. They lived in a harsh environment. The Highlands were a beautiful sight, but also dangerous. The rugged land hid untold riches -- gold and silver, precious jewels and more -- among its craggy, snowcapped peaks. But throughout their history the Highlanders had little use for the wealth that could be mined in their homeland. Rather, the people of the Highlands remained focused on a cold, stark and unforgiving reality, one of constant threats and peril, particularly from the north.

For Nestor and the other Highlanders that reality had crashed down upon them just a decade before. In a valley to the east of where the squad of Marchers now hid rose the stronghold of the Highlanders, the Crag, a monolithic rock that thrust up out of the earth and the surrounding forest. Carved from the mountain, the redoubt was a formidable sight. The Highlanders had built their fortress on top of a long-dead volcano, taking great slabs of black stone from the plateau to form its walls. During the night, the citadel receded into the darkness, indistinct in the gloom. The Crag had never fallen to an enemy. Many an army had learned that lesson the hard way, leaving behind crushed bodies and broken spirits. Until that fateful day ten years before, when a traitor among the Marchers had aided the reivers during their surprise attack on the Crag. Supported by warlocks and dark creatures, as soon as the Ogren and Shades broke through the Crag's outer curtain, the reivers grasped that they had won, and that the fate of the Highlands was sealed. Nestor and many of the Marchers standing with him now and shivering in the early morning cold had lived through that day, a day of shame and infamy. Talyn Kestrel, the Lord of the Highlands, had died that day. Refusing to escape, he fought until the very end in the Hall of the Highland Lord. His son, Benlorin Kestrel, met a similar fate at his camp in the northern peaks. Consequently, the Kestrel line had been broken, or so it had appeared.

Led by the Dunmoorian Lord Johin Killeran, who served as the High King's regent, from that point forward the reivers had assumed control of the Highlands. The High King had wanted the Highlands outright for himself, but there were still questions about the grandson. Did he die that night as well? Or had he survived the attack? A body had never been found. Therefore, according to the law set down during the time of the first High King, a decade-long regency was required. If no legitimate claimant stepped forward prior to the end of the stated time period, then the Highlands would revert to the High King for administration and rule. Although unhappy with the forced delay, it did not stop the High King, through his selected regent, from doing as he wished within the Highlands, much to the detriment of the Highlanders themselves, who reeled from the shock and loss of what had happened that fateful night and set the Highlands on a path of terror and oppression.

Nestor smiled to himself, remembering those not so long ago dark days. Hope had been lost during that desperate time and he, much like many of his people, had felt cast adrift, their thoughts only of survival, not vengeance. For with none of the other Kingdoms strong enough or willing to aid the Highlands against the expanding dominance of the High King, Killeran and his so-called Army of the Black Sword had been given free rein by Rodric Tessaril to do as charged. Enslave the Highlanders and force them into the mines so that the High King could extract the wealth that he needed to increase his power and achieve his larger objectives. For almost ten years the scheme had worked well for the High King and his sycophants. Until the boy appeared. The boy first known as the Raptor. The boy who aided the Highlanders whenever possible and killed dark creatures with ease. At first, Nestor, staying close to family in the passes of the northern Highlands, had taken the stories that had begun to spread among the peaks as no more than the fantasies of a desperate people, a people slowly being crushed under the heel of the High King. Even though the Marchers had the will to continue the fight, they didn't have the numbers to defeat the thousands of reivers that had flooded into the Highlands as part of the Army of the Black Sword and, more importantly, they had no way to defend against the Dark Magic of Killeran's warlocks.

But with time, as the stories continued to proliferate among the Highland towns and villages, and Nestor began to find evidence of the Raptor's work sprinkled among the Highland peaks – a small village saved from a reiver patrol thanks to the sharp shooting of a near perfect archer or the remains of several Ogren hamstrung and beheaded – he had started to believe, his hope returning once more. For Nestor and many others, that boy who had become the Raptor had shifted from myth to reality, in fact a new reality that held the promise of a better future for the subjugated Highlanders. The same boy who became a constant thorn in Killeran's side, burning down his primary fort and in the process reigniting the fire for freedom that now blazed in the breast of every Marcher. The boy who just a few months before had become the Lord of the Highlands. The Lost Kestrel was no longer lost. The grandson of Talyn Kestrel had returned to the Highlands to take his rightful place, and woe to any who opposed him, as the honorable Marchers had a saying: "A debt is owed."

With the return of the Lord of the Highlands, the Marchers began collecting on those debts, starting with the Army of the Black Sword, which had pushed deeper into the Highlands seeking to quell the uprising before it gained a momentum that could not be stopped. Killeran's reivers had failed miserably. What a glorious day that had been, thought Nestor, allowing his mind to drift just for a moment even as his eyes scanned his surroundings in an unerring arc, paying particular attention to the gulley that ran beneath where the Marchers hid among the evergreens. With the last of night still upon them, there was nothing but shadows to stare at among the bracken below.

Even though Ogren and Shades had been used in support of the reivers, the Marchers under the command of Thomas Kestrel had destroyed the Army of the Black Sword against the walls of a Highland village named Anselm, which was located at the very edge of one of the northern passes. Since that time, the Marchers had harried and harassed any reivers foolish enough to remain in the Highlands, driving them out or, as Nestor preferred, killing them. For the Marchers sought to pay their debts, and they owed the reivers a huge sum for the pain, misery, and death Killeran's lackeys had spawned in their homeland since the fall of the Crag.

Yet even with one victory attained, other challenges remained. Dark creatures from the Charnel Mountains continued to cross the barren Northern Steppes, seeking to gain a foothold in the Highlands for their master, who stirred once more. It was because of that threat, one that had troubled the Highlands for centuries, that Nestor and his Marchers waited patiently among the trees, bows in hand, several long, steel-tipped arrows stuck point first into the rocky soil and within easy reach. The Shadow Lord sought the Kingdoms for his own, and when his Dark Horde descended from the north the Lord Thomas and every other Highland chief, Nestor included, believed that the black-hearted bastard would seek to avoid the Breaker, the massive, granite wall to the west that ran from the Highlands to the coast and the Winter Sea. Three hundred feet in height and one hundred feet in width, the Breaker was constructed after the Great War by the Kingdoms as a way to defend against the Dark Horde, believing that the massive barrier would prevent the Ogren and Shades, Fearhounds and Mongrels, and the other terrifying, monstrous dark creatures that obeyed the Shadow Lord from threatening the Kingdoms once again. Yet Nestor scoffed at the naïve and misplaced hopes of those who had thought a stone wall would eliminate the need to defend against such an ancient evil. The Shadow Lord was not a fool. He had simply adopted a different strategy, seeking different routes into the west that would allow him to bypass the Breaker. Thus, the importance of the Highlands to his plans as an alternative path into the Kingdoms. Because of this threat, the new Highland Lord had charged Nestor and his Marchers with protecting the northern Highlands while he made his formal claim to the Highland throne during the Council of the Kingdoms.

Nestor hoped that all had gone well in Eamhain Mhacha, understanding the danger that Thomas, Coban, Oso, and the other Marchers had ridden toward. A danger that was difficult to defend against because more often than not politics hid your enemy in plain sight up until the instant you felt the dagger slide into your back. Much better to be here in the Highlands where you had no doubt about what you were fighting for and what you were fighting against.

"On my command," whispered Nestor, his eyes tightening as he glimpsed finally the movement that he had been expecting. The several dozen Marchers raised their bows in unison, the pull back on their strings barely making a sound as the biting wind swept up from the Northern Steppes, finding a path through the ravines and gullies leading up to the higher passes.

Large shapes had appeared just below the Marchers in the gloom of the early morning, the sun yet to find its way over the towering, rugged mountain peaks to the east. Bunched together, the huge creatures struggled up the slope of broken brush and loose rock, unaware or uncaring of what waited for them at the top.

"Release!"

The arrows flew through the morning mist, almost all finding a target. Roars of anger and pain echoed off the surrounding spires of rock. Below the Marchers some of the large shapes had fallen to the ground, never to rise again. But only a few, as these creatures were difficult to kill because of their armor and toughened hide, often requiring an arrow through the eye to ensure a clean kill, and to ask that of the Marchers in the dim light of the morning would have been unfair.

"Nock!"

The Marchers immediately heeded Nestor's command, pulling free the arrows they had stuck in the dirt by their feet and fitting them to the taut strings of their bows.

"On my command!"

The Marchers pulled back on their heavy bows, now seeking individual targets. The dark creatures below them had separated, their once orderly march having dissolved into a maelstrom of uncoordinated activity. Several of the beasts roared in rage and began to climb the slope toward their attackers.

"Release!"

A second flight of arrows arced through the air, all striking true this time as the monsters emerged from the grey murk in their rush to confront their tormentors. The dark creatures roared in rage as they struggled up the loose rocks of the incline, several using the broken brush to pull themselves up in order to avoid sliding back down the steep slope. Twice the size of a man, their heavily muscled bodies covered in fur, Ogren were truly hideous creatures. Their massive shoulders and upper body sometimes proved too heavy for their spines, forcing them to walk hunched over. Their chiseled, beast-like faces looked as if they had been carved from rock. Long, sharp tusks protruded from their lower lips to curl around their cheeks. They lacked intelligence, but their strength and viciousness more than made up for that shortcoming. Ogren were efficient soldiers. They enjoyed killing, and given the opportunity they ate what they killed, no matter what it was. A single person did not willingly fight an Ogren, not if they wanted to live. But the Marchers had mastered how to fight dark creatures such as these.

"Nock!"

The Marchers responded a third time to Nestor's command, ignoring the Ogren as they hauled themselves closer, several resembling pin cushions as arrows sprouted from their chests and thighs, the wounds seemingly having no effect on the enraged beasts.

"On my command!"

The Marchers raised their bows once more, sighting on individual targets, selecting the Ogren that had scrabbled closest to the Marcher line.

"Release!"

The third wave of arrows had a devastating impact at such a close distance, the steel-tipped shafts of wood tearing through Ogren eyes and mouths as the Marchers targeted where the beasts were most vulnerable. Almost all of the Ogren closest to the Marchers fell to the ground, an arrow embedded in their brains. But not every dark creature unfortunately. Therefore, Nestor judged that it was time to go.

"Retreat!"

The Marchers quickly began pulling back, following Nestor as he trotted off to the south. The Highland chief took great pleasure in the fact that they had hurt the Ogren raiding party badly with none of his Marchers the worse for wear. But the dark creatures were too many for the Marchers to stand and fight, and the beasts would be after them in an instant. In fact, he could hear several of the Ogren already pulling themselves to the top of the slope, their roars of triumph sending a shiver through his body and giving him a greater sense of urgency as the monstrous beasts began the chase.

"Come on my lads!" encouraged Nestor. "Come on my lasses! No one for an Ogren cook pot tonight."

The Marchers responded with a burst of speed. Increasing their pace, Nestor and his fighters ran across the rocky terrain, understanding the price they would pay if caught.

A tall man stood unmoving within the shadows of the forest, looking out from his place of concealment among the evergreens and birch trees at the verge of a small plateau. The field of long grass funneled toward him, constricted by two large, stone outcroppings that loomed above the wood on both sides. This would do nicely, he thought. Nicely, indeed.

He wore brown breeks and a dark blue shirt that covered a slim body. Though he did not look it, he had a deceptive strength. The cloak he wore not only helped to ward off the chill, but it also swirled around him, its green and brown colors allowing him to blend in perfectly with the environment. His piercing blue eyes held an intensity that would have frightened most men and were accentuated by the sharp features of his face. The short black beard flecked with grey gave him an almost dastardly appearance. If anyone had the courage to tell him so, he would have smiled and thanked them for the compliment.

"They come," said the diminutive woman standing next to him, who wore a similarly designed cloak so that she would remain hidden among the trees as well. She had used the Talent to scan their surroundings, having expected their quarry to arrive shortly after sunrise.

"It's about time," replied the man. "I'm tired of waiting." He glanced down at the beautiful woman who had stolen his heart so long ago. No more than five feet tall, she carried herself like a giant. As she swept her dark, chestnut hair away from her face with a quick swipe of her hand, she revealed deep blue eyes. Eyes that the tall man had often gotten lost in time and time again, much to his pleasure. In his mind, saying she was beautiful did not do her justice.

A massive shadow approached from behind, only the bright yellow of its eyes visible in the gloom of the forest. The growl that emanated from its throat sounded like the rumble of thunder.

"Yes, I know you had a part to play in putting this all together, Beluil," said the tall man, turning toward the wolf as it stepped out of the murk. The wolf stood as tall as a pony. Covered in a thick, black fur, he was invisible in the night, except for the streak of white fur that crossed his eyes. "Are you and your packs ready?"

Beluil growled once more, stretching his jaws in anticipation of what was to come and revealing his sharp teeth in the process.

"Then off with you, you big furball. We'll meet in the center."

Beluil dashed back into the trees straight away, lost from sight in less than a second.

"I'm glad that wolf is a friend," said Catal Huyuk, the hulking warrior stepping forward to stand next to his companions. He stood a head taller than most men, and his dark brown face disguised his age. His leathery skin showed him to be a man who had spent most of his life in the outdoors, and that he wasted little time in towns or cities. His long black hair was held back from his face by a knot of leather at the base of his neck. He was dressed in the leathers of a woodsman with a huge sword strapped to his back and a wickedly curved axe hanging at his waist instead of the expected bow and quiver of arrows. "Because I would hate to be his enemy."

"Yes, indeed," replied Rya. "Our grandson has a habit of acquiring dangerous friends."

"That's why I like him so much," rumbled Catal Huyuk. "He keeps things interesting and fun. Makes you feel alive."

"Fun?" asked Rya Keldragan, eyebrow raised quizzically.

"What could be more fun than killing dark creatures?" replied Catal Huyuk.

"It's time," said Rynlin Keldragan, ending the banter around him, his gaze fixed on the far side of the field. "They're only a few hundred yards from the entrance and coming fast."

"Good," said Catal Huyuk, who pulled his battle axe free. Even the largest of men would struggle to use the heavy weapon effectively, yet the Sylvan Warrior flipped it from one hand to the other as if it were no more than a child's toy. "I haven't been in a good fight in days."

Nestor cursed as he ran through the forest, ignoring the branches that scraped at his face and body. He had started out leading his Marchers through the fractured and jagged terrain as they sprinted from one copse of trees to the next after their ambush of the Ogren raiding party. But that hadn't lasted long. The younger and faster Marchers had sped ahead, and he had urged them on.

Now he was the last one, and he had larger things to worry about. Much larger. A handful of Ogren had closed in on him since the chase began, the foul beasts now no more than a few hundred feet behind and coming fast. The rest of the dark creature raiding party followed just seconds behind, ravenously pursuing their prey, pushed on by hunger and rage. Roars blasted through the small forest, the Ogren calling to one another as they continued to hound the Highlanders.

Peeking quickly over his shoulder to gauge his distance from the closest Ogren, the veteran Marcher stumbled on some loose rock, tumbling to the ground and slamming into the base of a fallen tree. Nestor hauled himself up rapidly, thankful that he hadn't injured anything except for his pride, but also realizing that his clumsiness had cost him greatly. The five Ogren that had raced ahead of the other dark creatures approached in a line, having caught up to him. The beasts bellowed in triumph as they brandished their short swords and axes, strings of spittle hanging from their curved tusks. Nestor pulled his sword from its scabbard across his back, relieved that it was still there after his tumble. There was no point in running. He'd never make it now. The Ogren were too fast. Better to die like a Marcher.

One Ogren charged forward, wanting the kill for itself. Nestor set himself, preparing for the attack and hoping that he could put up a good fight at least for a time. If he could delay the Ogren, even for just a couple minutes, then perhaps the time earned would aid his Marchers in their escape. The Ogren raised its battle axe above its head, thinking to bring it down on top of his smaller opponent and split him in two. Raising his sword in a two-handed grip, Nestor sought to deflect the blow, but he knew with some regret that he had little chance of success, the dark creature's blow too powerful.

At the last second, Nestor ducked down, hearing the distinctive thrum from behind him as three arrows in rapid succession streaked through the space he had just been occupying. The first arrow struck the beast in the chest, the second in the thigh, but those only enraged it. It was the third, driving through its cheek into its brain, that finished the job. The massive beast crashed face first to the ground, dead before it hit the rocky soil. The other Ogren watched in disbelief, then bellowed in anger and rushed forward.

A tall Highlander stood above Nestor, offering a hand. Nestor gladly accepted it and quickly regained his feet.

"Come on, old man," said Aric. "We're almost to the plateau. Once there, it's just a straight run across. Can you do it without falling?"

Not bothering to reply, though several pointed comments crossed his mind, Nestor ran through the forest, dodging trees, rocks and other obstacles that sought to take him down, until finally breaking out onto the wide stretch of grassland that he saw narrowed just ahead between two rocky outcroppings. Aric stuck close to his heels, apparently wanting to make certain that Nestor didn't have any more problems during their attempted escape.

Blasted children, Nestor thought. Stronger. Faster. Thinking they knew more than you. Much too confident. Not understanding the value of experience. The Highland chief pushed the thoughts from his mind. Yes, he was old. But he could still fight and lead. And he'd need to thank Aric once they escaped the Ogren. The young stripling had saved his life, and for that he owed him a debt.

"There they are," rumbled Catal Huyuk, pointing to the two Highlanders sprinting through the long grass and striving for the trees at the far side.

"The Ogren are gaining," said Rya. "They're not going to make it."

Nestor and Aric didn't bother to look behind them. The Marchers were well aware of the danger that pursued them. Four Ogren were no more than one hundred feet behind them and gaining with every step, the beasts' long strides allowing them to make up the ground in seconds. The remainder of the Ogren raiding party, almost five dozen in all despite their previous losses, followed after them, intent on the chase and not paying attention to their surroundings.

"They don't need to make it," said Rynlin. "They just need to get a little farther. We need the last of the Ogren into the gap. Otherwise, the trap fails."

"Marchers to the ready," Catal Huyuk ordered. Nestor's Marchers, all of whom had made it safely across the grassland into the small forest at the far side, stepped to the edge of the wood. Bows in hand, an arrow already on the string, they placed a half dozen arrows each into the soft earth in front of them, ready to launch on command. Nestor and Aric were agonizingly close, but it was too late. They weren't going to reach the safety of the trees by just a small margin. The Ogren were only a dozen feet behind them now.

"They're through the gap," confirmed Rya.

"Now!" shouted Rynlin.

He and Rya stepped forward, seizing hold of the Talent and allowing the natural energy of the world to flow through them. Several other Sylvan Warriors followed them out from the trees. Maden, almost as tall as Rynlin, wore a sword at his hip. Though it appeared as if his features were carved from granite, he always had a ready smile, and he wore it now as balls of white energy danced across his hands. Gavin of Ferranagh, a short man with a long, white beard that he looped in his belt to keep out of the way, emerged next. Followed by Brinn Kavolin, an extremely tall, slender man. He had a sharp, angular face and dark brown hair that continually threatened to fall into his eyes. Right behind him came the twins, Elisia and Aurelia Valeran from Kashel, the only difference between the two being the color of their hair, Elisia's a midnight black and Aurelia's a shocking white.

Just as the lead Ogren was about to stab his sword into Nestor's back, a bolt of white light shot over the Marcher's head and blasted through the chest of the pursuing Ogren. Nestor had ducked the blow he felt coming, sliding through the grass and then tumbling past the men and women who stepped from between the trees and faced the onrushing Ogren. Once again Aric helped him to his feet, and they watched in astonishment and delight as more bolts and balls of white energy slammed into the charging dark creatures, blasting through their wide chests and leaving a sickly smell of burning meat to drift on the wind.

"Release at will!"

Catal Huyuk's craggy voice cut through the commotion. The Marchers lined up behind the Sylvan Warriors released their first flight of arrows, and then another, followed by another. The men and women of the Highlands each sent a half-dozen shafts into the sky in less than a minute. The arrows flew through the air in an almost continuous stream, the flow thick and heavy, forcing the Ogren to halt their attack. Most of the arrows found their target, slamming into the Ogrens' heavily muscled bodies, although few found their killing mark. But that was not the intention. The Marchers simply wanted to cause confusion among the Ogren, and they swiftly did, as the huge beasts, many with two or three shafts protruding from their chests or legs, looked around uncertainly, not sure whether to continue their attack or seek to escape.

The decision was made for the slow-witted Ogren when a howl echoed off the two rocky outcroppings. A massive black wolf, a stripe of white across his eyes, sprinted at the head of more than a hundred wolves that streamed through the gap leading onto the plateau, their shining eyes intent on their prey. Launching himself into the air, Beluil slammed into the back of an Ogren, forcing it to the ground. Before the dark creature could bring its short sword to bear, the rusty blade stuck beneath its chest, the black wolf tore into the beast's throat with his sharp teeth. The growls and howls of the wolves added to the almost overwhelming din as they broke off into groups of three or four and tried to separate the Ogren, nipping at the back of its legs and seeking to bite into a calf or hamstring. Once disabled and on the ground, the wolves could easily finish the task or leave it to their allies, as the Marchers, having dropped their bows and pulled their swords, charged into the melee, Catal Huyuk leading the way as he cleaved an Ogren's head from its shoulders with the first swing of his giant battle axe.

In just a few minutes, it was over, the bodies of the Ogren scattered across the trampled long grass of the plateau. Marchers and Sylvan Warriors walked among the dark creatures, ensuring that none survived.

Rynlin watched the entire exercise with a grim smile, knowing that the lack of mercy was necessary. He was pleased. The trap had sprung exactly as planned with none of the Marchers, Sylvan Warriors, or wolves seriously injured. Smiling in satisfaction, a shriek above him pulled him from his thoughts and his gaze to the sky. A large raptor circled above. Dipping its wing, the large kestrel glided across the battlefield screeching in triumph, then tilted its wings to catch the wind coming through the gap between the two rocky promontories, which had served the purpose of the Marchers and Sylvan Warriors so well by guiding the Ogren toward the defenders of the Highlands. Rynlin watched the raptor sweep past. Its strong wings, spanning seven feet, propelled it higher into the air. The white feathers speckled with grey on the bird's underside blended perfectly with the sky. When visible, the raptor was a dangerous predator. When hidden, it was deadly, shooting down through the thin air like an arrow, its sharp claws outstretched for the kill. Much like he and his allies had just done, Rynlin thought.

"What should we do with the bodies?" asked Nestor, coming to stand next to Rynlin. The grizzled Marcher looked none the worse for wear despite his struggles of the morning, though he did appear a little winded.

"We'll burn the bodies," said Rynlin. "If your Marchers could help us move them into a pile, it won't take long."

"Give me a moment to take some of the heads," said Catal Huyuk, as he strode past them toward a dead Ogren lying in the grass just a dozen feet to their front.

"Why does he want the heads?" asked Nestor.

"As a warning," replied Maden, the tall Sylvan Warrior wiping black Ogren blood from his sword onto the grass. "Catal Huyuk is a quiet man, letting his axe do most of the talking for him. But he still knows how to make a statement."

"A man after my own heart," replied Nestor. "We need to have him visit the Highlands more often."

2. UNEXPECTED SHADE

The young Marcher stood in the shadows of the early morning, concealing himself behind a tree, his senses attuned to the sounds and movements of the forest waking around him. He could tell that something was not right. He could feel it in his bones. Danger lurked in these woods, and it was stealthily approaching the Marcher camp. But what it was, the Marcher didn't know for sure. Kylin Stonebreaker, better known as Oso, stepped silently from behind his tree and glided to another, not making a sound. A bear of a man, still he could pad through the Highland thickets and forests like a mountain lion with no one the wiser.

Oso nodded to his right, catching Coban Serenan's gaze. The veteran Marcher, burly and stout with grey hair and a mustache that hung below his chin, hid behind a tree as well. The craggy-faced warrior flicked his eyes to the gap between the two birch trees. They could both sense it. Darkness approached. Something evil. Slowly. Quietly. The two Marchers waited patiently, muscles tense, ready to spring, though not feeling the need to rush. Time seemed to drag on, every passing minute feeling like an hour, and still the stench of wrongness came closer.

After several more minutes passed, and concluding that the evil was almost even with their position, Coban leapt out from behind the tree, swinging his sword in a deadly arc. The clash of steel on steel broke the quiet of the early morning. Coban immediately jumped back as his opponent twisted his grip, allowing the Highlander's blade to slide off his own so that he could lunge forward with the speed of a snake's strike. Coban barely escaped, the tip of his adversary's sword sliding past his side with just a finger's breadth to spare.

The veteran Marcher slowly stepped back from his opponent, his gaze never leaving the black sword that tracked him, knowing that a single scratch from that blade would mean an excruciating death. The Shade followed after as if there was nothing to fear, its sinuous, graceful movement almost mesmerizing. Stories of the dark creature that crept toward him played through Coban's mind. Supposedly a Shade had once been a man who, in accepting the gifts and dominion of the Shadow Lord, had been corrupted by Dark Magic in service to his master. The Shade's white, faintly translucent skin gave it a ghoulish cast, its long, greasy, dark hair hung down his forehead, almost covering its milky white eyes. For a moment Coban thought it might be better to die from a touch of the Shade's corrupted blade, preferring not to be a casualty of the dark creature's more sinister habits. Shades no longer ate like a normal man. Instead, for sustenance they drank the spirits of their victims, leaving only desiccated corpses in their wake.

The Shade lunged forward once more, Coban parrying the strike and returning the attack with a backhanded blow. The Shade recovered unnaturally fast, catching Coban's blade with its own. But the Shade failed to stop the second blade that sliced through its neck. The dark creature stood there for a moment longer, not realizing it was dead until its head slid from its shoulders and its body crumpled to the ground.

"Took you long enough," muttered Coban, breathing heavily, though more from the tension of the situation than from the exertion expended.

"I was just waiting for the right moment," protested Oso.

"If you had waited any longer, I'd be the one lying dead in the dirt."

A disturbance in the air behind them made both Coban and Oso turn quickly. A second Shade stood in back of them, sword raised above its head prepared to strike. But the creature never completed its swing. Rather it was held in place by the sword protruding through its chest. The two Marchers jumped back quickly as the Shade fell toward them, sliding off the blade and falling to the ground next to its partner.

Thomas Kestrel, not too tall but able to capture the attention of all around him with a presence that demanded respect, stepped out of the shadows. He swung the Sword of the Highlands down in a two-handed stroke, cutting off the Shade's head in a single swing.

"Just wanted to make sure," Thomas said, pushing his long, sandy brown hair from his face and revealing his brightly glowing green eyes. "Maybe next time you two could focus a bit more on what's going on around you rather than arguing like two old men with nothing better to do."

Thomas bent down, using the Shade's cloak to wipe the blood from his blade. Then, upon sheathing his sword in the scabbard on his back, he walked deeper among the trees, ignoring the two Marchers who had kept their gaze down, somewhat embarrassed by their failure to identify the second Shade and not knowing what to say. But they were certainly thankful that Thomas had been there to eliminate this dark creature that could have taken their lives with ease.

The Lord of the Highlands, recognized as such by the Kingdoms just the day before, continued to walk through the forest until he came to a small glade. He was on edge this morning, but not because of the dark creatures so intent on killing him and his Marchers. He was used to it by now, an all too frequent occurrence and a hazard that could not be avoided. He grasped hold of the Talent, using the natural magic of the world to search around him one more time. Confirming that there had been only two Shades trying to sneak into the Marcher camp, he released the Talent and strode to the top of a small hill.

He closed his eyes, allowing the early morning sun to warm him after a cold night. He and his fighters had accomplished a great deal since leaving the Highlands. Appearing unexpectedly at the Council of the Kingdoms, they had thwarted the High King's plans. Just the look on Rodric's face when King Gregory of Fal Carrach had declared him the Lord of the Highlands had made the arduous journey across Dunmoor to Armagh worth it. But though he had been recognized as the Lord of the Highlands, thereby ending the ten-year regency administered by the High King, there was still more to do. So much more. As he did every day, he wondered if he had the strength and the wherewithal to do what needed to be done. Thomas opened his eyes once more, realizing that whether he did or not, it didn't matter. His grandmother's favorite saying played through his thoughts: *"You must do what you must do."* And so, he would.

A screech to his left drew his attention. In the tallest tree at the edge of the clearing, Thomas stared into the sharp gaze of the kestrel. Why the large bird had left the Highlands, he didn't know. But he could suspect. The raptor peered at him intently, its orange and white feathers sparkling as the sun's rays illuminated the bird. The raptor perched on a thick branch majestically, its sharp talons digging deeply into the wood.

For several minutes, the two surveyed one another, Thomas almost losing himself in the sharp gaze of the bird that held a special place in the hearts of the Highlanders. He knew this kestrel. Their paths had crossed before, most recently when he visited the Roost, the tallest tower in the Crag. And before that when Rynlin and Rya had taught him how to use the Talent in order to shape change so that he could take on the trials to become a Sylvan Warrior. After he had assumed the form of a kestrel himself, this kestrel had stayed by his side as he had flown among the peaks of the Highlands for the first time. There were other times as well that he remembered encountering a kestrel similar to this one, and he had no doubt that he and this kestrel were connected in some way. Staring into the raptor's sharp eyes gave him a feeling of calm, filling him with a fortitude and sense of purpose that had proven difficult to find this morning. Until now. It was almost as if this majestic bird, knowing of the challenges to come, sought to share its strength with him. As Thomas continued to stare at the kestrel his confidence began to grow. Then with a shriek that tore through the early morning, the kestrel launched itself from the branch into the sky. But rather than fly east toward the Highlands, Thomas watched the imposing raptor instead head west toward the fortress of Eamhain Mhacha.

Thomas tracked the raptor until it was no more than a speck in the sky, then turned when Oso walked out from between the trees.

"Thank you for what you did back there," said Oso, coming to stand next to him. "You're right. We should have assumed there was more than one Shade."

"A lesson for all of us, Oso. Never assume. But if you do, assume the worst."

Oso nodded, agreeing with his friend, and grateful for the gentleness of the rebuke.

"You seem a bit distracted. Is there anything I can do?"

Thomas smiled, glad for his friend's support. "No, Oso. Though I appreciate the offer."

"Worried about today, I take it."

"A bit, yes. I'd rather take on the Dark Horde than deal with what's to come this afternoon."

"It'll go well, Thomas. The other Kingdoms have acknowledged you as the Lord of the Highlands. They can't take that away from you."

"Yes, I know. Nevertheless, although I may have been acknowledged as Lord of the Highlands, I assume there are several rulers who have yet to accept that fact. Therefore, I expect that today's visit to Eamhain Mhacha will be more dangerous than killing a couple of Shades."

3. DECISIONS

Kaylie sat on the windowsill of her chamber, looking out over the shimmering Heartland Lake. Her sharp, smoky blue eyes tracked a heron as it glided over the gentle waves, searching for the best place to seek its morning meal in the shallow water by the shore. Pushing away the strands of her long, black hair that the gentle breeze spun before her face, she enjoyed the solitude and quiet with which her day had begun, knowing that would all change in just a few hours.

She did not particularly like staying in the Keep of Eamhain Mhacha, finding the ancient, stone citadel oppressive and disheartening. The palace of the High King rose above the city and overlooked the Heartland Lake, while the city itself had its own wall that continued along the road leading to the fortress, protecting anyone making the short journey between the two. The port jutted out into a small bay, with the city on one end and the cliff on the other. A sea wall ran the length of the bay, except for a small opening that allowed ships to pass through. An additional section of the sea wall could be swung into place to close the gap, effectively sealing the port and fortress from attack.

The citadel towered over the bay. The cliff rose five hundred feet from base to top. The walls of the fortress added several hundred feet more. In the shape of a perfect circle, three concentric walls protected the main portion of the castle. The first outer curtain stood a hundred feet tall, with the second and third of the same height behind it. If invaders actually made it past the first wall a grass-covered space between that and the second wall awaited them, and again between the second and third. The children living in the bastion often played there, unaware of the land's true purpose. The soldiers of Armagh had dubbed the immaculately groomed lawns between the walls the Killing Fields. There was no beauty associated with the fortress, only a strict, deadly functionality.

No, she definitely did not like visiting the capital of Armagh. Nevertheless, she did enjoy the view. Kaylie's thoughts drifted to yesterday's fateful afternoon. Her eyes had barely left Thomas as he went through the process of being declared the Highland Lord. Physically he appeared much the same. Unassuming, yet with an obvious strength and determination, a purpose rare in someone so young. Even with the Marchers arrayed behind him, many frighteningly imposing, everyone's gaze had remained fixed on the charismatic, intense Highland Lord.

She could only imagine what scars had been added to his body and his psyche since she had last seen him balanced on the edge of the Tinnakilly parapet. Kaylie still blamed herself for his capture and subsequent torture, despite Rya's claims to the contrary. She remembered leaving Thomas after he won the archery contest at the Eastern Festival, walking back to her chamber with a smile on her face, pleased that she was to meet with him again the next day.

But after that the only memory she had was kneeling in the mud in the Tinnakilly courtyard watching Dunmoorian soldiers, followed by Lord Chertney, taking a beaten Thomas to the dungeon. Ragin Tessaril had stood above her, crowing about his success and thanking her for her help in his capture. She didn't know how they got there, or what had happened, yet she immediately felt responsible. Rya had explained that someone strong in Dark Magic, likely Lord Chertney, had manipulated her mind and her perceptions, compelling her to do as he wished. But the guilt had entrenched itself within her, becoming a part of her that she couldn't seem to let go.

Relief had flooded through her upon seeing Thomas stand in front of the High King, making his claim for the Highland throne. Observing him, she saw the toughness in Thomas, how what he had gone through had helped prepare him for this moment. Yet she felt shame as well for what had occurred, and she still did not know how to make it up to him. In fact, she doubted that she ever could. Moreover, she feared that he wouldn't want to speak to her, blaming her for what had occurred during the Eastern Festival.

Jealousy had also taken hold when she saw Corelia Tessaril, daughter of the High King, openly appraise Thomas, as if she were examining an item at auction, as something to acquire. She didn't know if she were more afraid of what would happen to Thomas if Corelia got her claws into him, or if Thomas actually demonstrated an attraction to the Armaghian princess. Just thinking about it made her blood boil.

Her confrontation with Corelia yesterday afternoon during the ruckus following the declaration of the Highland Lord only increased the intensity of her anger. Corelia's knowing smile and then her predatory expression appeared before her every time she closed her eyes. But worst of all, she remembered word for word what the Princess of Armagh had said when Kaylie had asked Corelia if Thomas would be interested in her: "I'm absolutely certain. I have much to offer him, Kaylie. Much indeed. More, in fact, than you."

Those words had stung deeply and much to her annoyance

had burrowed under her skin. She was stronger than that. But what was she to do? Stay to the side, afraid of how Thomas might view her? Or take a risk that might prove more painful than she could bear?

An ear-splitting screech ripped through the early morning silence, breaking her train of thought. Kaylie followed the sound to its source, watching in awe as a massive kestrel settled on the ledge of the tallest tower of the Eamhain Mhacha fortress. Its orange and grey feathers sparkled in the early morning sunlight, its razor-sharp claws digging into the stone as if the majestic raptor could never be dislodged. Kaylie was entranced. The bird's proud gaze suggested that the raptor had made the palace of Eamhain Mhacha its own, much like Thomas had done the day before. Confident. Never backing down from a challenge. Direct. Kaylie decided that she would adopt the same approach. She didn't know if she could take the pain of possible rejection, but she decided that it was worth the risk.

I hope you enjoyed the first three chapters. To keep reading *The Claiming of the Highlands*, Book 7 of *The Sylvan Chronicles*, order your copy today from Amazon or PeterWachtBooks.com.

This short story is a prelude to the events in my series *The Tales of Caledonia* and is free to readers who receive my newsletter.

Join Peter's newsletter and get your FREE short story at www.PeterWachtBooks.com.